Sarina stole a quick look at Bashir's wound and asked, "Can you walk?"

"Not without help," he said. He ___ ____ opening a pouch on his suit to retrieve h___ _____ __ke me ten minutes to fix it."

S____ ___ ____ ___ ____ _____ ____ and lifted him to his ____ _____ ___ ____ ____ ____ ight now." She reache_ ___ ____ ___ ____ ____ ___tton that opened the trai_ ___ ____ ___ _ get off this train and into the city's tra_____ion system. If it's like most cities' transit networks, it probably has old tunnels that are no longer in use."

He let Sarina help him out of the train and down to the tracks. Once they were on foot, it was easy to see that her prediction had been correct: there were many levels of tunnels and several lines running parallel to one another. A few had obviously fallen out of use and been allowed to sink into darkness and disrepair. Within a few minutes of abandoning the train, they had retreated deep into a long-forgotten corner of the Breen city.

Limping along with his arm draped over Sarina's shoulders for support, Bashir asked, "What if they find traces of my DNA on the train?"

"They won't."

"How can you be sure?"

Somewhere above and behind them, a powerful explosion quaked the bedrock and rained dust on their heads.

Sarina smiled. "Let's just say I took a few precautions."

STAR TREK®
TYPHON PACT

ZERO SUM GAME

DAVID MACK

Based on *Star Trek*
created by Gene Roddenberry
and
Star Trek: Deep Space Nine®
created by Rick Berman & Michael Piller

POCKET BOOKS
New York   London   Toronto   Sydney   Salavat

Pocket Books
A Division of Simon & Schuster, Inc.
1230 Avenue of the Americas
New York, NY 10020

This book is a work of fiction. Names, characters, places, and incidents either are products of the author's imagination or are used fictitiously. Any resemblance to actual events or locales or persons, living or dead, is entirely coincidental.

First Pocket Books paperback edition November 2010

POCKET and colophon are registered trademarks of Simon & Schuster, Inc.

For information about special discounts for bulk purchases, please contact Simon & Schuster Special Sales at 1-866-506-1949 or business@simonandschuster.com.

The Simon & Schuster Speakers Bureau can bring authors to your live event. For more information or to book an event, contact the Simon & Schuster Speakers Bureau at 1-866-248-3049 or visit our website at www.simonspeakers.com.

Cover art and design by Alan Dingman

Manufactured in the United States of America

10   9   8   7

ISBN 978-1-4391-6079-4
ISBN 978-1-4391-9164-4 (ebook)

For Marco and Margaret:
thanks for everything.

Historian's Note

This story takes place in mid-2382, more than a year after the events depicted in the *Star Trek Destiny* trilogy and roughly three years after the events of the film *Star Trek Nemesis*.

In war there are no winners.

—Neville Chamberlain, speech, 1938

APRIL 2382

1

"*Intruder alert! Lock down all decks! This is not a drill!*"

The warning repeated and echoed through the corridors of the Utopia Planitia Fleet Yards' command facility. Red lights flashed on bulkhead panels, and pressure doors started to roll closed, partitioning the space station.

Ensign Fyyl tried to block out the cacophony of deep, buzzing alarms as he sprinted toward his post, phaser in hand. Was it an attack? Fyyl had no idea what was happening. The skinny young Bolian was less than a year out of Starfleet Academy and until that moment had counted himself lucky to have been posted to the security detail on a platform orbiting Mars, one of the safest assignments in the Federation. Now it seemed as if he was in the thick of the action—the last place he'd ever wanted to be.

He stumbled to a halt in front of a companel. With trembling fingers he punched in his security code, confirmed his section was secure, and requested new orders. A multilevel schematic appeared on the display. In real time, sections of the station switched from yellow to green as deck officers and patrolling security personnel such as Fyyl checked in. Then a number of sections turned red, and the

chief of security directed all his teams to converge on the
intruder.

Here we go, Fyyl thought, sprinting from the compartment
to the nearest intersection. Courtesy of the station's active sensor network, the junction's airtight hatch slid open
ahead of him and rolled shut behind him once he'd passed
into the next section. Through the windows lining each
tube-shaped passage he saw other security personnel moving toward the core ring ahead.

Then he winced at the searing flash of phaser beams
slicing through the air and steeled himself for the worst as
he charged through the next doorway into the thick of a
firefight. Pressing his back against a bulkhead, he snapped
off a pair of quick shots in the same direction he saw other
Starfleet personnel firing. Through the smoke and blinding
ricochets, he couldn't see if he hit anything.

Fyyl ducked as a volley of electric-blue bolts blazed
past him in the other direction. Two of his fellow Starfleet-
ers collapsed to the deck, their eyes open but lifeless, their
limbs splayed in the awkward poses of the dead. His heart
pounding, Fyyl returned fire into the smoky darkness,
trusting his training over his instincts, which told him to
run and hide. Several meters ahead of Fyyl, visible even
through the dense gray haze, a red warning light flashed.

Someone behind him shouted, "Fall back!"

Terrified and tripping over his own feet, Fyyl struggled
to turn away from danger.

The corridor lit up like a sun, swallowing Fyyl and
everything around him in a flash of light and heat beyond
measure.

• • •

"There's been an explosion inside the station," declared Lieutenant Vixia, the half-Deltan operations officer of the *U.S.S. Sparrow*. "They're venting air into space."

Commander Evan Granger leaned forward in his chair as he eyed the vapor jetting from a ragged wound in the hull of the command base. "Take us to Red Alert. If they don't get that breach sealed in twenty seconds, get ready to close it with a force field from our shield generator."

Beyond the decades-old space station, nearly two dozen half-constructed starships lay moored in their spacedock frames, mere shells of the vessels they were meant to become. Spread out beneath them was the shallow, dusky curve of the Martian surface, its crater-scarred face dotted with the gleaming lights of cities.

"Jex, any update from the station?" Granger asked his tactical officer.

The short young Bajoran man replied, "Not yet, sir." He tapped at his console. "I'm still picking up heavy comm chatter from inside the station. Sounds like the intruder's still alive and on the move."

"Prep a tractor beam. Be ready to snag any ship or escape pod that leaves that station without clearance."

"Aye, sir." Jex began entering new commands on his console, then stopped, his eyes widening with alarm. "Another explosion inside the station."

Granger looked at the *Sparrow*'s main viewscreen. Before the young commanding officer could ask Jex for more details, he saw all he needed to know: a massive conflagration had ruptured the station's lower core, and a crimson fireball now surged toward the small patrol vessel.

"Evasive!" Granger cried out, gripping his chair's armrests in anticipation. "All power to shields!" No sooner was the order spoken than the blast rocked the *Sparrow*. For several seconds stretched by fear and adrenaline, there was nothing for Granger to see on the main screen except static and a hellish cloud of flames, and nothing to hear but a deep roar of thunder against the hull.

The quaking ceased, and in the hush that followed Granger heard all the sounds of the bridge with perfect clarity: the soft chirps of feedback tones, the low thrumming of impulse engines beneath his boots, the gentle hum of ventilators.

"Damage report," he said. "Jex, any casualties?"

"Negative, sir. All decks secure."

Vixia said over her shoulder from the ops console, "Shields holding, sir."

"Jex, hail the station, see if they need medical personnel or damage-control teams. And see if you can find out what the hell just happened over there."

Sitting back, Granger wasn't sure anyone would ever give him or his crew a true account of what had just occurred, but as he watched the station continue to burn, he wasn't certain he really wanted to know.

"Do I even *want* to know what just happened at Utopia Planitia?"

Admiral Leonard James Akaar's rhetorical question

reverberated off the walls of his office on the uppermost level of Starfleet Command and gave way to a pained silence that none of his half dozen assembled peers seemed eager to disturb.

A tiny, throat-clearing cough snared Akaar's attention. He turned his glare toward Admiral Alynna Nechayev, a trim, middle-aged human woman whose blond hair had begun to show the slightest traces of turning silver in the months following the previous year's Borg invasion. "Preliminary reports," she said with the practiced calm of a political veteran, "suggest that the fleet yards' command station was sabotaged as a diversionary tactic, to conceal the theft of classified data from its main computer."

Troubled looks passed among the other admirals in the room. Akaar got up from his desk and took his time stepping out from behind it. He towered over the other Starfleet flag officers, and his broad chest and shoulders made it easy for him to part their ranks as he moved to stand in front of Nechayev. The svelte woman held her ground, tilting her head back to meet his gaze as he loomed over her and asked, "What was stolen?"

"The schematics for slipstream drive."

Akaar's jaw clenched. He sighed. "Everyone else, get out."

Nechayev stood with her hands folded behind her back as the other admirals left the room. As the door slid closed behind the last person to exit, Akaar inquired, "How much do we know for certain right now?"

"Not as much as we'd like," Nechayev said. "We're fairly certain the spy was a civilian engineer named Kazren. His dossier lists his species as 'Dessev,' but he appears to be the first of his kind we've ever met. He gained access to the main computer on Utopia Planitia's command station at 1431 hours, using stolen credentials and specialized tools to fool the biometric sensors." She stepped over to a companel on the wall and called up a series of classified reports from Utopia Planitia. "The first explosion he set off helped him evade capture while he transmitted a locator signal. The second explosion appears to have been planned to disable the station's shields and conceal his beam-out."

Settling back into his chair, Akaar asked, "Beamed to where?"

Punching up a new screen of graphs and data, Nechayev said, "Sensor readings from the station and its patrol ship, the *Sparrow*, suggest there was a cloaked Romulan vessel waiting nearby to pick Kazren up."

"How did a cloaked vessel get past our perimeter defenses?"

"We didn't think the Romulans had this kind of cloak yet." Nechayev pointed out an isolated section of the graph. "Judging from these readings, I'd say the Romulans have put phasing cloaks into active service."

Akaar frowned. "If that's true, they could be roaming at will throughout Federation space."

"I know," Nechayev said, "but right now we have a bigger problem. If the Typhon Pact develops their own version of the slipstream drive, we'll lose the only tactical advantage we have left—and with it, our only hope of keeping this cold war from turning into a real one."

All at once, Akaar understood why Edward Jellico,

his immediate predecessor as Starfleet's chief admiral, had always seemed to be on the verge of a migraine. Massaging an oppressive ache that throbbed in his temples, he said in a somber tone, "Can you give me the room, please, Alynna? . . . I need to call the president."

2

President Nanietta Bacco rubbed the sleep from her eyes as she asked her secretary of defense, "Is this as bad as Starfleet says it is, or are they overreacting?"

"I don't think they've exaggerated the threat, Madam President," said Raisa Shostakova, a short and squarely built human from a high-gravity homeworld. "Otherwise, I wouldn't be standing in your bedroom at three a.m., waking you from a sound sleep."

"Don't be silly, Raisa," Bacco said. "I haven't had a *sound sleep* since I was sworn in." She stood and cinched the belt of her robe around her waist. Another visitor signal buzzed at her door. "Come in."

The door slid open. Bacco's chief of staff, Esperanza Piñiero, hurried inside, followed by the director of the Federation Security Agency, a lanky but dignified-looking Zakdorn man named Rujat Suwadi. Heavy dark circles ringed Piñiero's brown eyes, but the white-haired Suwadi carried himself with a crisp, alert demeanor that did little to endear him to the Federation's sleep-deprived head of state. "Sorry we're late," Piñiero said, sounding short of breath. She brushed a sweat-soaked lock of brown hair from her eyes and added, "The transporter network is all backed up because of the elevated security status."

"I know," Bacco said. "Raisa filled me in about the breach on Mars. Do we know for sure who hit us?"

Piñiero threw a look at Suwadi, who replied, "Not with absolute certainty, Madam President. However, the preponderance of evidence suggests a Romulan vessel facilitated the spy's escape."

Shostakova said, "I've ordered Starfleet to step up patrols along our border with the Romulan Star Empire. If they were involved—"

"Then that ship could be bound for any of a dozen nearby worlds aligned with the Typhon Pact," Suwadi cut in.

Piñiero noticed a pointed look from Bacco and took the cue to ask Suwadi, "How likely is it that the Typhon Pact was involved in this?"

"Extremely probable," Suwadi said with confidence. "They are the only power in local space with the resources and motivation to perpetrate such an act."

"That we know of," Shostakova added, apparently hedging her bets against the unknown. Her comment seemed to irritate Suwadi.

"Well, yes," he said, rolling his eyes at her. "It wouldn't be *possible* to speculate on the capabilities of entities we don't even know of, would it?"

In the interest of preventing an unproductive feud between the intelligence chief and the secretary of defense, Bacco interjected, "Actually, an unknown entity *was* involved in the breach. What species was the spy?"

Piñiero plucked a thin padd from her coat pocket and

glanced at its screen. "Admiral Akaar says the spy called himself a 'Dessev.' Whatever the hell *that* is." Narrowing her eyes at Suwadi, she added, "Have *you* ever heard of these people?"

Suwadi's mouth wrinkled into a grimace. "No. To the best of my knowledge, there might not even be such a species. It is entirely likely that the infiltrator misrepresented himself entirely—from his given name to his world of origin." He sighed. "Clearly, more stringent controls are required in our hiring process for civilian employees at high-security facilities."

Bacco wondered if it would be impolitic to slap the Zakdorn in the back of the head. "*Really? Are you sure?*" She cast an intense glare at her chief of staff. "Esperanza, initiate full security reviews of *all* personnel at facilities that require clearances higher than level five—Starfleet *and* civilians."

"Yes, Madam President."

"Suwadi, I want to know what the hell you're doing now that the barn is burning and the horses are gone. Are we looking for the stolen plans? Digging up background on the spy? Tell me you're not just standing there looking smug."

The intelligence chief shifted his weight awkwardly back and forth as he replied, "Well, I've been in contact with my opposite number at Starfleet Intelligence, and they appear to have taken the lead on researching the background of the spy known as Kazren. As far as tracking down the plans—"

"Let me guess," Bacco interrupted. "Starfleet's already moving on that, too?" She exhaled angrily and shook her head. "Once again, I am reminded of why we need the military. You can go, Mister Suwadi. I'll call if I need you." Suwadi stood and blinked a few times in surprise, his jaw moving up and down despite no words issuing from his mouth. Bacco added, "I said, *you can go.*"

Verbally lashed into retreat, Suwadi nodded at his president, backpedaled three steps, then turned and made a swift exit. As the door closed behind him, Bacco turned her focus toward Piñiero. "How do we spin this for the media?"

"An accident. It's a shipyard, an industrial environment. Mistakes happen, and sometimes the best safeguards fail."

Bacco nodded her approval. "Good. Tack on some verbiage like, 'Our hearts go out to the families of those who were killed in the explosion, and we pledge our support to those who were wounded, blah blah blah.' That ought to keep the vultures in the press pool happy for a while."

"Okay, so we throw FNS a bone," Piñiero said. "We still need to talk about the political fallout. If the Typhon Pact *was* behind this, its ambassador will start talking tough as soon as she thinks she has us at a disadvantage."

"Then we have to keep *her* on the defensive," Bacco said. "But how do we stop Tezrene from feeding the *real* story to the press?"

Piñiero shrugged. "We play dumb and pretend to carry a big stick."

"I'm listening," Bacco said.

Shostakova nodded. "So am I."

"Even though we can't admit the data theft occurred, the Typhon Pact knows that losing the monopoly on slipstream is a big deal for us. And they know the kind of losses we took in the Borg invasion. What we need to do is make them *think* that we have some other ace up our sleeve—one so devastating, they don't even want to *know* what it is, much less see it in action—and that we're prepared to use it on whoever we find out bombed the Utopia Planitia shipyard."

Shaking her head, Bacco walked toward the door. "And what if we end up provoking the Typhon Pact into a shooting war?"

"I don't think we're there yet," Piñiero said as she and Shostakova fell into step behind Bacco and followed her into the hallway. "If they were ready to go head to head, they wouldn't be pulling this cloak-and-dagger shit."

Bacco threw a look over her shoulder at Shostakova. "Do you agree?"

"Yes, ma'am," Shostakova said. "For the moment, at least."

Plodding toward the kitchen, Bacco asked, "What does *that* mean?"

Shostakova replied, "It means that I think we have a very short grace period in which to act. The Typhon Pact might be playing catch-up with us on a technological level, but if they have those plans, it won't take long. At best, we have a few months before this goes from an embarrassment to a disaster."

"Then talk to me about response plans." Bacco crossed her kitchen, moving on a direct course for the replicator. "If the clock's ticking, what's our play here? Diplomacy? Direct military engagement?"

Piñiero and Shostakova swapped apprehensive glances,

and then the defense secretary said, "Neither. I think we need to look at covert options."

The suggestion wasn't unexpected, but it left Bacco desiring a moment to think things through. With a touch of her fingertip, she activated the replicator and said, "Decaf coffee, French roast, black and hot."

As the beverage took shape in a whirl of light and with a pleasing sound, Piñiero lifted one eyebrow at Bacco and asked, "Decaf?"

"Thank my doctor for that," Bacco grumbled. "He says my blood pressure's up again. You know how it is." Aiming a sour look at the youthful brunette, Bacco added, "What am I saying? Of course you don't—you're not even fifty yet." She picked up her coffee from the replicator and sipped it, wrapping her hands around the white mug to warm her cold fingers. Leaning against the countertop, she asked Shostakova, "When you say 'covert options,' are you talking about Starfleet Intelligence or Federation Security?"

"Starfleet. If this were a strictly internal matter, I'd say keep it on the civilian side. But if we're facing off with the Typhon Pact, we'll need to take action on foreign soil, and Starfleet is better equipped for that."

"Maybe, but they're also more culpable. If we send civilians to an enemy planet, we can disavow them if they get caught or killed. If we send Starfleet personnel, it's an act of war. So why risk a military op?"

"Because only Starfleet has the resources to mount a covert insertion and extraction mission on this short a timescale," Shostakova said. "I assure you, Madam President, if a better option were available, I'd recommend it."

Bacco took another sip of coffee and savored the tendrils of warm vapor that snaked into her nostrils and opened her sinuses. "Okay, Raisa, give Starfleet Intelligence the go-ahead. If the Typhon Pact is trying to build a slipstream-drive starship, SI is authorized to do whatever is necessary to stop it."

Piñiero said, "Ma'am, I'm not sure that broad a license is—"

"*Whatever* is necessary, Esperanza," Bacco repeated, silencing her chief of staff. "They hit us at home, killed our people, and stole our property. If they try to use it against us, I want them shut down with *extreme* prejudice. SI is cleared to proceed with a full-sanction black op. Understood?"

"Yes, ma'am."

"Good. Now get out of my house. I have to bullshit the Federation Council about this in forty minutes, and I'd like to shower first."

AUGUST 2382

AUGUST 2382

3

Julian Bashir sat alone at a small table on the upper level of Quark's bar. He had been nursing a *raktajino* for the better part of an hour; it had long since gone cold, and his last sip had left a bitter aftertaste. His closed-off body language—hunched forward over his drink, elbows on the tabletop, outer arm raised to block his peripheral vision and avoid accidental eye contact—was deliberate. For reasons that even Bashir himself failed to grasp, he had a habit of visiting the social hub of space station Deep Space 9 when he wanted to be left in peace.

In the old days such a ploy would always have back-fired. Sooner or later, one of his friends would stop by and join him, disregarding his halfhearted protests. But that had been when he'd still *had* friends on the station, at a time when his attempts at seclusion had been just transparent invitations for solace. Looking around the Ferengi-owned restaurant, gaming emporium, and embassy, Bashir saw only strangers and passing acquaintances.

Miles O'Brien had left DS9 with his family years earlier, after the end of the Dominion War, to help in the rebuilding of Cardassia Prime. Garak, of all people, had been appointed Cardassia's ambassador to the Federation.

Benjamin Sisko, after returning from his brief sojourn with
the Prophets—the nonlinear-time entities that had created
and resided within the Bajoran wormhole to the Gamma
Quadrant—had gone to live on Bajor and never returned to
active duty on the station. Odo had not yet come back from
his pilgrimage to commune with the Founders on some remote world in the Gamma Quadrant. The Jem'Hadar ob-
server Taran'atar likewise had not returned, having been
designated a persona non grata by Starfleet Command after
he attacked and nearly killed Captain Kira and Ro Laren
before becoming an outcast even from his own people.

It had been more than a year and a half since Ezri Dax
had accepted a transfer to the *U.S.S. Aventine* as its second
officer—only to become its commanding officer as the result of a battlefield promotion, when her captain and first
officer were killed during an early battle of the Borg invasion. To fill gaps in her ship's roster, she had poached three
of Deep Space 9's best young personnel: command officer
Sam Bowers, engineer Mikaela Leishman, and Dr. Simon
Tarses, who had excelled as an attending physician under
Bashir's tutelage.

A sharp, nasal voice from the bar's lower level pierced
the white noise of the crowded dining room, interrupting
Bashir's maudlin reminiscence. "Doctor! Another *raktajino*
for you?"

"No, thank you, Quark," Bashir called back, shaking
his head at the Ferengi bartender, who also served as his
people's ambassador to Bajor, now a member world of the
United Federation of Planets.

Quark nodded once at Bashir, began wiping down the

bar, and then mumbled under his breath, "That's fine. It's not as if I'd rather have *paying* customers at that table."

An ordinary human being would not have overheard Quark's sarcastic grumbling from the busy bar's upper level, but Bashir was far from ordinary. Born with severe developmental delays, he had lagged behind his peers until the age of six, when his parents—in violation of Federation law—took him to a clinic on an alien world for a program of genetic resequencing and enhancement. Over the course of two months, young Julian was transformed into one of humanity's elite. He had been made smarter, stronger, and more dexterous, and gifted with keener senses, faster reflexes, and greater stamina than most human beings could ever hope to possess.

They gave me everything except the ability to be happy, Bashir brooded. He considered ordering another *raktajino* just to vex Quark, but then he noted the time and realized his daily hour of exile from the station's infirmary was nearly over. Abandoning the dregs of his caffeinated Klingon drink, he left the restaurant through a portal on its upper level and strolled to the nearest staircase.

The crowd on the Promenade was denser and slower moving than usual, no doubt because of an upcoming Bajoran religious festival that had become a major draw for tourists.

To think that when I came here thirteen years ago, most of the Federation had never heard of Bajor. Now they take vacations here. That rumination brought Bashir up short, and he stopped halfway down the stairs to the Promenade's main level. *Have I really been here* thirteen *years?*

He continued down the stairs and caught his reflection on one of the shops' windows as he passed by. His hair had started to thin a bit on top, and much of it was showing signs of gray, as was the close-cropped beard he had grown recently. His fortieth birthday had passed without much more than a celebratory subspace comm from his parents and an automated message from the station's computer. Some days he could almost ignore the sensation that time was catching up with him, but he was only months shy of turning forty-one and keenly aware that while he might to some eyes still appear youthful, he would never again be young.

Worst of all, he had in recent months been haunted by a feeling he had kept at bay most of his adult life but that now seemed to hold him in its grip. He was, in a word, lonely.

The doors of the infirmary parted as he approached, and he trod with light steps as he entered the dimly lit medical center. All the biobeds were empty, and most of the displays were in standby mode. That was the way Bashir liked to see his professional domain: unoccupied. Unlike the other tenants of the Promenade, Bashir felt most successful when no one needed to visit his place of work.

He passed his office and stole around the corner into the intensive-care ward. At the far end of the spacious room, a single biobed was illuminated by a soft, orange-hued overhead light. Lying comatose in the bed and attached to a complex array of life-sustaining technologies was Captain Elias Vaughn, who had come to Deep Space 9 years earlier as its first officer. He had served briefly as its commanding officer before his passion for exploration had inspired him to transfer to starship command—a decision that had proved fateful and tragic.

Sitting in a chair beside the bed was Vaughn's daughter, Lieutenant Prynn Tenmei. The young woman held a slender padd, from which she read to her father in a low, dulcet voice. "'The ship's prow cleaved the black water,'" she said as Bashir drew closer, "'and the sails snapped over Wade's head, filled with gusts driven by the inferno on shore. All around him huddled the weak and frightened, the orphaned and dispossessed—while behind him, the second land he had come to love and call home burned, torched by the Wights of Scarden. *Never again*, Wade vowed, his hands closing into fists. *Never again*.'" Tenmei scrolled to the next page of text as Bashir sidled up behind her shoulder. "'Wade turned his back on the fire. In the distance, lightning danced on the edge of a storm. Sea spray kissed his face as the deck rolled under his feet. Confronted by a darkness with no horizon, he finally understood what it meant to fear the future.'" She turned off the padd, looked at her father, and added, "End of chapter twenty-four."

Bashir asked, "Book two of *The Twilight Kingdoms*?" Tenmei nodded, and Bashir continued. "I read that trilogy as a boy. It's amazing how well it holds up, even after all these centuries. I guess one could call it timeless."

"My mom used to read it to me when I was about nine or ten," Tenmei said. "I don't know if Dad ever read it, but I thought he might like it."

The coldly rational part of Bashir's mind wanted to point out that Vaughn was probably no longer capable of liking or disliking anything, as he had shown no evidence of higher brain function since being wounded eighteen months earlier during a battle against the Borg. However, the more compassionate part of Bashir's personality knew that this was a subject to be broached delicately with Tenmei, who had lost her mother to Borg assimilation nearly a decade earlier.

Tenmei looked up and fixed Bashir with a bitter glare. "I know what you're going to say."

"I haven't said *anything*."

She stood, set her padd on her chair, and leaned over her father. "I'm not ready to give up on him," she said, finger-combing unwashed wisps of Vaughn's white hair from his forehead. She pressed her honey-brown palm to the old man's gaunt, pale cheek. "He wasn't meant to go out like this."

Voicing his reply with care, Bashir said, "You mean free of pain and with a loved one by his side? There are worse ways to go." Suppressing a flood of undesirable memories, he added, "Believe me, I've seen them."

"So have I, Julian."

Bashir saw no value to pressing the point or provoking an argument. He nodded once, turned, and started to walk away. He paused and turned back as Tenmei said, "I'm not clinging to some fantasy that he'll wake up on his own." Her eyes glistened with tears. "I know he won't. But you've done so much under such worse conditions—replacing Kira's heart, rebuilding Ro's spinal cord, not to mention what you did to save Bowers that time . . ." Wiping her eyes with the back of one hand, Tenmei sniffled to clear her sinuses and then swallowed hard. "I'm just saying, you've worked miracles before."

"Prynn, your father's *a hundred and eight years old*. Kira, Ro, and Bowers are all in the primes of their lives. And to be honest, I had help with Ro and got lucky with Sam." He took a few steps toward Tenmei and softened his tone. "I've done all I can for your father, Prynn. I'm sorry, but my medical advice is the same now as it was a week after his surgery: you should let him go."

His words made Tenmei recoil and turn away from him. Her lips pressed together and twisted with grief, and a single tear escaped as she squeezed shut her eyes. In a constricted voice, she protested, "I can't." She hurried past him, heading for the exit. "I'm sorry, Julian. I just can't." She left shaking her head in mute denial.

Bashir made no attempt to go after her. It wasn't his place. He walked over and stood beside Vaughn's bed. The captain's vitals were faint but steady, his blood chemistry was good, and his brainwave monitor was blank. As much as Bashir wanted to disconnect Vaughn from the dignity-stealing life-support machines that were sustaining his frail old form, that decision belonged to Tenmei, who was Vaughn's only surviving family member. Until she gave permission to turn off the machines, Vaughn would lie there, in limbo.

He couldn't blame Tenmei for her choice. *She's smart enough to know what's right and weak enough not to choose it,* he lamented. *But that could describe any of us, at one time or another.* Walking back to his office, he reminded himself, *My job is to heal—not to judge.*

Settling into his chair, his mind filled with the clutter of routine tasks that he knew were soon to arrive on his daily action plan: vaccination updates for the children at the station's schools, physicals for all Starfleet personnel with surnames or official identities beginning with *K* or *L*, and a review of his staff's reports of health-code violations inside all food service and paramedical businesses—except Quark's place, which, as a foreign embassy, was exempt.

So much for the excitement of "frontier medicine," he chided himself, recalling his original reason for requesting assignment to Deep Space 9 after he'd graduated second in his class at Starfleet Medical. *I guess the frontier inevitably becomes an extension of home once you colonize it.* He snorted with cynical derision. *Conquer it, sanitize it, and homogenize it. That's the Federation way.*

Just as he was about to get a head start on the next month's paperwork, a man's voice announced from an overhead speaker, *"Ops to Doctor Bashir."*

"This is Bashir. Go ahead, Jang."

"The captain wants to see you in ops on the double, sir."

Cocking one eyebrow with mild interest, Bashir replied, "On my way."

Bashir stepped off the lift into Deep Space 9's busy Operations Center—known to the crew simply as ops. As he descended the stairs to the main deck, Lieutenant Jang Si Naran—a Thallonian man with deep red skin, a goatee, and a shaved pate adorned in the back by a long braid of black hair—tilted his head sideways toward the commander's office, which was up two more flights of stairs, elevated above the rest of ops. Through the transparent panels of the office's doors, Bashir could see only the back of a tall, dark-haired man in a Starfleet uniform.

Eager to find out why he'd been summoned, Bashir took the steps two at a time and bounded off the staircase with a smooth stride that carried him through the parting doors and into the commander's office.

"Thanks for coming so quickly, Doctor," said Captain Ro Laren, who had been promoted to command of the station after Vaughn applied for and received a transfer to command a starship on an exploration mission. The tall, striking brunette dipped her chin as she looked at her other guest. "This is Commander Aldo Erdona from Starfleet Intelligence." Erdona extended his hand to Bashir.

The intelligence officer's grip was firm. "Good to meet you," Bashir said.

"Likewise, Doctor." Erdona gestured toward the chairs in front of Ro's desk. "Shall we sit down? We have much to discuss."

Ro settled into the chair behind her desk while Erdona and Bashir took the seats opposite hers. Bashir asked, "What can I do for you, Commander?"

"I'm here to recruit you for a special assignment."

"Something medical in nature, I presume?"

The intelligence officer shook his head. "Covert ops."

Bashir inhaled sharply, frowned, then looked away and cleared his throat. "That's not exactly my area of expertise."

"Actually, I read the after-action report of your mission to Sindorin, and—"

"Hardly my finest hour."

Ro scowled. "Let him finish, Doctor."

Chastised, Bashir gestured at Erdona to continue. The commander nodded once and then resumed speaking. "Based on what I've read in your file, you have precisely the sort of skills and capabilities we need for this mission."

After cracking a polite smile in response to Erdona's flattery, Bashir replied, "I find it hard to believe that Starfleet Intelligence really needs *me* so badly when it has its own specially trained field operatives."

"We suffered losses during the Borg invasion, just like the rest of Starfleet," Erdona said. "We're shorthanded and spread thin, gathering intel on the Typhon Pact. But even if we weren't, I'd still be here talking to you."

"Why?"

Erdona sighed. "Did you read in the news a few months ago about the explosion at the Utopia Planitia Fleet Yards?"

"Yes." Bashir thought for a moment and then continued. "It wasn't just an industrial accident, was it?"

"What I'm about to tell you can't be discussed with anyone not involved in the mission. Understood?" Ro and Bashir nodded. "The explosion was part of an exit strategy by a spy who stole the designs for slipstream drive. There's evidence that a phase-cloaked Romulan ship was involved in the extraction of the spy, which suggests this was an act of espionage by the Typhon Pact."

It was sobering news, but it had not answered Bashir's question. "I still don't see what this has to do with me."

"SI began monitoring shipping activity throughout the Typhon Pact's territories. We were looking for patterns that suggested they were gathering matériel and components for the construction of a slipstream system. Three weeks ago, we correlated our latest updates and found what we think is a secret shipyard, hidden on a world inside Breen space." He leaned forward, picked up a padd from Ro's desk, activated it, and handed it to Bashir. "We're looking at a planet called Salavat, in the Alrakis system. It's not much more than a half-frozen chunk of rock, but it's been getting quite a bit of cargo traffic from the Breen and the Romulans lately. We haven't found much beyond a few small installations on the surface, but we think that's because the real action is underground."

"As in, a concealed shipbuilding facility," Ro said.

"Exactly," Erdona said. "We have eyes on every shipyard in the Typhon Pact, so we know they aren't building a slipstream prototype at any of them. But this world is where they've been shipping critical parts for a chroniton integrator—which is the secret to making slipstream work without slamming into stars, planets, or other ships at a hundred thousand times the speed of light."

Folding a hand over a fist, Ro asked, "If you know that's where they're making the prototype, why not just send in a fleet and frag the planet?"

"Tempting," Erdona said, "but ultimately self-defeating. We're in no condition to start a shooting war with the Typhon Pact, Captain. Besides, just because they're building the prototype there doesn't mean that's the only place they have the plans. But it does mean that's where they're doing their research—"

"And updating the schematics with new data," Bashir said, catching on, "as they figure out how to make the drive work with their ship designs."

Erdona nodded. "Very good, Doctor. That's this target's real value. Consequently, we've been ordered to initiate a full-sanction op to—"

"Excuse me," Bashir said, "a what?"

"A full-sanction operation. It means whoever we send in has a license to kill, authorized by the president herself." Erdona gave that a moment to sink in before he continued. "As I was saying, we don't just want to take out the shipyard—we also want to sabotage the stolen data and all its backups."

Ro sounded skeptical as she asked, "And how much time do you think that'll buy you? They'll figure out slipstream sooner or later, with or without our plans."

"True, but it'll take them a lot longer without," Erdona said. "Our best estimate is that sabotaging this program will buy us another decade of monopoly on slipstream, by which point we hope to have rebuilt the fleet and expanded our reach to new regions of the galaxy. But if we don't shut down the Typhon Pact's slipstream project before it launches a prototype, the Federation will become a second-rate power in less than a year. What happens after that, I don't think any of us want to find out."

"On that much we can agree," Bashir said. "But I still don't see why you think I'm the right man for this job."

"Our knowledge of the Breen is still limited," Erdona said. "We can barely translate that machine-speak of theirs, and their culture's a total blind spot. Remote observation has yielded almost no usable intel about their society or their biology. Whoever we send to Salavat needs to be more adaptable than anyone we currently have available. Our agent will have to be able to think and react at superhuman speeds. And because of the cold temperatures, higher gravity, and thicker atmosphere on Salavat, we'll need someone with great strength and endurance. Last but not least, we need someone who can fit inside a suit of Breen armor."

Now Bashir understood why Erdona had come to Deep Space 9. He was recruiting Bashir for the same reason the doctor had been tapped to go to Sindorin: because he was genetically enhanced. "I see," he said in a measured tone. "Forgive me if I seem less than thrilled at the prospect of being dropped alone onto a Breen planet, especially when you have no idea what you're sending me into."

"Well," Erdona said, raising his eyebrows, "you wouldn't be going in *alone*. As for *what* you'd be getting into, we've brought in some experts who might be able to shed some light on that—assuming you're willing to commit to the mission." Apparently sensing Bashir's reluctance, Erdona added in a more supplicative tone, "The fact is, Doctor, we need you. Your enhanced abilities give you a better chance than any other agent to survive this mission. If you turn us down, we *will* go forward without you, but . . . frankly, I don't like our odds."

Bashir threw a look at Ro, who shrugged and said, "Your call, Doctor."

Resigning himself to answering duty's summons, Bashir said, "All right, Commander. Let's go meet your experts."

4

"Oh, no," Bashir said as Erdona led him into the guest quarters where the "experts" stood waiting for them.

Jack—seven years older, a few hairs grayer, but no less manic—flashed a crazy-eyed smile as he waved at Bashir. He'd also retained his trademark rapid-fire speech pattern. "Bet you weren't expecting *us*, were you? Hm? Hm? Hm?"

Standing beside trim, goateed Jack was his portly, graying companion in captivity, Patrick. Looking like an abashed cherub, the childlike man in baggy gray pajamas waggled the plump fingers of one hand at Bashir and mumbled, "Hello."

Before Bashir could reply, he felt a hand firmly grip his left buttock. He leaped forward in surprise and pivoted to see Lauren, the third and final member of the genetically enhanced—and profoundly damaged—trio that some of his former colleagues had taken to calling the Jack Pack. Leaning against the wall, the buxom brunette gave Bashir a salacious smirk and purred, "*Love* the beard. Very sexy."

Bashir glared at Erdona. "I'm out." He turned to leave.

Erdona grabbed Bashir by one shoulder and stopped him. "I know about your history with these three, but—"

"Then you know they shouldn't be here."

The look on Erdona's face told Bashir he'd struck a nerve. Clearly, Erdona knew that Jack, Patrick, and Lauren had—like Bashir—been subjected in early childhood to genetic resequencing. Unlike Bashir, however, the members of the Jack Pack had suffered severe negative side effects. Jack had become a violent, malignant narcissist; Patrick's emotional development arrested at a four-year-old level; and Lauren filtered all her interactions through her delusional libido.

Adopting a soothing mien, Erdona said, "Let's be reasonable, Doctor. You know as well as I do that Jack and his friends possess remarkable insight when it comes to analyzing raw intelligence, especially as it pertains to alien cultures." With a firm nudge, he made Bashir turn to look at Jack and Patrick. "They say they have new information about the Breen—information we *need*, Doctor."

Something in Erdona's manner—an odd inflection in his voice, perhaps some minuscule hesitation, or maybe a fleeting microexpression—captured Bashir's attention. Bashir sensed that Erdona had omitted something important, and as he noted the awkward body language between Erdona and Jack, Bashir had a flash of intuition. "Oh, I see," he said with unfiltered cynicism. "The *real* reason you need me isn't that I'm enhanced—it's that Jack and his friends won't reveal their information to anyone but me." Looking Jack in the eye, he added, "Isn't that right?"

Jack responded with frantic applause and a psychotic gleam. "Bravo, Doctor! Well done! Way to use those synapses!"

Lauren stepped toward her peers, stroking Bashir's arm

as she passed by, and shot him a smoldering look. "You never fail to *impress*, Julian." She fell into place beside Patrick, who bounced from foot to foot like an overexcited toddler.

Bashir shook his head at Erdona. "This is ridiculous."

Jack screamed, "This is life and death, Doctor!" Noting that everyone in the room had recoiled from him, he mumbled a meek "Sorry."

Interposing himself between Bashir and the Jack Pack, Erdona said, "I know this looks bad, especially after that business with them trying to sell us out to the Dominion, but I promise, Doctor, we've been keeping *very* close tabs on them this time. They made breakthroughs in hours where our people hadn't made any progress in *years*. Now they tell me they've made a major discovery, but they won't tell me what it is unless you're one of the agents being sent to Salavat." Leaning closer, Erdona lowered his voice to a whisper, "I can have Starfleet Command make it an order, Doctor, but I'd rather you *consent* to help us."

Conflicted and more than a bit irritated, Bashir looked over Erdona's shoulder at the trio. Jack shrugged. Patrick giggled. Lauren blew him a kiss.

Bashir sighed. "Okay, fine. Let's get this over with."

Jack poked Lauren's arm several times in quick succession. "See? See? Told you he'd do it. Told you. Knew he would. Said so." Lauren rolled her eyes and strutted away from her pestering cohort, leaving Jack with no one to torment but Patrick. After a momentary pause, a chastened Jack jabbed his index finger into the balding man-child's fleshy shoulder and said in a softer voice, "See? Told you."

The prospect of being cooped up with three lunatic-savants filled Bashir with dismay. Casting a fearful look at Erdona, he asked, "How long is this briefing supposed to take?"

"At least a few hours," Erdona said. "There's a lot to cover."

Across the room, Lauren sat on a short couch and patted the cushion beside her as she called out to Bashir, "You should make yourself *comfortable*, Doctor."

Erdona glanced at Lauren, then asked Bashir, "Does she ever run out of innuendos?"

Bashir chuckled. "Are you kidding? *Innuendo* is her primary language." Gesturing toward the sitting area, he added, "We should get to work."

"Not yet," Erdona said. "I don't want to go through all this twice, so I want them to brief your partner at the same time." He stepped to a door that linked the Jack Pack's quarters to the next one in the section and pressed the visitor signal. As soon as the channel opened, he said, "Ready to start when you are."

A familiar, feminine voice replied over the comm, *"Coming."*

The moment Bashir heard it, he felt his pulse quicken. *No*, he told himself, trying not to get his hopes up. *It can't be* . . .

Then the door opened, and it *was*.

She was more beautiful than Bashir had remembered. Her blond hair was still long and straight, and she carried herself with poise and grace. Gone was the shy young woman who, because of a botched genetic resequencing, had languished in a decades-long semicataleptic state as a member of the Jack Pack, until an experimental surgery by Bashir had set her free. In her place was a mature, confident, genetically enhanced adult—a professional who was in every way at least Bashir's equal and in some respects his better.

Her gaze met Bashir's, and she flashed a jubilant grin. "Hello, Julian."

For a few seconds he stood dumbstruck with equal parts surprise and joy. Recovering his wits, he smiled warmly at his long-absent lost love, "the one who had gotten away," and replied in a voice that quaked as if he'd just hit puberty. "Hello."

Everyone in the room fell silent, and Bashir realized that his reunion with Sarina Douglas had become the focus of attention.

"All right, then," Erdona said, glossing over the moment by slapping Bashir's shoulder and steering him toward the sitting area. "Let's get to it."

As Bashir and Erdona walked over to join Jack, Patrick, and Lauren, Sarina sidled up to Bashir. "Suave as ever, Julian. And to think"—she nodded at Erdona—"Aldo was afraid this would be *awkward*."

"For a species you know nothing about, you had quite a deep file on the Breen," Jack said. He paced in front of a vid screen with his left hand tucked into his right armpit and his right hand hovering in front of his face. Nibbling on a ragged fingernail, he continued his spiel. "Did you know you captured one of their starships three years ago? Says so in one of those classified memos from Starfleet. Found it adrift in the Ravanar system." He let out a derisive chortle. "*Adrift.*"

Lauren interjected, "Starfleet slang for 'disabled by Special Ops.' They probably sabotaged its life-support systems while it was docked at Arawat."

Bashir said, "Can we stay focused on the Breen, please?"

Patrick replied with mild confusion, "Their biology makes no sense."

"What he means," Jack said, "is that it's *inconsistent*. You have *four* totally different physiological profiles for Breen, did you know that? Hm? Hm? You've got one report that says they're humanoids with canine snouts—"

"Purely speculative," Bashir said.

"Because of the armor," Lauren said. "We know."

Jack continued. "Another says their bodies are sacks of ammonia with skeletons and they just go *poof* at temperatures above fifteen degrees."

"*Poof,*" echoed Patrick.

Jack added, "That's from your own Major Kira—"

"*Captain* Kira," Patrick said, correcting him.

"Actually," Lauren said, "it's—"

"*Enough,*" Bashir snapped, in no mood to be reminded of another friend and colleague who had moved on and left him standing still. "Stay on topic. Is that all you have on Breen physiology?"

"Hardly," said Lauren. She held up a padd. "A Klingon file says they're silicon based, but Starfleet thinks they're carbon based. One file says the Breen have four-lobed brains and no blood, and another says they have no organs at all."

Jack tossed three padds across the table in quick succession to punctuate his sentence fragments: "Two genders. Asexual. Hermaphroditic."

"Schizophrenic is more like it," Patrick said.

"If this was *really* their physiology, they'd have no use for Class-M worlds," Jack said. "They'd be all over Class-P worlds. But they colonize Class-M planets almost exclusively. Why would they do that? Hm? Hm?"

Bashir traded a weary look with Erdona and shrugged. "To be difficult?"

Perhaps noting the Starfleet officers' waning patience, Sarina asked Jack, "What's your hypothesis about the Breen's physiology?"

"Wouldn't *you* like to know?"

"Yes," Sarina said, favoring Jack with a disarming smile, "I would."

"Oh," Jack said, his defensive façade crumbling. "Um, okay. I—we—think the Breen are humanoids. Well, *most* of them, anyway."

Erdona and Bashir sat forward almost in unison. "Hang on," Bashir said. "Are you suggesting there's more than one kind of Breen?"

"You're not seeing the big picture," Jack said. "It's bigger than that!"

"Lots bigger," Patrick said.

"It's *massive*," Lauren said, in what Bashir could only imagine had been intended as an open-ended double entendre for anyone willing to infer it.

"This goes beyond biology," Jack said, growing more excited. "Beyond blood or no blood, bones or gelatinous cartilage. It's all in those speech vocoders." He turned his gaze toward the ceiling. "Computer, play Breen speech extract one four alpha." A harsh metallic screech filled the room. It made Bashir think of dueling drills and grinding gears. "Pause playback!" Pointing at the ceiling, Jack exclaimed to Bashir, "There! Did you hear that?"

"Hear what?"

Lauren replied, "That's not organic syntax, it's artificial. It's the kind of signal a universal translator creates when it parses one language into another."

Erdona seemed even more befuddled than Bashir. "So . . . the Breen language is computer generated? What, are they androids?"

Jack waved his hands furiously on either side of his head, and a snarl of mad frustration twisted his face. "No, no, no! You're totally *missing* it! We're saying there *is* no Breen language! Those vocoders aren't for translating or amplifying—they're for scrambling. They *hide* the speaker's true language!"

Sarina asked, "To what end?"

"It's how they hide," Patrick said. "From each other."

"I don't understand," Bashir said.

"He means," Lauren said, "that Breen society is based on misinformation and obfuscation, inside and out. They hide their true natures from each other as well as from outsiders."

"Wait," Sarina said. "You just did the same thing Jack did—you referred to the Breen in a plural manner, implying they have more than one nature."

Lauren cocked one eyebrow and rolled her head in a

dismissive gesture. "Well, of *course* they do. That's what we're saying. It's the whole *point.*"

Jack stepped in front of Lauren, figuratively stealing the spotlight, as he said, "Pay attention, this is important: there is *no such thing* as Breen physiology because *Breen* is not a species. *Breen* is an arbitrary social construct." He looked almost giddy in the wake of his revelation, as if he were expecting applause or perhaps the serenade of a celestial choir, and then his glee turned to a tantrum in the making when he was rewarded with naught but silence. "Didn't you hear me?"

"We heard you perfectly, Jack," Sarina said. "It's just taking us all a moment to catch up to you. I'm sure you understand."

"Of course," Jack said with a curt nod. "I forget sometimes how *slow* you all are compared to me." Lauren cleared her throat, and Jack rolled his eyes as he added with a bitter note of mild contrition, "To *us.*"

Commander Erdona walked over to the companel on the wall, studied its data, and asked, "How many species do we think the Breen comprise?"

"At least a dozen," Patrick said. "Maybe more."

"All appear to be essentially humanoid in form," Lauren said. "But even while wearing all that armor and speaking through those ridiculous vocoders, they exhibit subtle variations in their body language."

Jack was pacing again. "Preferred distance while speaking to a subordinate, reactions to the presence of superiors, the way they shift their weight while at rest—all dead giveaways. Plain as day, really. Can't believe you missed it, Julian."

"Indeed," Bashir deadpanned. "I'm mortified."

"Ignore him, Doctor," Lauren said. "Even though you spent weeks as a prisoner of the Breen, you wouldn't have seen any differences. The Breen segregate their starship crews and base personnel. We saw the differences only after we compared dozens of recordings made over a span of decades."

"The real giveaway is that not all Breen armor has working coolant packs," Jack said. "Ninety percent of them are just for show."

Sarina looked at Bashir and Erdona. "This is our way in," she said. "If the Breen use those suits and helmets to mask their identities even from one another, we can modify two sets of armor and practically walk right in."

"That's what I'm saying," Jack interjected. "They're *ripe* for infiltration."

"Modify the helmets' translators to turn your voices into Breen noise, and vice versa," Lauren said. "Even in a crowd of Breen, no one would know."

Patrick said, "Plus, the suits are made to mask the wearer's vital signs!"

Erdona nodded. "SI could even hide some gadgets in the armor—vacuum support, tools, compact rations, medicine, that kind of thing."

Bashir got up, stepped away from the others, and turned to look back at them. "Have you all lost your minds? You call yourselves 'the smartest people in the galaxy,' but the best plan you can come up with is to put on a pair of stolen Breen uniforms and try to walk in the front door of a secret military installation?"

Affecting an indignant pose, Jack replied, "Do you have a better idea?"

"A *much* better one," Bashir said, heading for the door. "I'm out."

A few minutes after Bashir had returned to his quarters, the door signal buzzed. He turned away from the view of stars outside his windows and said, "Come in."

The door slid open, and Sarina stepped inside. "That was a dramatic exit."

"Call it a bookend to your dramatic entrance," Bashir replied. She moved toward him, and Bashir stepped away from the windows and met her in the middle of the room. "This isn't quite how I'd imagined our reunion."

"So, you *have* imagined our reunion," Sarina said.

"At least a thousand times."

She grinned. "I can picture it. You'd come to the Corgal Institute to give some keynote speech, and between applause lines you'd sweep me off my feet. And I, having pined and pined for you, would swoon and fall into your arms."

"Now you're making fun of me."

Her grin widened. "Yes, I am." She leaned forward and hugged him. He wrapped his arms around her, grateful that she was really there. Resting her head against his, she said, "I missed you, too, Julian."

"That's nice to hear," he said, admiring the subtle fragrance of jasmine in her hair and basking in the gentle warmth of her body. "But is it true?"

She let go of him and stepped back to arm's length. "You don't believe me?"

"Let's just say that I know you had a lot of other things on your mind."

"My mind can handle a lot of things at once," she said, flashing a crooked smile. Turning serious, she continued. "I know that six years ago, I wasn't able to be the woman you wanted me to be. And I'm sorry for that."

Bashir shook his head. "You have nothing to be sorry for. I'm the one who should apologize to you. I was your doctor. No matter how strongly I was attracted to you, I should have restrained myself. I should have realized that you weren't ready for a romantic relationship. . . . I put my feelings ahead of your needs."

"Only for a moment." Sarina stepped forward and caressed his face. "I remember *every second* of our time together with perfect clarity, Julian. I've replayed those mo-ments over and over, and . . ." Her voice faltered, and her eyes glistened with tears. "And I realize how much it must have hurt you to let me go. I didn't understand then how deep your feelings were. I couldn't comprehend it. Now I do." Tears rolled from her eyes. "I'm sorry."

It was a struggle for Bashir to retain even a modicum of composure. Though his time with Sarina years earlier had been brief, it also had been the most intense connection he had ever felt with another person. No other woman with whom he had ever been involved—not Melora, not Leeta, not even Ezri—had been so effortlessly brilliant, so innately attuned to his way of seeing the world as Sarina was. As he had confided to Miles O'Brien during his first blush of attraction to Sarina, she was the woman whom Bashir had waited his entire life to find.

And there she stood, right in front of him, her blue eyes looking into his as he gently stroked the tears from her cheeks with the back of his hand.

"So," he said, pausing to collect his thoughts, "what now?"

"That's up to you. I'm going to Salavat with or without you, but I'd rather it be with you."

He let go of her and backed up a step. "You can't be serious! You'd actually risk your life on Jack's harebrained costume ploy?"

"First, it's not as bad a plan as you think it is. Second, there's more to it than just slipping on two sets of armor and ringing the Breen's doorbell." Leaning forward, she said with a conspiratorial gleam in her eyes, "Trust me."

He crossed his arms. "I'll need more to go on than *that*."

"Such as . . . ?"

"Such as why you're working with Starfleet Intelligence in the first place."

Sarina nodded. "I knew *that* would come up."

"Of course you did, you're a supergenius."

"So are *you*. And I know you've done intelligence work before. So why are you so against it? Did the Sindorin mission sour you?"

Bashir waved his hands. "I asked why *you* were working with Starfleet Intelligence. Last I heard, you'd been granted a research fellowship at the Corgal Institute."

She sighed. "That was *six* years ago, Julian. And the fact is, I exhausted my possibilities at Corgal about a year after that. They had neither the staff nor the facilities to support my work."

"What about the Daystrom Institute? Or the Vulcan Science Academy?"

"Both were interested in my work and had the infra-structure to pursue it," she said with a nod, "but neither offered me a position. Basically, I got the same reception from them as I did from the handful of people who showed any *romantic* interest in me during the last six years: curiosity at first, followed by fear when they found out that I had been genetically enhanced." She continued as she took a curving path around Bashir. "About four years ago, I was approached by an officer from Starfleet Intelligence. He—"

"What was his name?" interrupted Bashir, fearing that Sarina might have been approached by Section 31 agent Cole, who had tried to recruit Bashir.

"Darwyn Friel. Is that important?"

"No. Sorry. Go on."

Standing in front of the replicator, she said, "Chai, hot." As her drink materialized, she continued. "Friel made a good case for why people like us ought to join SI. Our enhanced skills and reflexes make us better suited to field operations than most other members of Starfleet—human or otherwise." She took her tea from the replicator and carried it toward the sofa. "We can go places and do things that others can't, and make better tactical decisions in less time."

"Just because we *can* do a thing—"

"—doesn't mean we *should* do a thing. I know that. But I believe we have an obligation to use our superior abilities in the manner that best serves our society *and* our principles. Tucked away in some lab or toiling on some space station, there's only so much you and I can do." She sat down on the sofa.

Bashir shook his head. "No, that's not true. I've made major contributions from here and aboard the *Defiant*. As a scientist, you could cure diseases, develop new energy sources, invent technologies never even dreamed of—"

"And as an SI operative, I might prevent a war that kills billions, stop a coup that would condemn a world to generations of political oppression, or help the Federation keep its rivals in check without resorting to bloodshed. As elite field agents, we have a chance to make a real difference in a time of crisis, for Starfleet *and* the Federation. Besides"—she sipped her tea—"I thought you'd want in on this mission for its exploration value alone. Think about it: we'd be getting an inside look at the Breen—not as prisoners but moving among them. As far as we know, they've *never* allowed outsiders to visit one of their planets, not like this. All they've ever permitted was a handful of diplomats and trade negotiators in a few isolation facilities on their ice cube of a capital."

It *was* tempting; Bashir admitted that much to himself. The promise of adventure certainly appealed to him. Coupled with the prospect of spending an extended period of time in close company with Sarina, it was all but irresistible.

He asked, "It would be a temporary assignment?"

"That's my understanding," Sarina said.

"And how, exactly, are we to infiltrate this hidden Breen shipyard?"

Sarina lifted one shoulder in a coy shrug. "If you want to find *that* out, you'll have to commit to the mission. Operational security. I'm sure you understand."

I'm going to regret this, Bashir thought.

"All right," he said, "I'm in. Let's go get fitted for some armor."

5

Thot Keer stood on a scaffold beneath the bow of his half-assembled fast-attack cruiser prototype and gazed into a firefall of sparks. Glowing motes rained down from a team of hull welders working high above him. The torrent cascaded over his shoulders and ricocheted off his armored chest and the snout of his helmet.

My masterpiece will need a name, Keer realized. *Something fitting.*

An electronically processed voice squawked inside his helmet. *"Command to Thot Keer. Do you read me, sir?"*

"Yes, Trez. What is it?"

"Our visiting dignitaries insist on meeting with you. I told them you were busy, but they were quite adamant."

Masking his annoyance with boredom, Keer asked, "Where are they now?"

"In your office, sir. Should I have them escorted back to their quarters?"

Keer began the slow walk back to the airlock. "Not necessary, Trez. Tell them I will be there momentarily. Keer out." As he crossed the catwalk, Keer was thankful for the magnetic pads in the soles of his boots. They kept his footing solid as he traversed the microgravity environment that surrounded his work in progress.

Massive floodlamps focused blinding light on the dart-like starship, the reflection from which illuminated the rough-hewn stone interior of the classified shipyard. The rocky walls were reddish-brown and studded with shimmering hunks of crystal and glittering patches of metallic ore. There had been times during Keer's years of service to the Confederacy when he had envied starship designers who worked in open space beneath a curtain of starlight; this was not one of those times. As claustrophobic as this wholly enclosed drydock had seemed to him when he'd first arrived, he had to admit that he also found it beautiful in a peculiar way that so far he had been unable to describe to anyone else.

At the end of the catwalk, he keyed his security code into the panel beside the airlock door, which slid open. As soon as he stepped inside, he felt the pull of normal gravity, and the magnets in his boots automatically disengaged. The outer door closed behind him, the chamber pressurized in seconds, and the inner door opened, permitting him ingress to the command center for the shipyard. It was a short walk to the lift, and a few minutes later he was standing in the doorway of his office, facing the two newest impediments to his success.

"Thank you for seeing us," said General Valnor, a Romulan who had come on behalf of the Tal Shiar—the intelligence apparatus of the Romulan Star Empire—to monitor Keer's progress. Valnor nodded in the direction of his companion, a high-ranking Gorn military officer known as an *ozuk*. "Ezgog and I trust you and your team are making swift progress on the prototype."

"Yes," said Thot Keer. "Thank you for your confidence." He hoped that adopting a dismissive attitude toward his unwelcome visitors might cut the meeting short, but his experience with Romulans kept him from being optimistic.

Valnor narrowed his eyes. Despite being middle-aged, he sported a full head of jet-black hair and an intense demeanor. "My people took a great risk to extract your field operative from the Federation's shipyard," he said. "We also honored your requests for his privacy while we ferried him here. I should think our actions would serve as evidence of our good faith in this joint endeavor."

"Your people have honored the terms of our agreement to the letter," said Keer. "So have mine. We provided an operative who could and did access the plans, and we are constructing the prototype, as agreed."

Ezgog's voice was as rough as his fangs were sharp. "But you have not been sharing your prototype's test data," said the Gorn archosaur.

"Because that was not part of our agreement," Keer replied. "You pledged to provide us with the requisite rare ores and finished components. We promised you six operational cruisers in return."

"The imperator insists that you share your research into the slipstream drive, so that we may begin training crews to operate it," Ezgog said.

"Unfortunate, then, that your imperator failed to specify such terms when the parameters of our partnership were set."

The Romulan stepped between Keer and the Gorn. "Friends, there is no need for us to argue—or to be bound by the unnecessarily narrow language of politicians. I'm certain that if we discuss this in a rational manner, we can arrive at a mutually beneficial arrangement that allows for greater cooperation."

"Our arrangement is already one of mutual benefit," Keer said. "If you wish to see it changed, that is a job for diplomats. I am an engineer and a soldier. Amending treaties is not part of my job description."

"Forgive me," Valnor said, "but you are being most unreasonable. My people and Ezgog's are both skilled shipwrights. If you would share the design schematics and your latest notes, our engineers could help you. It might shave days or even weeks off the schedule." Adding a touch of soft menace, he said, "Time is a factor for this project, in case you've forgotten."

Keer resented Valnor's insinuation that he and his crew were unequal to the task of finishing the prototype. "I have not forgotten," he said. "And I *am* on schedule—assuming we end this meeting now so I can return to work."

A low growl rolled behind Ezgog's razor-sharp grin, and Valnor's taut smile was no less threatening. "As you wish," the Romulan said. He followed the Gorn to the door. After Ezgog stepped outside, Valnor looked back at Keer. "For your sake, Keer, I hope you remain on schedule. Because if you do not, I assure you that I *will* amend the terms of our partnership."

Valnor walked away, and Keer pressed a button to close and lock the door, just in case the Romulan or his reptilian pet decided to come back. He blamed politics for this state of affairs. In the past, Keer knew, he would have been free to spend a few years developing slipstream technology without drawing the attention of the Confederacy's galactic neighbors. But now the Breen were yoked to the Romulans' paranoia, the Gorn's ambition, and the Tholians' xenophobia.

All I ever wanted to do was build great starships, Keer reflected. *If I had known it would mean dealing with politicians, I would have become a chef.*

6

"Energizing," said the *Defiant*'s transporter operator, whose name Bashir had not had time to learn during the ship's four-day, high-warp jaunt to the edge of Breen territory. With a sidelong glance at Sarina, Bashir muttered, "Here we go."

Seconds later they stood cocooned in luminous columns of whirling particles. The cramped transporter bay of the *Defiant* faded to white and, as if between synaptic pulses, gave way to a state-of-the-art transporter room aboard the *Vesta*-class slipstream starship *U.S.S. Aventine*. Three people stood facing the platform. Two were familiar to Bashir; he had never before met the third.

"Welcome aboard," Captain Ezri Dax said as Bashir and Sarina stepped off the platform. "It's good to see you again." To Sarina she added, "Both of you." She gestured toward her first officer, a tall human man with brown skin and a broad smile. "Miss Douglas, I don't think you've met my XO, Commander Sam Bowers." Bowers shook Sarina's hand. Nodding at a dark-haired Takaran woman with delicately scaled green skin and a lieutenant's rank insignia, she added, "This is Lieutenant Lonnoc Kedair, my chief of security. Lonnoc, this is Doctor Bashir of Deep Space 9 and

Sarina Douglas of Starfleet Intelligence." Kedair seemed content to acknowledge Bashir and Sarina with a half nod.

Everyone stood silent for a moment, and then Bashir noticed that Dax and Sarina seemed to be studying each other. Finally, Sarina said, "I trust you've been fully briefed by SI on our mission profile."

"Yes," Dax said. "We've coordinated with Special Ops to develop an insertion strategy that should help you avoid too many awkward questions once you're inside Breen space." Glancing at her officers, she added, "Sam and Lonnoc handled the particulars, so I'll let them walk you through it."

Bowers held up one hand to interrupt. "First things first, Captain. We should get Doctor Bashir and Miss Douglas—"

"Forgive me, Commander," Sarina cut in. "I know I'm not uniformed, but SI *has* commissioned me as an acting lieutenant for the duration of this assignment. Since I know from your service record that you can be a stickler for protocol, I thought you might want to know."

To Bashir's surprise, Bowers seemed put at ease rather than irked by Sarina's correction. "Ah," Bowers said. "Very good. Thank you, Lieutenant."

"You're welcome, sir."

"As I was saying," Bowers continued, "we should get Doctor Bashir and Lieutenant Douglas to their quarters, conduct an inventory to make certain all their gear has been transferred from the *Defiant*, and reconvene in conference room one at 1700 hours."

"Sounds like a plan," Kedair said. "With your permission, sir, I'll see to their equipment." Upon receiving a nod from Bowers, Kedair left.

The first officer said to Dax, "I can escort them to quarters if you—"

"That's okay," Dax said. "Report to the bridge and relieve Mister Helkara. I'd like a chance to catch up with Julian and Sarina."

"I understand," Bowers said. "I'll be on the bridge if you need me." To Bashir he added, "Good to see you again, Julian—it's been too long."

"Definitely," Bashir said. "Let's tip a few pints after the briefing."

"You're on." On his way out the door, Bowers smiled at Sarina. "Pleasure meeting you, Lieutenant."

"Likewise, sir," Sarina said. "See you at 1700."

Dax took Bashir and Sarina each by an arm and ushered them toward the door. "C'mon," she said, "let's get you two settled in, shall we?"

The trio's stroll through the *Aventine*'s sleek corridors was casual and brief, and Dax filled the time with small talk. She asked Julian about their old acquaintances and asked Sarina in general terms about her transition from scientific researcher to covert intelligence operative. It was all very polite and professional, which only fed Bashir's suspicion that Dax's veneer of politesse concealed a swift current of lingering bitterness from their failed romantic relationship several years earlier—a topic he had not yet broached with Sarina.

They arrived at a door, and Dax unlocked it. "Here's your stateroom," she said to Sarina. "Your bags will be along shortly. If you need anything, you're cleared to use the internal comms."

"Thank you, Captain," Sarina said, echoing Dax's formality. As she stepped past Dax and entered her quarters, she added, "See you at the briefing."

The door closed, and Dax took Bashir's arm. Tugging him back into motion, she led him to the next door on the opposite side of the passageway. "For you, our finest accommodations."

"As always, you spoil me."

Dax unlocked and opened the door. Bashir walked inside and looked around at the spacious suite. From the doorway, Dax said, "I trust you can find your way to conference room one by yourself?"

"If I get lost, I'm sure Sarina can show me the way."

"No doubt." She took a step back and mustered a feeble smile. "I should get back to the bridge. Let Sam know if you need anything."

Bashir nodded. "Will do." Dax walked away, and the door slid closed.

I suppose that could have been a lot more awkward, he thought. He turned slowly, acquainting himself with the layout and furnishings of the room and committing it all to memory in case he should be forced to navigate it in the dark. The door signal buzzed, and he turned toward the entrance. "Come."

The portal slid open. Sarina walked in, took a quick look around, and then asked, "So, why didn't you tell me you'd been involved with Dax?"

"How did you . . . ?"

"Are you kidding? You both got tense when you saw each other. And the way she put herself between us while we walked from the transporter room? A classic divide-and-conquer move. Did you two have a bad breakup?"

He rolled his eyes and let slip a rueful chuckle. "To say the least."

"You'll have to tell me all about it sometime." She moved past him and admired the warp-stretched starlight outside the sloped windows of his suite's main room. "Nice view." Throwing him a look of mock innocence over her shoulder, she added, "My quarters don't have any windows."

Bashir smiled at her transparent angling for an invitation. "Would you rather stay here with me? I have more than enough room."

She batted her eyelashes and said in a playful voice, "A real gentleman would offer to *trade* quarters."

"Perhaps," Bashir said, "but rank has its privileges."

"I see." She strolled toward the door. "I guess that includes sleeping alone."

"It doesn't *have* to . . ."

She smirked over her shoulder at him as she left. "It does now."

"Outfitting you two with modified Breen armor was the easy part," said Lieutenant Kedair. "The hard part was concocting cover identities for you."

Heads bobbed in silent acknowledgment around the conference room's long, oval table. Dax sat at the head, flanked by Bowers and Kedair. Bashir and Sarina sat together with their backs to the wide transparent-steel window. Opposite them sat the *Aventine*'s chief engineer, Lieutenant Mikaela Leishman, another of Bashir's old colleagues from Deep Space 9 and the *Defiant*.

Sam Bowers leaned forward and folded his hands on the table. "Working with Starfleet Special Ops, we've developed an insertion strategy around the *Guernik*, a Breen vessel captured a few years ago in the Ravanar system. We're going to use it as a stand-in for another Breen vessel, the *Sitkoskir*, which was destroyed in the Draconis Sector last month by the Klingons."

Kedair added, "Because both the *Guernik* and the *Sitkoskir* were privateers, we suspect their crew manifests might not have been as closely monitored as those aboard official Breen military vessels." She nodded at Sarina. "With help from your three peculiar friends, we think we've figured out how to spoof Breen identity cards, and we've encoded your armor disguises with chips that will identify you as members of the *Sitkoskir*'s crew."

Bashir cocked an eyebrow as he asked, "What if the Breen government figures out that our cover identities are forgeries?"

"In that case," Bowers said, "you'll both probably be killed as spies. But not until a Breen military vessel picks you up, which is our second challenge."

"This is where the *Guernik* comes in," Kedair said. With a look, she cued engineer Leishman to join in the briefing.

Activating a viewscreen on the bulkhead behind her, Leishman said, "When we reach the edge of Breen space, you'll be placed aboard the *Guernik*, which is waiting for us inside a sensor blind, along with an unmanned Orion corsair." Images of the two alien starships appeared on the viewscreen. Leishman continued as a computer-animated dogfight between the ships played out in slow motion. "Both have been fitted with extensive remote-control systems and programmed to play out a series of combat maneuvers. Though their weapons are at full power, none of the shots they fire will actually hit. Instead, we'll be triggering a number of controlled demolitions to simulate battle damage."

Bashir asked, "Why are their weapons at full power?"

Kedair replied, "To make sure the Breen cruiser patrolling that sector detects the battle. We want it to register as authentically as possible on their sensors."

"You two," Leishman said, resuming her presentation, "will ride out the mock battle inside one of the *Guernik*'s escape pods. Yours will be the first pod ejected. Once you've reached minimum safe distance, we'll self-destruct the *Guernik* and the corsair, making it look as if they've destroyed each other. The remaining pods from the Breen ship will be decoys caught in the blast radius, explaining why there are no other survivors from the ship."

Sarina asked, "What if some of those pods survive the blast? Or if the Breen patrol ship recovers the *Guernik*'s sensor logs?"

Bowers said, "The other pods are rigged to self-destruct, and we've programmed the *Guernik*'s logs with the mock battle. If the patrol ship recovers anything from the wreckage, it should corroborate their own sensor readings."

Kedair added, "We've outfitted your pod with a transponder recovered from the *Sitkoskir*, so you'll appear to be survivors of that ship. It ought to make your cover story a bit more plausible if you don't come from a ship that's already been missing for three years."

"So," Bashir said, "Lieutenant Douglas and I will wait inside the pod for a Breen patrol to pick us up. How long should we expect to be adrift before the patrol ship rescues the pod?"

"Approximately six to eight hours," Bowers said.

"And once we're aboard, how do we know they'll take us to Salavat?"

Anxious looks passed between Kedair and Bowers. Kedair frowned and said, "That part's a gamble. Salavat is the closest Breen colony to the coordinates we've picked for your mock battle, and it's also the home port of the patrol ship we're trying to lure. Unless the patrol ship has orders to proceed somewhere else, its most likely destination after picking you up should be Salavat."

Bashir shot a concerned look at Sarina, who maintained a perfect poker face. "For now, let's operate on the assumption that the patrol ship brings us to Salavat," he said. "What's our exit strategy?"

"You'll be given recall beacons," Bowers said.

Leishman explained, "High-power, superlow-frequency subspace burst transmitters. Like the ones used on cloaked Klingon starships. We'll be able to read it from distances of up to thirty light-years."

"The *Aventine* will be standing by on the Breen-Federation border," Dax said. "As soon as we get your recall signal, we'll hop in at slipstream velocity, beam you out, and make a run for it."

"We'd rather not spark a shooting war," Bowers added, "so try to keep a low profile and get someplace remote before you trigger the beacon."

Bashir replied, "We'll do our best. Captain, how soon after we call for extraction can we expect your arrival?"

Dax shrugged. "If everything goes according to plan? Five minutes."

"And if everything *doesn't* go according to plan?"

"Then possibly a bit longer."

"What if we lose the beacons?" asked Sarina. "Can we see the specs on the signal in case we need to find an alternative transmission method?"

"Sure," Leishman said. "It's all in your briefing packet."

"Final details," Kedair said. She picked up a padd from the table and tapped in commands, changing the display on the viewscreen behind Leishman to show cutaway schematics of Breen armor. "We've taken the Breen life-support gear out of your disguises and replaced them with human-tailored systems. The suits will protect you from vacuum, submersion, heat, and cold, and they should offer you some limited defense against projectile and directed-energy weapons."

Bashir said, "So it's a closed system?"

"Only when it needs to be," Leishman said. "Most of the time you'll breathe normally while it replenishes its air supply. But if the suit's sensors detect toxins within twenty meters, or if you get submersed or lose air pressure, it'll switch over automatically unless you override it."

The image on the screen enlarged the helmet design. "Inside your helmets are holographic heads-up displays," Kedair said. "These will provide you with our best available real-time translations of written Breen languages, superimposed over your field of vision. We've also scrounged up a fair amount of Typhon Pact currency, as well as some older Breen currency, in case you need it." Zooming back out to a full shot of the armor, Kedair added, "Airtight pockets will contain tools, compact medkits, and compressed rations. Myoelectric fibers will amplify your strength. Make sure you review your briefing packets before you deploy."

Bowers asked the room, "Any further questions?" No one spoke, and he nodded. "We rendezvous with the *Guernik* in twelve hours. Doctor, Lieutenant, good luck. Meeting adjourned. Crew dismissed."

As everyone left the conference room, Dax caught Bashir by his sleeve. He turned and faced her. She said, "Dinner. My quarters, 1900."

"See you there," Bashir said.

Dax let go of his sleeve, and Bashir followed the other officers out of the room. In the corridor, he caught up to Sarina, who he was certain had heard Dax's invitation but was saying nothing about it. Rather than pretend it hadn't happened, he asked under his breath, "What do you think? Am I having dinner with a friend or with my ex?"

"Both," Sarina said, "and also a captain, so mind your manners and make sure you wear a clean uniform."

The door to Captain Dax's quarters sighed open at Bashir's approach, and he entered to find Dax attired in civilian clothes and standing over a table set with a formal dinner service. Soft music, which reminded Bashir of Betazoid-influenced jazz, filtered down from overhead. All that was missing was the meal.

Looking up at Bashir, Dax said with a smile, "Right on time, as always."

"I do like to be punctual," he said, meandering toward her and the table. "I hope you'll forgive me for arriving empty-handed. Your replicators wouldn't let me whip up a bottle of wine or a bouquet of flowers."

Dax rolled her eyes. "That would be Sam's doing," she said. "I never knew he was such a stick-in-the-mud until I made him my XO."

"I guess that's just the way it is with people. Who they are depends a lot on *where* they are and whom they're with."

"True," said Dax, who seemed a bit more contemplative than usual. She gestured toward a chair. "Have a seat. I'll get our food."

Bashir pulled out a chair from the small dining table, which he noticed felt out of place in the main room of Dax's quarters, as if it had been a last-minute addition. He sat down. "I feel honored. It's not every day one is served by a captain."

She chastised him with a look over her shoulder while she stood at the replicator. "When I'm out of uniform, I'm just Ezri." Holding two plates of coq au vin with sides of sautéed asparagus, she joined Bashir at the table. "In fact," she continued, "I apologize for not telling you to wear civvies." She smiled. "Now I feel underdressed."

"Nonsense," Bashir said. "You look wonderful, as always."

"Kind of you to say." She walked back to the replicator. "What do you think would go best with this?"

"Something robust," Bashir said. "A Pinotage, or perhaps a Malbec."

"Pinotage it is," Dax said, keying her request into a manual interface beside the replicator. Moments later, an open bottle appeared with two glasses. She brought them back to the table and offered the bottle to Bashir. "Care to do the honors?"

"Certainly." He filled her glass and then his own as Dax settled into her chair and sampled her dinner. He put down the bottle. "It's been a long time since we were alone together like this."

Dax swallowed and replied, "True." She sipped her wine. "I'm sorry if this seems weird or kind of out of the blue, but it just seemed like you and I had so much unfinished business, and what with . . . you know . . ." Her voice trailed off.

"Me leaving on a possible suicide mission?"

She let out a short nervous laugh. "I guess, yeah." She collected herself. "I just thought it might be the right time for me to say some things I should've said a long time ago, before I left Deep Space 9."

"Things such as . . . ?"

"Such as, 'I'm sorry, Julian.' For starters." Looking down at her plate, she continued. "I know I didn't make things easy for you. I guess part of it was that I didn't understand how profound a change I was going through until I was deep in the middle of it. And by then it was too late for me to undo what I'd done."

"I know," Bashir said, "and I understand. It can't be easy to adjust to such a massive change in self-image, to take eight past lives and make them your own. To become more than the sum of your parts."

Recoiling slightly, Dax paraphrased Bashir's turn of phrase. "The *sum of my parts*? Where did *that* come from?"

He tried to downplay the statement with a one-shoulder shrug. "Just something Sarina said a long time ago, after she first met you."

Dax's mood darkened, and she became quiet. "Of course. I see."

"See what?"

"You still have a crush on Sarina, don't you?"

The question left Bashir feeling defensive. "I remain attracted to her and interested in her. My feelings for her go far beyond mere infatuation."

"So you're in love with her—and acting as her partner on a high-risk undercover intelligence mission? Don't you see a few potential *complications* with this scenario, Julian?"

He reined in a snort of laughter. "You're one to talk! Or have you forgotten how you attached yourself to my mission to Sindorin? And don't try to tell me that was different, because we both know that's a lie."

Dax threw her napkin on the table. "You want to know what's the same about the Sindorin mission and this one, Julian? You are. You've always loved playing spy, and I think this is more of the same."

"Oh, really?" Dropping his own napkin beside his plate, Bashir stood up. "You think I'm here to play a game? To satisfy some adolescent appetite for adventure?"

"No," Dax said as Bashir loomed over her. "I think you're here to impress Sarina. But just because you're genetically enhanced, that doesn't make you qualified to do intelligence work."

"Funny, that's what some people have said about your status as a joined Trill and your readiness for starship command. According to our critics, *neither* of us is qualified for our current duties." He walked to the door, stopped as it slid open in front of him, then turned back toward Dax. "You were offered a chance to expand your horizons, and you took it. I plan to do the same." As he made his exit, he added, "With or without your approval."

7

The first twelve blasts that rocked the escape pod left Bashir feeling ready to vomit. The second dozen slammed him and Sarina against each other and pinned them to the bulkheads. One salvo after another rumbled through the hull of the *Guernik* and shook the sealed, claustrophobic pod. "So much for Leishman's promise we wouldn't feel a thing," Bashir said between bouts of violent shaking and thunderous noise. "I'm starting to hate this plan."

Sarina seemed to be enjoying the rough ride. "It'll hurt less if you don't tense up. Just relax and pretend you're a spring." She lifted her arms and spread her legs in a fair impression of Leonardo da Vinci's famous "Vitruvian Man." Floating in the pod's zero-gravity environment, she used her fingertips and toes to keep herself bouncing lightly around the middle of the pod. Bashir emulated her pose and focused on staying limber.

A hull-rattling explosion quaked the ship, and Bashir followed Sarina's lead, bending at the knees to absorb the pod's momentum, springing back, and then bending at the elbows once he made contact with his hands. As the effects of the latest barrage faded, he and Sarina hovered once more in the pod's center, tenuously maintaining their equilibrium. He exhaled with relief.

"Nice trick," Bashir said.

"It makes for a lot fewer bruises, anyway." Looking around, Sarina seemed concerned. "I still wish Leishman had let me check her demolitions plan."

"Relax. Just because she's not genetically enhanced, that doesn't mean she's incompetent. I served with her on the *Defiant*. She's a great engineer."

Cacophonous noise roared around them. "For your sake and mine," Sarina said, "I hope she's as good as you say she is." She peeked inside her helmet and checked its built-in HUD. "Two more minutes of this before we eject."

"That's not so bad," Bashir said, even though he knew full well that under the right circumstances, two minutes could feel like—or even be—a lifetime.

A sudden jolt launched them upward, and Bashir heard a hollow clang as Sarina's head made impact against the pod's sealed airlock hatch. She winced, then squeezed her eyes shut as she pressed a hand to the top of her head.

Bashir reached out with one hand and steadied her. "Are you all right?"

She opened one eye and glared at him. "I'm starting to hate this plan."

Dax sat with her legs crossed in the *Aventine*'s command chair, presiding over the tense but generally quiet labors of her bridge crew. Commander Bowers was directing the mock battle that the crew was waging by remote control and monitoring on the main viewscreen. "Stand by for final salvos," he said.

At the helm, Lieutenant Tharp guided the movements

of the Breen privateer *Guernik* with his left hand and controlled the Orion corsair with his right. "Both ships are in position," he said. "Initiating final attack patterns in ten seconds." Watching him pilot both sides of a dogfight, Dax mused that this was the first time she had realized the youthful Bolian flight controller was ambidextrous.

Leishman sat at the engineering console, where she monitored and triggered the demolitions packages that were slowly tearing the remote-guided vessels to pieces. Her actions were being coordinated with those of Kedair, who was in charge of firing the two ships' weapons in a series of painstakingly choreographed near misses that would, they all hoped, deceive the sensors of a distant Breen patrol ship, which had already been detected en route at maximum warp.

"Charges twenty-one through thirty armed and ready," Leishman said.

"Weapons locked," Kedair replied.

Lieutenant Oliana Mirren, the *Aventine*'s senior operations officer, was generating a series of sensor shadows intended to create the illusion of full crews inside the two battling ships. It wasn't clear whether Breen sensors were accurate enough at long range to pick up such details, but Dax had insisted her crew not err by underestimating the intelligence or capabilities of the Breen military. Helping the lithe brunette calibrate her sensor illusions was the ship's senior science specialist and second officer, Lieutenant Commander Gruhn Helkara. "Reduce crew complement on the corsair by nine percent," the slim Zakdorn man said. "We need to simulate casualties in real time."

"Already on it," Mirren said. "Just waiting for the plasma fire Leishman triggered to spread past frame ten." She silenced a chirping alert on her console. "Fire confirmed in forward sections, reducing crew signatures."

Tharp declared, "Final attack runs are under way at full impulse."

"Look sharp," Bowers said. "Leishman, send the *Guernik*'s SOS now, and stand by to eject our agents' pod."

Kedair said, "Weapons firing in five seconds."

"Eject pod," Bowers said. "Launch the decoys."

"Pod's away," Leishman replied. "Decoys released."

"Firing," Kedair said.

"Detonate all charges," Bowers said.

A brilliant flash of light turned the main viewscreen white for a moment, and then the radiance faded into the dark curtain of stars.

Mirren worked at her console as she reported, "Both ships destroyed, sensor ghosts terminated. The pod is undamaged and clear of the blast radius."

"Good work, everyone," Dax said. "Secure from Yellow Alert and begin radio silence. Mister Tharp, set course for the edge of the Black Cluster. Mirren, keep our sensors on the escape pod. I want to know the moment the Breen pick it up." Swiveling her chair toward her chief of security, she continued, "Lonnoc, monitor all transmissions from the Breen patrol ship. If they don't buy our ruse, we'll need to extract our people on the fly."

"Aye, sir," Kedair said, "standing by for Plan B."

Bowers made a quick circuit of the bridge and passed out compliments to each member of the crew as he went.

When he finished, he stepped into place beside Dax's chair and asked in a confidential tone of voice, "And now . . . ?"

"Now we wait," Dax said, "and pray this doesn't go hideously wrong."

Bashir and Sarina spent the first few minutes after being ejected from the *Guernik* treating their various bruises and abrasions with the portable medkits included with their modified Breen armor. Then they passed the remainder of the first few hours savoring the blissful silence of being adrift in deep space.

For once resisting his urge to fill the quiet with idle chatter, Bashir was surprised when, apropos of nothing, Sarina asked him, "What did you and Dax fight about?" He considered lying but then decided there was no point denying the facts. Sarina possessed an uncanny ability to interpret others' body language and microexpressions, probably thanks in part to all the years she had spent in the company of the Jack Pack.

"She doesn't think I'm qualified to be here," he said.

"Do you agree with her?" Noting the pointed reaction her question provoked from Bashir, Sarina continued, "I ask only because it seems to be bothering you."

He sighed. "I don't care if she doubts my abilities. I know full well what I'm capable of. What upset me was that she questioned my motives."

"Because of me?" She read the answer in his glum expression. "Well, at least she's consistent. But I have to be honest with you, Julian. She might not be entirely wrong." Before he could protest, she continued, "What I mean is, I know that if anyone but me had asked you to do this mission, you probably would've said no. And that makes Dax think I'm taking advantage of you."

More worried than he had been before, he asked, "Are you?"

"Maybe a bit. But the part of this that she—and you—seem to be forgetting is that if I hadn't been the one chosen for this mission, SI probably wouldn't have asked you to be part of it. I had to *insist* on meeting with you." She shuffled around until they sat side by side, and she nestled herself under his arm. "I don't care if Dax thinks you're the wrong man for the job, because I know you're the right one. And whether you're here just for me or—"

"I'm not. In my life I have done many stupid things for many stupid reasons, but I've never risked my life just to impress a woman."

That drew an amused smile from Sarina. "That's good to know. Now I feel like I can count on you to do really stupid things for all the *right* reasons."

"Precisely." They laughed softly for a moment, and then the mirth tapered to an uneasy silence. A somber mood settled over Bashir. "I know this is the wrong time to be thinking about this, but this mission could very well be a one-way ticket for us. There's no telling how much or how little room for error we'll have once we're among the Breen. And if they find us—"

"Don't dwell on that," Sarina said. "The best thing you can do is relax your mind and pay attention to your senses and your instincts. Feel the rhythm of their culture and try to stay aware of who other people seem to be listening to, or pushing around, or ignoring." She grinned. "Treat it like a game of Simon Says."

He responded with a grim chortle and looked at Sarina. "In Simon Says, the losers don't get shot in the head."

"They do in the original Klingon version."

That time he laughed, even though he knew it was just gallows humor. "I'm glad you're able to keep a sense of humor about all this."

"Well, *someone* has to. Otherwise, this mission won't be any fun at all."

Bashir leaned his head back against the pod's bulkhead. "No fun? We'll be surrounded by some of the most notoriously paranoid aliens the Federation has ever met, while trying to locate and break into a hidden military base so we can destroy a prototype starship and sabotage the stolen data. And we get to do all that with no backup and no defined exit strategy. How could this not be fun?"

"Now you're getting into the spirit," Sarina said. "If you get depressed again, just remember that we have no idea if we'll be able to eat Breen food or use their waste-removal technologies, and that'll put a smile back on your face."

"I'm feeling better already." A comm unit built into the side of the pod screeched with metallic-sounding noise, turning Bashir's and Sarina's heads. Bashir said, "So soon? It's been less than four hours."

"Captain Dax warned us the patrol ship was closer than we'd expected. Apparently, they're also faster than we expected." She picked up her helmet and lowered it into place. "Time to suit up."

Bashir donned his helmet, and immediately the metallic noise from the comm speaker was rendered into a masculine voice speaking in uninflected English: *". . . is the Confederate frigate* Torzat. *We have received your distress signal. Respond and confirm your status."*

Sarina nudged Bashir. *"Go ahead. They're waiting, but not for long."* The secure comm inside his helmet rendered her voice as normal, but only because his and Sarina's suits had been programmed to let them communicate privately without fear of being overheard by the Breen.

He reached up and opened a reply channel. *"Torzat, this is Pod Nineteen of the privateer* Sitkoskir. *There are two of us aboard."* Checking the pod's status display, he added, "All systems stable, homing beacon coordinates verified."

"Acknowledged, Sitkoskir *Nineteen. Stand by for our tractor beam. We'll have you aboard in a few minutes.* Torzat *out."*

The channel went quiet. The pod lurched, and then a deep vibration resounded through its hull. Moments later, from outside, came the sounds of mechanical grapples seizing hold of the pod, and the dull scrape of the tiny emergency vehicle touching down on a hangar deck.

Bashir drew a deep breath and mentally prepared himself for the worst.

Sarina grabbed his knee and gave it a playful squeeze. *"Here's where the fun begins,"* she said, just before the pod's main hatch was opened from the outside.

8

Bashir stayed clear of the pod's hatchway as a Breen military officer helped Sarina out of the escape craft. She clambered over the side and into the helping hands of several other Breen personnel. As soon as the way was clear, Bashir followed her. The ship's crew assisted him as well, and he found himself standing beside Sarina in the hangar of a Breen warship, surrounded by half a dozen of its crew.

"I am Chot Jin, executive officer," said the one standing apart from the others and closest to Bashir and Sarina. Recalling the mission briefing, Bashir recognized *chot* as a senior military rank roughly equivalent to a commander. "You two are lucky to be alive. Identify yourselves."

Sarina replied, "Minh Sann, comm technician."

"Ket Rhun," Bashir said, "biologist."

He and Sarina had selected cover occupations that played to their strengths. Bashir didn't know enough about Breen physiologies to pose as a medical doctor, but he knew enough about xenobiology to pass himself off as a junior scientist.

Jin beckoned one of his men, who stepped forward and scanned Bashir and Sarina with a small handheld device.

"IDs confirmed," the crewman said to Jin. "No signs of injuries or radiation exposure. Cleared for boarding."

"Very well," Jin said. He looked at Sarina and Bashir. "We are near the end of our patrol cruise. If we drop you off at Salavat, will you be able to continue on your own from there?"

Sarina and Bashir glanced at each other—a futile gesture, since they were unable to exchange glances through their snout-shaped helmets. "Yes," Bashir said as he looked back at Jin.

"Do you have any objection to sharing quarters?"

"No," Bashir said.

"Good. We will notify you when it is time to debark. I estimate we will reach Salavat in just over ten hours." Jin nodded at another crewman. "Venz, put them in the spare quarters on deck six."

"Yes, sir." Venz stepped away from his shipmates and motioned for Bashir and Sarina to follow him. The pair walked behind the Breen crewman. As they crossed the hangar deck, Bashir clandestinely scouted his surroundings. As his eyes focused on various bulkheads and portals marked with Breen symbols, his helmet's HUD translated them into English words and Arabic numerals, providing him with a real-time tutorial in the Breen's written language.

Venz led Bashir and Sarina through a few turns in the ship's corridors and then into a turbolift that took them up two decks. The ship's passageways and conveyances were dimly lit and bereft of obvious design touches. Everything about the ship felt generic, as if it had been created with the intention of not expressing any kind of cultural identity. *That would mesh with the Jack Pack's hypothesis*, Bashir ruminated as he followed Venz. *If the Breen are trying to hide the fact that they're a multispecies society, their starships would have to be as free of cultural design artifacts as possible.* It seemed to Bashir like a sensible response to a peculiar cultural need, but in his opinion it also made for a boring aesthetic.

They stopped at a door. Venz unlocked it. "Stay inside unless you are summoned," he said as the door slid open. "Do not wander the ship without permission and an official escort."

"We understand," Bashir said. He entered the narrow, spartan quarters, and Sarina followed him.

"If you need anything, use the comm next to the door controls." Venz shut the door without waiting for Bashir or Sarina to reply.

The duo pivoted and surveyed their close quarters. It contained two bunks, one stacked above the other; a nook that seemed designed for waste removal and processing; a food slot; and a tiny cloister with a single seat and a short table. Bashir activated his private comm channel to Sarina. "Cozy," he quipped. "I'd hate to see the accommodations in steerage." He lifted his chin toward the cloister. "A mess hall for one?"

"I think it's a dining alcove," she said. *"Apparently, the old saying that 'a Breen always eats alone' wasn't so much a proverb as an observation."*

Bashir bent down to remove his boots. Sarina's hands snapped out and grabbed Bashir's arms. *"Don't,"* she said as she let go. *"Your suit is the only thing masking your true biosigns. If you take off any part of it, the ship's internal sensors might flag you as an intruder. We have to stay fully covered and use the secure comms until we're concealed somewhere on Salavat."*

"We can't even take off our *boots*?"

"Not unless you feel like going from this two-bunk sardine can to a Breen prison camp." She sat down on the lower bunk. *"On the bright side, our cover identities seemed to work, and so did our disguises. Once we reach Salavat, we should be in good shape for the next phase of the mission."*

"Assuming the next phase of the mission is a nap, I'd heartily agree."

She stretched out on her claimed bunk. *"Why not grab some shut-eye here? We do have ten hours to kill."*

"I can't sleep while wearing *this*," Bashir said. "My own breathing sounds downright asthmatic inside this helmet."

Sarina chuckled. *"Ah, the curse of genetically enhanced neural pathways. Having some sensory-integration issues?"*

"Very funny," Bashir said. "I just can't get comfortable wearing all this."

Folding her gloved hands behind her head, Sarina said, *"But you did take vacuum-survival training, right? You learned to sleep in an environment suit."*

"It's different when you're weightless," Bashir said.

"If you say so." Sarina stared at the underside of the bunk above hers while Bashir continued to tug at his armored disguise in an unsuccessful effort to make it less uncomfortable. He was experimenting with loosening the waistband when Sarina said, *"Hang on. I know why you can't relax*

and fall asleep, and it has nothing to do with that suit being too snug."

Halting his efforts at adjusting his disguise, he said, "Really. Tell me."

"Because you had to leave Kukalaka behind."

"That's ridiculous," Bashir said, overcompensating to mask his surprise that she was correct. Much as it pained him to admit it, he missed his stuffed bear, a keepsake of his childhood. He had owned the now-threadbare plush toy nearly all his life, and over the decades he had stitched or patched nearly every square centimeter of its fuzzy body. Most of the time it occupied a place of honor on the desk in his quarters, but sometimes after a rough day he still took comfort from clutching Kukalaka under one arm while he slept.

Despite his best effort to act aloof, he sighed. His helmet's vocoder translated the sound as a staticky crackling. "Okay, maybe it's a little true." His shoulders sagged as he looked at Sarina. "You think I'm crazy, don't you?"

"Crazy? No. Adorably broken, maybe—but not crazy."

"Oh, good," he said, climbing into his bunk. "Imagine my relief."

Dax looked up as Lieutenant Mirren reported, "The Breen ship has recovered the escape pod, Captain." The operations officer swiveled her chair to face Dax. "They've resumed their previous course and are en route to Salavat at warp six."

Looking over her shoulder at Kedair, Dax asked, "Has the Breen patrol ship made any long-range subspace transmissions since picking up the pod?"

Kedair shook her head. "No, sir. They seem to have resumed radio silence."

Bowers leaned toward Dax and said sotto voce, "That's a good sign."

"Maybe," Dax said. "At the very least, it's not an obviously *bad* sign, and for now that's good enough." Had the crew of the patrol ship recognized Bashir and Sarina as impostors, they likely would already have contacted their command base to request further orders or arrange for the transfer of their prisoners.

Dax thumbed a switch on her chair's armrest and activated her log recorder. "Captain's Log, supplemental. Have observed a skirmish between two unidentified vessels: a Breen privateer and an Orion corsair. Both ships appear to have been destroyed in the conflict. Only one escape pod, from the Breen vessel, appears to have weathered the battle. The pod was recovered inside Breen space by a Breen military patrol. No further data is available at this time." She switched off the recorder and uploaded the file to Kedair's console. "Lieutenant, compile today's logs and send a batch transmission back to Starfleet Command."

"Aye, sir," Kedair said, playing her part in their well-rehearsed mission plan. Signal traffic within the Federation was always being monitored by its rivals, just as, in return, the Federation used passive listening stations to eavesdrop on its interstellar neighbors. Suspecting that her log would be intercepted, Dax made it as innocuous as possible while ensuring that the admiralty and the Federation's leaders would understand its hidden meaning regarding their espionage mission.

After a few moments' work, Kedair looked up from her console. "Batch transmission away, Captain." Dax nodded in acknowledgment, and work on the bridge resumed its normal, quiet rhythm.

Only minutes later, however, a worried murmur from the ops station caught Dax's attention. Bowers was hovering over Mirren as the two of them argued in tense whispers. Curious, Dax got up and joined them. "What's up?"

Mirren deflected the question with a pointed glance at Bowers, who replied, "It looks like a sensor ghost, Captain. Probably just a gravitational-lensing effect caused by our proximity to the Black Cluster."

"That's one explanation," Dax said. She turned her gaze toward Mirren. "Something tells me you have a different hypothesis. Let's hear it."

Calling up a series of enhanced sensor graphs on her console, Mirren said, "I think it might be evidence of a cloaked ship shadowing our movements."

Dax asked, "Klingon or Romulan?"

"Based on the gravitational artifacts, I'd say Romulan, sir. Most likely a side effect of the artificial singularity a warbird would use as its main power source."

"Send your analysis to Kedair and Helkara," Dax said. "I want them to have a look at this before we start drawing conclusions." As Mirren sent her data to the security chief and sciences specialist, Dax walked back to confer with Kedair and Helkara, who had already begun their own analyses. "Thoughts?"

Kedair looked up. "It's not conclusive."

"But it's definitely not good," Helkara said, punctuating

his opinion with a frown. "Stellar phenomena can produce gravitational effects like these, and they can also emit these sorts of particles—but few stars do both. And the odds of a singularity as small as this one surviving in nature without evaporating or rapidly swelling in size are astronomical." He shook his head. "I'd lay odds that we've got a Romulan warbird on our tail."

Dax and Bowers traded worried looks. Returning to the command chair, Dax said, "Kedair, Helkara, review our sensor logs. Start with the most recent and work your way back. I need to know where and when we picked up this shadow."

Helkara and Kedair nodded and set themselves to the task. Bowers sidled over to Dax and muttered, "If that warbird saw us stage the fight between the privateer and the corsair, our agents' cover story is blown."

"In which case," Dax said, "we'll have to decide whether to cut and run or find a way to neutralize that warbird without starting a war."

Telegraphing his doubt with raised eyebrows, Bowers replied, "Easier said than done, sir. Warbirds don't usually fly solo. If we see one, there are probably two more waiting in the wings. And it's not that I don't have faith in our ship and crew, but I don't think even we would last long against three warbirds."

"Calm down, Sam," Dax said. "*Anticipate* problems, but don't feel like you need to *invent* them. Right now we have *one* warbird to cope with. Focus on that and worry about its possible wingmen later."

"One crisis at a time, eh?"

"Precisely. Now hop to it. I need those sensor analyses on the double."

"Aye, Captain." Bowers busied himself by looming alternately over the shoulders of Kedair or Helkara, keeping watch over their backward search through the ship's sensor archives. Minutes later, Bowers returned, flanked by Kedair and Helkara. "We've got something," Bowers said.

Helkara said, "The first sign of that 'sensor echo' occurred five minutes before the Breen patrol ship entered weapons range."

"We suspect that a Romulan warbird, or maybe something smaller, is acting as an advance scout for the Breen patrol ship," Kedair said. "They probably scan ahead and try to prevent their allies from blundering into an ambush."

Dax nodded. "Smart tactic. I'll have to remember that."

"The good news," Bowers said, "is that based on Kedair's projections of the cloaked ship's most likely flight path and velocity, it would've been too far away to detect our ruse during the staged battle."

"Good," Dax said. "Chalk that up as a lucky break, then." She walked toward the helm as she continued. "Unfortunately, now that we have a shadow, it'll probably stick with us. And that's going to be a problem." She looked over Tharp's shoulder at his console. "Lieutenant, call up a star chart that shows this and all adjacent sectors."

"Aye, sir," Tharp said as he obeyed Dax's command.

The starmap appeared on Tharp's console, and Dax studied it for a moment while a scheme took shape in her imagination. "Adjust our patrol route." She pointed at a destination along their path. "Skirt closer to the Koliba system. Put us within half a light-year of its outer comet ring by the day after tomorrow."

Tharp looked nervous as he glanced up at Dax. "Are you sure, sir? Koliba's a major port for the Breen fleet."

"I'm aware of that, Lieutenant. The Breen built a port there because the Black Cluster practically surrounds that system, making it almost impossible for us to spy on it without showing ourselves right on their doorstep."

Bowers asked, "You mean, like *we're* about to do?"

"Exactly as we're about to do," Dax said. "Lonnoc, tell Starfleet Command about this change to our flight plan. And be sure to use Encryption Protocol India Seven Kilo White."

Kedair wore a confused expression. "Are you sure, Captain? The latest update from Starfleet recommends using Victor One Delta Red."

"You have your orders, Lieutenant."

"Aye, Captain."

Dax settled back into her chair as her crew set to work on the course change. Bowers returned to her side, his persona of calm masking his dire concern. "You know that cruising that close to their port is like daring them to come and get us."

"I know," Dax said. "Now let's see how badly they *want* us."

9

President Bacco could tell that Councillor Bera chim Gleer of Tellar, in a rare display of respect for the office of the Federation presidency, was struggling not to raise his voice as he protested, "This is an unconscionable display of executive arrogance, and one unbecoming the president of the Federation!"

"I know you feel strongly about this, Councillor," Bacco said, "and it really does warm my heart to see you and Councillor T'Latrek on the same side of an issue for a change, but insulting me won't change my mind about vetoing this bill."

Bacco's statement was met by a surge of overlapping protests from three of the four members of the Federation Security Council who were gathered on the other side of her desk: Gleer, of course, as well as Kellerasana zh'Faila of Andor, and Tomorok of the Rigel Colonies. Sitting beside them in solidarity and also in silence was T'Latrek of Vulcan. The hubbub ended when T'Latrek lifted her hand and said, in a cool and measured tone, "If you veto our bill, Madam President, I will introduce a motion to overturn your veto."

"And I will second that motion," said zh'Faila.

"As will I," Gleer added.

Folding her hands atop her desk, Bacco leaned forward and smiled. "I would expect nothing less, Councillors. But before you cross the Rubicon on this issue, I think it's only fair to warn you—you don't have the votes to overturn my veto."

Tomorok replied, "Oh, but we do, Madam President, I assure you."

"Are you sure? I hope you're not counting on Betazed's vote." Though it would have been impolitic to admit it, Bacco took great satisfaction in watching her visitors' facial expressions shift in the span of a breath from righteous certitude to shocked dismay. "Yes, I had a *long* talk with Cort Enaren about the need to extend the Starfleet Operational Security Act for another ten years. I also had a *lovely* chat with Councillor Krim, so I wouldn't tally Bajor's vote in your column just yet, either. And I think you'll find that Councillor Beltane is a proponent of strong national defense—and of robust counterintelligence programs."

Gleer sprang to his feet. He shook with impotent fury. "This is a disgrace, Madam President, and an affront to an open society! If I have to, I will take to the floor of the council and fight this bill with my every breath!"

"I'm sure you will," Bacco said. "Heaven knows I've seen you do it before."

"This isn't over, Madam President! I'm—"

The Tellarite's tirade was cut short by the buzzing of Bacco's desk intercom, followed by the dry baritone of her elderly Vulcan assistant, Sivak. *"Forgive the interruption, Madam President, but Admiral Nechayev and Chief of Staff Piñiero need to meet with you on urgent business."*

Bless his heart and his pointy little ears, Bacco thought, grateful for any excuse to end her verbal wrestling match with her four visitors. "Very well, Sivak. Please show them in." She switched off the intercom and met the dubious stares of her guests. "Councillors, I apologize for this abrupt ending to our discussion, but I need to ask you all to step out, please."

The four councillors were silent as they walked to the door, which slid open ahead of them. Gleer was the last one out, and he paused in the doorway and looked back. As the Tellarite opened his mouth to speak, Bacco said, "I know, Gleer—this isn't over. Good luck with your veto. Now get out." He scowled and stormed away. A moment later, Esperanza Piñiero strode in, followed by Admiral Alynna Nechayev. The two women were like night and day—Piñiero an olive-skinned brunette and Nechayev a pale blonde.

Skipping any pleasantries, Nechayev said, "We've just heard from Captain Dax on the *Aventine*. Our two agents have been successfully inserted into Breen space and are on their way to Salavat. Unfortunately, we have a new situation developing with the Breen."

Bacco replied, "A *new* situation? For Pete's sake, Admiral, we haven't even finished dealing with the *current* situation." Collecting herself, she continued. "Sum it up for me: What's gone wrong this time?"

"Dax's ship is being tracked by a cloaked Romulan warbird that's working with the Breen military," Nechayev said. "If the *Aventine* can't shake off its Romulan shadow, it might prevent the extraction of our agents."

Piñiero asked, "How does Dax plan to deal with this?"

"She's taking her ship deeper into the sector between the Breen Confederacy and the Black Cluster," Nechayev said.

"Whoa," said Piñiero. "Isn't that a bit risky? That'll put her within less than a light-year of the Koliba system."

Nechayev nodded. "Yes, ma'am. If I understand Captain Dax's intentions, I'd say she's trying to goad the Typhon Pact into a fight. Personally, I doubt the Breen will cross their border, even with this kind of provocation—but if the Romulans are involved, that's another matter. And if it goes wrong, there'll be major political fallout." With a look of mild contrition, the admiral added, "Just thought you'd want a heads-up, Madam President."

"First the security bill, now this. You Starfleet types just *love* to make my job more difficult, don't you?"

"All part of the service, ma'am."

"I'm sure it is. Thank you, Admiral, dismissed. Esperanza, get Safranski in here, and make it fast. If Dax flushes our diplomatic ties with the Typhon Pact down the crapper, our secretary of the exterior deserves to know why."

10

The door of Bashir and Sarina's quarters unlocked with a soft clunk and slid open. Chot Jin leaned in and said, "We have reached Salavat. Follow me to your shuttle." He stepped back and pivoted just enough to block the corridor and make it clear in which direction he intended for them to walk.

Bashir clambered down from the top bunk. His back ached, and he winced at his own body odor, which had built up inside his suit. Breathing shallowly did nothing to make the stink less offensive, but it reduced the quantity of bad breath that he was adding to the problem with each exhalation.

Sarina slid her legs off her bunk. She seemed enviably limber and energetic to Bashir, whose limbs were stiff from his uncomfortable nap. He let her exit first, and then he followed, with Jin close behind, giving directions. Bashir's fascination with the fleeting glimpses he stole of the Breen ship's biomechanoid technology made it difficult for him to pay attention to Jin. Distracted by the alien ship's living technologies, Bashir missed a turn.

Jin's hand clamped down on the doctor's shoulder.

"That is a classified area," Jin said. "Do not deviate from

my directions again." He shoved Bashir back into motion behind Sarina. Forcing himself to tune out the ship's captivating details, Bashir focused on Jin's instructions and Sarina's back. A few turns later, they entered the ship's hangar bay, where, as promised, a shuttle awaited them.

Jin escorted them to the shuttle's open starboard hatch. "This vessel will take you to the main spaceport," he said. "There you will debark." He held up a fist in front of his chest and closed his open hand over it. "Night and silence protect you."

Hoping that the Jack Pack's analyses of Breen idioms and customs had been accurate, Bashir mimicked Jin's gesture and replied, "May darkness bring you fortune." He bowed slightly and waited. Jin reciprocated the gesture, turned, and walked away, the obligations of courtesy apparently fulfilled. Sarina stood at Bashir's shoulder, and they were quiet for a moment as they watched Jin leave. Then Bashir keyed his secure comm and said, "We should get on the shuttle."

"Right," Sarina replied, and they stepped through the hatchway. As soon as they were aboard, the pilot sealed the hatch and initiated the liftoff procedure. Bashir and Sarina were the craft's only passengers. Outside the cockpit's windshield, the dark gray hull of the hangar's interior gave way to black space speckled with stars. Sarina pretended to ignore Bashir as she said, *"Looks like someone wanted us off that ship in a hurry."*

"Good to know the Breen are as paranoid with one another as they are with outsiders," Bashir replied. "At least now we know it's not personal."

The journey to the planet's surface was brief. From orbit, Salavat looked like a gray ball of rock cloaked in lighter-gray ice. Closer to the surface, as the shuttle neared the spaceport, Bashir looked out across the desolate landscape and realized this world lived up to its first impression. Bleak plains of broken stone were blanketed with ice and slush and scoured by curtains of wind-driven rain. "For a colony world," Bashir said to Sarina, "it doesn't show much in the way of development." He nodded at the speck of a spaceport growing larger outside the cockpit's windshield. "If that's the center of town, don't blink or you'll miss it."

They suspended their conversation as the shuttle descended to a landing pad. It touched down with barely any sensation of contact, and the starboard hatch lifted open, admitting a spray of rain on a howling gale. The pilot looked back at Bashir and Sarina and said, "Get out." They scrambled through the hatchway and out into the storm. Trudging against a stiff and shrill headwind, Bashir noted that the spaceport amounted to little more than a few large, ramshackle buildings ringed by landing pads. A few other shuttlecraft were arriving, and several more stood on different pads, awaiting passengers.

Bashir nudged Sarina's arm and nodded at a handful of what looked like Breen civilians heading inside the spaceport. They wore helmets similar to those used by the Breen military and its privateers, but instead of armor they were attired in drab, utilitarian clothes, boots, and gloves. Every square centimeter of their bodies was covered. "If we follow them, they might lead us to the colony," he said.

"It's worth a try."

They trailed the quartet of civilians into a high-ceilinged facility that was alive with echoing footsteps and an oppressive droning caused by reverberations from the Breen's vocoders. A few armed Breen soldiers stood watch at various points on different levels of the facility. The place felt glumly efficient. Unarmed but uniformed Breen personnel ushered civilians through security checkpoints, verified identichips, and scanned both incoming and outgoing cargo and luggage.

Unable to see past the dense knot of people ahead of them at the security checkpoint, Bashir asked Sarina, "Can you see where they're going once they reach the other side?"

"No. But I don't see an exit on the other side, do you?"

"No," Bashir said.

He wondered if perhaps he and Sarina had taken a wrong turn. Though he hadn't thought of himself and Sarina as being in line for the checkpoint, when he tried to turn around, there were other Breen queuing up behind them.

From a walkway overhead, a Breen soldier pointed at Bashir and barked, "Keep moving forward!"

Sarina grabbed Bashir's arm and pulled him with her toward the checkpoint, a narrow passage flanked by Breen guards. *"Now we find out how convincing our identichips are."*

Their turn at the checkpoint was over in a moment. One guard passed a scanning device in front of Bashir and Sarina, and the other studied the readout on a small display. The forged identity profiles appeared on the second guard's screen, and he gave them a cursory once-over before waving Sarina and Bashir through the scanning station to a downward-sloped moving walkway that carried them away in a blur.

Sarina looked back. *"All right. We made it through."*

"Great," Bashir said, "but where are we going?"

Seconds later, he had an answer. The walkway leveled out and disgorged its passengers onto a broad thoroughfare—high above a chasm within which had been constructed a massive underground city. The subterranean metropolis was crisscrossed with bridges, walkways, cables, lights, and pipes, and it bustled with throngs of pedestrians and tiny antigrav-propelled 'bots that zipped to and fro. The air was heavy with food scents, hazy with smoke, buzzing with vocoder noise, and alive with music. Looking up, Bashir saw a dome of rough-hewn stone festooned with hanging lights, antennas, cabling, and loudspeakers that filled the air with booming announcements in a stentorian voice of authority.

"Well," he said, "now we know why Breen colonies always look so sparse. They're ninety-nine percent *underground.*"

Every twist and turn Bashir and Sarina explored led them deeper into the Breen's hidden metropolis, whose lower levels were packed with civilians, all garbed in simple garments of neutral colors—grays and beiges, with an occasional hint of dark brown—and snout-shaped masks that left Bashir wondering how the Breen were able to tell one another apart.

Most surprising to him, however, was the sultry

climate of the city's deepest environs. Heat surged up from
the pitch-black abyss that yawned in the center of the city,
and the streets were hot and teeming with activity, thick
with smoky haze and savory aromas. Atonal music wafted
from distant chambers and mixed with the squawking of
vocoders. A gaggle of short humanoids whose slightness
of frame led Bashir to speculate they might be adolescents
flowed around him and Sarina. As they passed, Bashir
noted that several of them were carrying swaddled infants
in pouches slung across their chests or balanced on their
hips. He looked more closely at one of the infants, hoping to glimpse an unmasked Breen face, but saw only a
smaller, less detailed version of the Breen mask staring
back at him.

Sarina beckoned Bashir with a sideways nod toward a
distant intersection. He followed her.

Though he was grateful for the information provided
by his mask's HUD, its constant intrusions into his field
of vision had begun to annoy him. Many of its notes
seemed superfluous to him, so he used his suit's internal
voice-command module to turn off certain notifications
and override the translation of selected symbols. Only
after he had done so did he realize why he had needed
to—he was starting to assimilate rudimentary elements of
the Breen language.

More elusive than the Breen's language were the tiny
nonverbal cues that seemed to serve as the basis for communication between individuals. Because of their ubiquitous use of masks, the Breen could not take their cues from
facial microexpressions, as did so many humanoid species

throughout local space. Instead, they appeared to have incorporated a subtle and complex form of sign language to augment their verbal interactions.

Observing exchanges of currency and goods, Bashir noted that body language also seemed to play a role in Breen discourse. Distance, angle, and even the specific posture of the head, torso, limbs, and extremities could convey meanings, telegraph emotional states, or be used to jockey for social dominance. It troubled Bashir to think that a nod at the wrong time or a nervous fidget could easily lead to him and Sarina being exposed and killed.

They neared a busy intersection beside a broad walkway that bridged the chasm. In the center of the crossroads stood a cluster of tall, four-sided obelisks made of black granite. The faces of each obelisk sported a computer interface. Sarina led Bashir through the crowd to the nearest open computer panel.

"*It's a public-information kiosk,*" she said, continuing to use their private comm channel. Breen symbols raced across the screen from right to left. "*It's moving too quickly for my HUD to translate.*"

Bashir huddled in close against her so that he could also see the screen. The flood of data crossing the display was a green blur. "What are you looking for?"

"*Lodging. We need to get off the street and set up a base.*"

She poked at the computer while Bashir watched and resisted the urge to shake his head. "Incredible. Here we are, hoping to infiltrate a Breen military base, and we don't even know how to book a *hotel room*."

Exasperation gave an edge to Sarina's voice. "*Think you*

can do better, Julian? Feel like taking over and showing me how it's done?"

"Is that a challenge? Are you saying you don't think I'm up to the task?"

"Do you answer every question with another question?"

"Move over." Bashir shouldered Sarina half a step left so he could access the touchscreen. He spent several embarrassing seconds trying and failing to keep up with and control the torrent of alien symbols speeding past. Finally, even though Bashir couldn't see Sarina's face, the weight of her stare became too much for him to take and he stepped aside. "Okay, I give up."

Leading him away from the kiosk, she said, *"It might be a few more days before the heuristic learning circuits in our HUDs can keep up with that thing."*

"What do we do for shelter until then?" He looked up at the walls of the city, which were honeycombed with dwellings aglow with amber light. "Knock on random doors and hope for the kindness of alien strangers?"

"Hardly. Maintaining a city this size underground requires infrastructure for power and ventilation. If we can find a way inside some of it, we can buy ourselves some time." She leaned against the bridge's railing and looked out and down. *"There, between levels. See those fans? I bet those are part of an air-filtering system. I bet we'll find maintenance hatches down some of those empty alleys."*

Nodding at a passing drone that flew past and dived into the darkness, Bashir asked, "What if those hatches are monitored? Or secured inside official buildings? I doubt a people as paranoid as the Breen would leave vital areas of their civil infrastructure accessible to the public."

Sarina started walking. When Bashir caught up to her, she asked, *"Would you say the Cardassians were paranoid in the years before the Dominion War?"*

"To say the least," Bashir said.

"But even they didn't take extraordinary measures to secure their old water-supply and waste-removal infrastructure, did they?"

"That's because they didn't need them after the introduction of replicators and matter reclamators," Bashir said. "Once they shut down the old plumbing, it was sealed off and forgotten. But the Breen's air system is open and active."

"But do you think a lot of Breen civilians are out to sabotage one of the key systems that keep them alive?"

"How would I know? I just got here." He eyed the spinning blades of a giant fan that filled the mouth of a tunnel dozens of meters below the bridge. "If I were the Breen, I'd be more worried about defending that system from outside attack."

Still walking at a brisk pace, Sarina replied, *"Let's assume you're right. Maybe the air system isn't the best place to hide. It's not our only option."* She led him into a narrow passage that had been excavated from the bedrock.

Sidestepping in pursuit, Bashir asked, "What's down here?"

Sarina pointed up. *"Something connected to those cables."*

Bashir looked up and saw that several groups of wires converged into the sliver of an alleyway. When he and Sarina reached its dead end, she turned on her palm beacon and used its beam to trace a path of ladderlike grooves cut into the rear wall. At its apex was a deep alcove containing a bulky piece of machinery to which all the cables were linked. Beside the device was a metal door.

"Ladies first." Bashir gestured at the ladder.

Sarina stepped aside. *"Age before beauty."*

It was an easy climb, but the alcove at the top was barely large enough for them both to stand in at the same time. Bashir pinned his arms at his sides to make room for Sarina while she used some of her SI-provided tools to disable the door's alarm and then pick its lock, which released with a hollow clack. To Bashir's relief, the door swung inward and into a long, gently curving passageway lit by widely set dim panels on its rocky ceiling. Its walls were lined with cables, power lines, and small components. It stretched away for nearly a hundred meters, past several intersections, before vanishing beyond its curve.

Bashir moved past Sarina and stopped a few meters inside. She stepped in, shut the door behind her, and used her tools to relock it. Tucking the tiny device back into its pocket on her disguise, she said, *"Don't worry about the internal sensors. They're tied to the alarms, which I deactivated."* She removed her helmet, and her sweat-soaked blond hair tumbled in a mess about her face as she sighed with relief and smiled. "Welcome to our new home away from home."

11

The image of space looked empty and serene as warp-distorted starlight stretched away from the center of the *Aventine*'s main viewscreen, but Commander Samaritan Bowers remained wary. He was reviewing a steady stream of tactical updates from Lieutenant Kedair and sensor analyses from Lieutenant Commander Helkara, who both were nearing the end of their second full shift on bridge duty.

Fast-moving sensor contacts that had originated in the Koliba system were on intercept courses for the *Aventine* as it cruised along the edge of Breen territory. Bowers counted seven Breen ships, including two heavy attack cruisers. Their combined firepower would be more than enough to destroy the *Aventine*, despite the improvements made to its shields during the previous year's Borg invasion.

Ideally, we'd outrun them, Bowers thought. Under normal circumstances, with slipstream drive, the *Aventine* could easily outpace the Breen ships. Unfortunately, the *Aventine*'s current course left it hemmed in on three sides by the Black Cluster, a region of collapsed protostars that was notorious for swallowing up starships that dared to venture too close to its brutal gravitational effects, and flanked by the approaching Breen battle group.

That left the *Aventine* with two ways to go: forward or backward.

Bowers eyed the tactical map beside the command chair, which showed Kedair's report about the Breen fleet, and then glanced at the navigational chart on the other side of the center chair. That display highlighted Helkara's enhanced analysis of the ship's latest sensor sweeps, all of which suggested that the Breen ships were not the only threat in the sector but merely the most obvious one.

A young Vulcan ensign holding a tray bearing a mug of hot coffee stepped up from behind Bowers, stopped beside the command chair, and said, "Sir."

"Thank you, Yeoman." Bowers lifted the mug from the tray. The ensign nodded and stepped away. Bowers sipped his sweetened coffee and wondered what advice he might give to the captain that could persuade her to move the ship clear of what he perceived to be an increasingly dangerous area.

At the rate we're going, they'll have us surrounded by the time we reach Cetareth, he realized. *Even if the Breen stay on their side of the border, it would take only a few Romulan warbirds to put us on ice for the rest of this op—and that'll leave no one to extract Bashir and Douglas.*

A voice filtered down from the ship's internal comm and interrupted Bowers's dark musings. *"Dax to Commander Bowers."*

Sitting up straighter, Bowers replied, "Go ahead, Captain."

"I want you to make a course correction."

He faced the navigational chart. "Ready, sir."

"*Drop us out of warp, bring us hard about, and retrace our path.*"

The order gave Bowers pause, and he exchanged perplexed glances with Kedair, Helkara, and beta shift flight control officer Ensign Erin Constantino. Though he was not in the habit of making his commanding officer repeat her orders, he decided that this directive needed to be verified. "Excuse me, Captain, but could you confirm that you wish us to double back?"

"*That's correct. And increase speed to warp nine. I want to see the Breen try to keep up, and I really want to see what those sensor ghosts on our aft quarter do when we start moving directly toward them.*"

The audacity of Dax's tactics made Bowers smile. "Aye, sir. Initiating course correction." He nodded at Constantino, who began executing the order.

"*One more thing,*" Dax said. "*I've sent Lieutenant Kandel to relieve you, so go get some rack time, and tell Kedair and Helkara to do the same. I think we're in for a rough day tomorrow, and I want you all rested.*"

"Acknowledged," Bowers said, and then he raised his voice to declare, "Alpha shift personnel, to your racks. Captain's orders."

"*See you in the morning,*" the captain said. "*Dax out.*"

12

Hiding in the maintenance tunnels and crawlspaces of the Breen's underground city had not been what Bashir would call an ideal situation, but it had served its purpose. He and Sarina had been able to shed their disguises for a few hours, clean themselves up a bit using personal hygiene kits hidden beneath the thigh guards of their lightweight polymer armor, and enjoy some unencumbered sleep.

After a few hours' rest, Sarina roused Bashir. "Time to get back to work," she said, handing him his helmet.

They ate a quick breakfast of Starfleet dry rations, donned their suits and masks, and set off to explore the city's infrastructure. Along the way, Sarina paused to install a signal tap in the city's information network. "Never know when this'll come in handy," she said as she spliced some cables into a small wireless transceiver. "If you need to patch in, it's transmitting an encrypted signal to our helmets on channel nine forty-one."

"Got it," Bashir said, making a mental note.

The path out of the maintenance tunnels led them into what appeared to be the subbasement of an industrial facility. Mechanical noise and chemical fumes filled the air. "Look for an exit," Sarina said.

Bashir pivoted slowly while straining to pierce the darkness. "There." He pointed at a familiar ideogram stenciled on a wall beside an open staircase. "I'm fairly certain that's the symbol for 'exit.'" He took point and guided Sarina through the maze of oversized machines. To his great relief, the sublevel seemed to be unoccupied, and they took the steps two at a time in hurried bounds.

At the top, Sarina halted him with a tap on his shoulder. "Let me check the door for alarms. We've been lucky so far, but we can't get sloppy."

He stepped aside and let her pass. She scanned the door with a small sensor and then inspected its edges and frame with her gloved fingertips. "It's clear." She unlocked it and cracked it open to see what lay on the other side.

Street noise and golden light seeped in through the sliver-thin gap between the door and its jamb. Fleeting shadows hinted at brisk pedestrian traffic outside. Sarina listened, and at the first sign of a lull she pushed the door open just enough to slip through. "C'mon," she said. Bashir darted out and looked around to see if they'd been observed. The few Breen civilians passing by did not seem to have noticed Bashir and Sarina's suspect emergence from a door marked with a symbol that meant "restricted area." Sarina closed and locked the door. "Let's get out of here," she said.

Purposeful strides and a minimum of conversation helped them blend back into the crowd of Breen pedestrians, which carried them away like a strong tide. They stayed close to each other, and Bashir let Sarina decide which paths to take at intersections. After they had walked for what felt like at least an hour, she stopped and ducked into a narrow alley beside a wide, brightly lit boulevard packed with retail merchants, food vendors, and what Bashir surmised were office complexes. Most of the stores were fronted by huge vid screens that displayed a steady torrent of product images and text messages accompanied by several competing streams of overamplified Breen machine-speak.

"This is just what we need," Sarina said as Bashir stole into the shadows behind her. "A variety of businesses and civilians who look like they hail from more than one social stratum. It's an anthropological gold mine."

"I don't understand," Bashir said. "What are we supposed to do here?"

"Just watch and listen. Use your helmet's sensors to eavesdrop on conversations, and pay attention to the speakers' body language, like we talked about last night. This street is about to become our master class."

"I thought we were supposed to be looking for the secret shipyard."

"If we don't learn the finer points of the Breen's language and culture, we'll be lucky to find our way back to the surface, never mind the shipyard." Turning her attention to the comings and goings of the street, she added, "We need to learn how to walk before we can run, Julian."

To Bashir, lurking and observing felt like a waste of time. He wanted to be in motion, in action, but when he tried to imagine where he would go and what he would do when he got there, he understood that Sarina was right. Their helmets' translators provided only a rudimentary grasp of the Breen language and no context at all for its cultural quirks. Spending some time spying on the locals would give the heuristic circuits in Bashir's and Sarina's suits more raw data, which would, in theory, lead to more accurate translations of verbal and printed communications.

None of which made eavesdropping on mundane interactions the least bit more interesting. Customers haggled with vendors about retail merchandise or asked questions about raw food for sale. Random conversations bled together: complaints about work schedules, insufferable supervisors, or slipping deadlines; small talk about ill-behaved children, ungrateful spouses, or music; people asking for directions, requesting transportation, or offering unsolicited advice.

Then a snippet of one-sided conversation caught Bashir's attention, though he was unable to tell which person in the crowd was speaking: *"I'd like to report unusual activity. Two individuals on Level Twenty-eight, Tyzil Sector . . . Merchants Circle, the nine hundred block. . . . They've been standing in an alley for a few hours. I don't know what they're doing, but they're acting strangely."*

Bashir nudged Sarina. "Someone's reporting us to the authorities."

"I hear them," Sarina said. "We should go." They merged back into the fast-moving crowd.

Somewhere far away but rapidly getting closer, a siren wailed.

On any world and in any language, Bashir knew that to be a bad sound.

So did Sarina, because she started running.

They bladed through dense knots of people blocking their way. More sirens wailed from other directions, ahead of them and from side streets.

Crowds stopped, congesting the streets and rendering Bashir and Sarina conspicuous by virtue of the fact that they were running. None of the civilians made any effort to stop them, but their passive obstruction of the streets was a major hindrance to the duo's escape.

A swarm of silvery antigrav drones converged a few blocks ahead of Bashir and Sarina, regrouped into a wedge formation, and started moving toward them.

Sarina stumbled to a halt, and Bashir skidded to a stop at her side.

"We have to get off the street," Bashir said.

"But we can't lead them to our hiding place."

From behind them, an amplified voice barked, *"Stop and submit!"*

Looking around for an escape, Bashir saw stairs beneath a sign that he now recognized as a marker for the city's mass-transit system. "This way!" Running, he elbowed one civilian out of his way and hip-checked another clear of his path.

Disruptor bolts ripped apart the sign above Bashir's head as he and Sarina sprinted down the stairs. Civilians scattered in a panic as several more shots screamed past the staircase. Bashir and Sarina dashed across the platform and through a massive scanning arch as civilians scrambled out of their path or dropped to the ground. The percussion of running footsteps echoed off stone walls and ceilings.

Warning alarms buzzed, low and angry, reverberating in the transit station and nearly drowning out the hum of an arriving maglev train.

Conditioned by years of living aboard a Starfleet-run space station, Bashir expected the doors of the train to open ahead of him as soon as it stopped. Instead, he collided with the train's closed portal and fell backward. In the fraction of a second between his head hitting the train door and his ass hitting the ground, a disruptor blast streaked by him and disintegrated half the door.

Sarina dropped to one knee, drew her own disruptor, and returned fire. Over the screech of weapons, she shouted at Bashir, "Get inside the train!"

He scrambled to his feet, leaped over the remaining half of the door, and somersaulted to his feet inside the train. Pivoting about-face, he drew his disruptor, shot out one of the train's windows, and laid down suppressive fire at their Breen pursuers. "Come on!" he called to Sarina. "I'll cover you!"

She snapped off a few more shots, then turned, ran to the half door, and hurdled over it. Breen civilians inside the train cowered and shrank from Bashir and Sarina. "We have to move," Sarina said. "Head for the driver's cab, and stay down." She ducked and hurried toward the front of the train, shooting out more windows as she laid down suppressing fire on the run.

Disruptor pulses peppered the train, showering the duo with sparks and shrapnel as ricochets slammed into the civilians around them. Bashir blasted apart the lock on the door leading to the first car of the train and pushed the door open. As he lurched into the next car, a flurry of energy blasts tore through the metal skin of the train, and a stray shot cut a searing wound through the top of his thigh.

He howled in pain but forced himself to stagger onward toward the driver's cab. Sarina rushed into the lead car and caught up to him. "Are you all right?"

"No," Bashir snapped. "Do what you have to do, I'll cover you."

While Bashir fired his disruptor in the general direction of their pursuers, Sarina charged to the driver's cab, shot off its lock, and yanked open the door. "Out," she said, pulling the driver by the front of his uniform and tossing him aside. To Bashir she added, "Hang on, this might get rough."

Gritting his teeth and wincing at the burning agony in his leg, Bashir replied, "I think that ship has sailed."

All of the train's doors opened, and over its PA system Sarina announced, "Attention, passengers: Everyone out—now!"

The civilians raced off the train and straight into the law enforcement personnel chasing Sarina and Bashir. As the last passenger scrambled out of the front car, Bashir noticed the driver still cowering on the floor. Bashir waved his disruptor at the driver. "You, too. Go."

"Thank you," the driver said and then fled at a full run.

"Here we go," Sarina said, closing the train's doors. The train lurched forward and accelerated with frightening speed. In seconds the whine of disruptor shots faded away, leaving only the quiet hum of the train's magnetic-levitation generators. Then Sarina leaned out of the driver's cab and said to Bashir, "Hit the deck and grab something heavy."

He dropped to the floor, wrapped his arms around a seat rail, and prepared for the worst. The train slammed to a stop as if it had struck a solid barrier, and the sudden deceleration hurled Bashir against the car's forward wall. All he could hear was the groaning of stressed metal as the train's emergency brakes strained to absorb its momentum. Then the bone-crushing pressure of the high-speed stop abated, and Bashir almost relaxed—until another pang of red-hot pain in his leg reminded him that he'd been shot.

Sarina stumbled out of the driver's cab and kneeled at Bashir's side. She stole a quick look at his wound and asked, "Can you walk?"

"Not without help," he said. He started opening a pouch on his suit to retrieve his medkit. "It'll take me ten minutes to fix it."

She thrust her hands into his armpits and lifted him to his feet. "We don't have ten minutes right now." She reached inside the cab and pressed a button that opened the train's doors. "We need to get off this train and into the city's transportation system. If it's like most cities' transit networks, it probably has old tunnels that are no longer in use."

He let Sarina help him out of the train and down to the tracks. Once they were on foot, it was easy to see that her prediction had been correct: there were many levels of tunnels and several lines running parallel to one another. A few had obviously fallen out of use and been allowed to sink into darkness and disrepair. Within a few minutes of abandoning the train, they had retreated deep into a long-forgotten corner of the Breen city.

Limping along with his arm draped over Sarina's shoulders for support, Bashir asked, "What if they find traces of my DNA on the train?"

"They won't."

"How can you be sure?"

Somewhere above and behind them, a powerful explosion quaked the bedrock and rained dust on their heads.

Sarina smiled. "Let's just say I took a few precautions."

13

Thot Keer knew that protocol and cultural taboos required him to accept the rebukes of his superior with quiet dignity, but the longer he worked on the slipstream project, the more fervently he harbored a secret wish to reach across his master's encrypted subspace channel and choke him to death.

"I have the utmost respect for your work on this assignment," said Thot Naaz, the director of the Breen Militia's secretive Special Research Division. *"However, the domo is demanding results sooner than expected."*

In his youth, Keer might have brashly asked, "Why?" Now he was old enough and cynical enough to guess at the truth: the Romulans and the Gorn were applying political and economic pressure in order to co-opt Keer's work. He was disgusted by the notion that his people's elected leader would yield so easily to the will of foreign powers, despite the Confederacy's vast arsenal and numerous technological advantages.

Choosing his words with caution, Keer said, "I have no wish to disappoint the domo or our allies, but the prototype is not ready for testing."

"So you said in your last report. Why, then, are you refusing aid freely offered by the Romulans and the Gorn?"

"Because their assistance comes at too high a price," Keer said. "Our security as a nation hinges now on our ability to serve as the technological innovator of the Typhon Pact. Not once in our people's history have we ever surrendered a military asset as valuable as this one."

Naaz tilted his head forward into an aggressive posture. *"We also have never before pledged ourselves to a multinational coalition. The Romulan Star Empire and Gorn Hegemony are not our rivals—they have become our allies."*

"Even allies can be rivals, in certain spheres of influence," Keer said. "Look at the Federation and the Klingon Empire, for example. Staunch allies—but the Federation has not shared its slipstream drive with the Klingons, has it?"

His vocoder crackling with the anger in his voice, Naaz replied, *"This is all beside the point, Keer. What matters now is whether you can have the prototype ready for testing in four days, as the domo has ordered."*

"I cannot," Keer said. "There are too many design flaws for us to proceed."

"What do you mean, 'design flaws'? This is already a proven technology."

Keer struggled to purge his voice of anger before he replied, "It has been proven only on a handful of specially designed Starfleet vessels. The more I study the slipstream formulas and engine schematics, the more certain I become that hull geometry plays an even more vital role in the application of this technology than it does in standard warp-drive designs."

"Are you telling me the problem is that your prototype is the wrong shape?"

"No, sir. I am saying the problem is that *all* our ships are the wrong shape. They are too wide, have too much mass, and are marred by too many hard angles." He patched in an image from the microgravity hangar outside his office. "As you can see, my crew is dismantling those sections of the prototype that I have flagged as being unsuited to the final configuration, which needs a more fluid aesthetic."

Naaz pounded his fist on the desktop in front of him. *"Have you lost your senses, Keer? Why would you take the prototype apart? And why* now?"

"I have no choice, sir. It needs to be stripped down to its spaceframe and retooled from the keel up. I have begun my calculations for a stable slipstream geometry that will work with our basic hull shape, but many changes will still be required. Resolving the variables in these equations will take considerable time, but until I have done so, it is not safe to proceed."

Keer's explanation was met by a long, bitter silence. Naaz turned his body a few degrees away from Keer, signaling his intention to distance himself from Keer's act of career suicide. *"Work quickly,"* he said. *"Our allies gave us only a limited window of exclusivity with this technology. If we fail to master it in a timely manner, they will move to seize control of it."*

"My staff and I are working as swiftly as we are able. If you could intercede with the domo to gain us more time, it would be appreciated."

"I will try, but it is not the domo who holds our hands to the fire."

"Understood. I will contact you as soon as I finish the

equations. If possible, I would be grateful if I could be kept apprised of events in the political arena."

Naaz's vocoder buzzed—a mechanical rendering of a derisive snort. *"Trust me, Keer. If our allies see fit to ruin my day, I will not hesitate to ruin yours."*

"Of that I have no doubt, sir."

Naaz terminated the transmission, and Keer switched off his terminal. He looked out his office window at the gutted prototype hovering before him.

I should be thankful I'm not rebuilding a complete starship, he decided. His directive was to produce a proof of concept—to solve the issues of quantum-slipstream field geometry as they pertained to Breen starship designs. Most of his prototype's interior volume was empty. It had barely enough habitable decks and compartments for a skeleton crew of engineers and designers to monitor its power output and engine functions. Once the redesign was finalized, they might be able to assemble a new prototype in six days. *But we have only four*, he reminded himself. *And I still haven't finished the redesign.* He drew a deep breath and focused on remaining calm. *Just prove it can work*, he told himself. *Turning this husk into a working starship is someone else's headache.* He sat down at his desk and called up the seemingly endless formula that governed the generation, manipulation, and controlled termination of a slipstream effect.

The digits and mathematical notations seemed to melt into a blur while Keer stared at them, and he knew he was in for a very long night.

14

Bashir kept his attention on the dermal regenerator in his hand and its progress repairing the wound beneath it, and he blocked out the unpleasant truth that it was his own leg he was treating. The pain-suppressing neural inhibitor diodes he had affixed on either side of the ugly scorch in his flesh helped; because he no longer felt his injury, he could pretend it wasn't his body he was fixing but someone else's. It reduced the task to an abstraction, a rote procedure.

A few meters away, Sarina stood guard at the hatch that linked the maintenance passages to the transit tunnels. Her disruptor was in her hand, held ready, and she had the door cracked open so she could watch and listen for trouble. She glanced back at Bashir. "How're you doing?"

"Almost finished. What's our next move?"

"I don't know about you, but I'm hungry."

He nodded. "Yes, running for your life tends to build an appetite." Brushing his fingertips over the new skin on his leg, he was pleased with his handiwork. "Good as new," he said, removing the neural inhibitors. Sensation returned to his thigh almost immediately. There was no serious pain, only a dull ache deep in the muscle and a strong tingling just under his epidermis.

"Go ahead and eat first," Sarina said. "I'll keep an eye out for trouble. When you're done, we'll switch."

"All right." Bashir dug out his rations, which consisted of a high-calorie, high-protein candy bar of his own invention, a pill that contained both a multivitamin compound and a booster for his immune system, and several generous sips of water recovered from his breath, perspiration, and urine and then filtered by his suit's life-support system—another detail he was trying to ignore.

After he finished, he put his gloves and helmet back on and joined Sarina at the door. "Your turn," he said. Sarina holstered her disruptor, and he drew his. She stepped behind the limited cover of some protruding pipes a few meters from the door, removed her helmet, and wolfed down her own meager dinner.

She returned to his side, once more submerged into her disguise. "Ready?" He nodded, and she reached past him and pushed the door shut. It locked automatically. "They'll be watching the tunnels. We need to find another exit."

They walked for more than two hours through what seemed to Bashir like endless catacombs. Sarina seemed to make random turns at intersections and climb or descend ladders at various junctions on a whim. As they neared a T junction, Bashir mustered his courage to ask, "Do you have any idea where we are?"

"Level Thirty-five, Gevat Sector, the industrial ring, behind the eighteen hundred block." She stopped, turned, and looked at him. "What? You thought I was making this up as I went along?"

"The possibility had crossed my mind."

"I wanted to get us a good distance away from our dust-up in Merchants Circle. The entire city's probably on high alert by now, so I thought we might want a less-trafficked area for our next public appearance." She turned the corner, led Bashir down a terminal passage to a heavy door, scanned it, and declared, "It's not locked." Bashir tensed as Sarina pushed the door open a few centimeters and scouted the area outside. "Looks clear," she said.

They stepped out into another nook set back from an alley and closed the door behind them. Bashir peeked around the corner and saw a narrow, dark street lined with windowless buildings. Deep vibrations coursed through the ground beneath his feet and made his teeth buzz. "What next?"

Sarina pointed at a nearby public-information kiosk. "I think we and our suits have learned enough to keep up with one of those—halfway, at least." The duo walked quickly but not as if they were in a hurry. Bashir wanted to swivel his head and scout the rooftops and corners for anyone who might be watching, but he knew that doing so would only attract attention. He stayed by Sarina's side and trusted in his hearing to warn him of danger.

The kiosk flashed to life at Sarina's first touch, its screen rolling with symbols and its speakers jabbering away with random commercial prattle until she silenced it with a quick poke at an icon along the screen's left edge. Echoes of the machine's synthetic blathering resounded down the deserted street, stoking Bashir's paranoia. Sarina tapped at the kiosk's interface and seemed to control it with a fair degree of skill.

"Can you actually read all that?" asked Bashir.

"Not all of it, but enough to ask the right questions." She punched in new instructions. "I'm asking it for a guide to military and government offices on Salavat." While the machine processed her request, she added, "In case you're curious, the name of this city is Rasiuk."

"Good to know. How many cities are on Salavat?"

"Judging from the results of my last query, at least a few dozen, maybe more. Not sure how many smaller settlements there might be." New information appeared on the kiosk's display. "Here we go. There's a military comm center here in Rasiuk. It's part of a government complex on Level Fifty-six, Elbis Sector."

Reading over Sarina's shoulder, Bashir asked, "What else is down there?"

"Not much. It's practically the bottom of the pit. Everything on that level is either military or a government black site." She blanked the kiosk's search screen and powered down the terminal. "If there is a secret shipyard on Salavat, the comm center's our best chance of finding it. That site should be tied into every other Breen military outpost on the planet, plus it'll have the decryption codes we need."

Sarina walked away from the kiosk and headed back the way they had come, to the maintenance passages. Walking beside her, Bashir said, "I hope you aren't planning on trying to walk in the front door of a Breen military base."

"Of course not. It must have a back door somewhere . . ."

• • •

Chot Nar entered her task pod, closed the door, and hoped that her supervisor and coworkers at the Breen Intelligence Directorate hadn't noticed her lethargic manner as she returned from her meal break. She was still adapting to working the second shift, to which she had been transferred only a few days earlier. For her the hardest part was transitioning to a new sleep schedule; despite the ease with which her peers seemed to move between shifts, Nar found it exhausting and disorienting.

She settled into her chair and keyed her authorization into her workstation to release the security lockout she had engaged before leaving for her break. Her computer powered up, and an alert appeared on her holographic display. She opened the message with a swooping gesture inside the holomatrix, expecting another of her supervisor's time-wasting manufactured emergencies.

It was an automated error notice from the urban surveillance network. As one of the BID's midlevel intelligence analysts, Nar performed troubleshooting and maintenance when something went wrong with its software or its firmware. Most glitches in the system were minor and easily repaired.

Best just to get it done and move on to something worthwhile, she told herself as she opened the alert's full log of the error. As soon as she saw the complete report, she froze. This was no simple malfunction, no inconsequential dropped bit of data. Nar had never seen anything like it, though she had heard of similar incidents happening in the years before she had been assigned to the BID.

She calmed herself. Nothing would be accomplished by getting emotional. The best response would be to obey established protocols. *Just follow procedure*, she admonished herself while launching an incident-report template. *Start with documentation. Nothing but the facts. Save the analysis for later.*

There were null values roaming the surveillance grid. They had appeared in random locations throughout Rasiuk over the past day. Interactive advertising panels, which were linked to the city's central database, contained sensors that detected the identichips of persons passing by on the street. The city's AI used the identichip codes to look up each citizen's purchasing history and economic profile, and it used that data to deliver targeted advertising tailored for maximum enticement. Similar advertising modules were built into the city's public-information kiosks, two of which had also registered null errors.

In addition to being used for crass commercial profit, the system was a key tool of the BID, which used the network to monitor the movements and habits of Breen civilians and construct virtual models to suss out suspect behavior.

Roaming errors were almost definitely not hardware or firmware related, Nar knew from experience. If the null values were in fact errors, the most likely cause would be a bug in the software of the central AI.

Nar launched a series of diagnostic programs. One scanned for viruses while another checked the main computer for physical damage or faulty connections. While the diagnostic applications compiled their findings, she pinpointed the null errors on a three-dimensional virtual map of the city and then linked them with a visible timeline to see whether they occurred in random locations.

The graph took shape in her holomatrix. She saw right away that there was nothing random about the errors. They moved in steady progressions down city blocks, lingered in the middle of major thoroughfares, and appeared and disappeared near maintenance access points. *That is not good*, she realized.

She created a secure channel using an encryption protocol to which, by law, she should not have had access. In minutes she had tapped into 249 remote surveillance cameras that had views of the streets where the null values had occurred, and she began downloading their memory logs from the relevant time periods. While the vid files compiled in her holomatrix, her diagnostic programs completed their analysis of the central AI.

The conclusion: no errors, no viruses, no malfunctions.

Whatever was causing the error, it was outside the system.

A majority of the vid files had finished downloading. Nar opened them in a pattern-recognition application. "Computer," she said, "initiate a search for visual commonalities among persons near terminals that reported null errors at each site during the referenced time frames."

Almost as soon as the program started working, Nar's holomatrix began to fill with side-by-side freeze-frames taken from different cameras. In each pair of images, two figures had been highlighted. Always the duo moved in close proximity to each other, and, in what Nar knew could not be a coincidence, they had been the targets of a security action that had ended in a public firefight and the hijacking of a civil rapid-transit train that was subsequently destroyed by high-power demolitions believed to be of Tholian manufacture—no doubt a deliberate act of misdirection intended to conceal the criminals' true affiliation.

Staring at the two paramilitary-style masks pictured in her matrix, Nar was stunned at the implications of her discovery. There were two ghosts in the machine, and it would be only a matter of hours before some other more senior analyst in the BID would make the same discovery in the course of searching the network's logs for clues to the two fugitives' identities.

She looked up the last reported error. It had occurred at an information kiosk in the industrial zone on Level Thirty-five. On a hunch, Nar accessed the search activity log for that kiosk and noted what the fugitives had been looking for.

It came as little surprise to Nar that they were seeking government and military facilities. She knew that going after the fugitives on her own was a dangerous proposition, but the alternative was to watch them be apprehended by some other BID operative who would in turn be richly rewarded with a promotion and maybe even a better residence assignment on one of the upper levels.

No, she decided. *I will not accept that.*

She uploaded an image of the fugitives to her personal

comm unit, programmed her computer to send her real-time updates of any new null-value errors in the network, and locked down her terminal. Her hands trembled as she opened the door of her task pod and slipped out. Getting out of the building would not be a challenge. Getting away with what she planned to do next would be.

15

The Mayday that crackled from the overhead speakers of the *Aventine*'s bridge was garbled and interrupted by bursts of white cosmic background noise: *". . . have struck . . . lost main power and life support . . . any ship, please respond . . . peat, this is the* S.S. Tullahoma *out of Nashira. We . . ."*

"Analysis," Dax said, swiveling her chair first toward Kedair.

The security chief looked up from her console. "The *Tullahoma* is a civilian freighter designed for the transport of perishable goods. She shipped out of Nashira five days ago with a mixed cargo of food and medicines bound for the Cardassian Union. Crew complement, approximately forty personnel."

Mirren chimed in from ops, "Based on the *Tullahoma*'s rated cruising speed of warp six, the coordinates of her last transmission are within her flight range from Nashira." Looking back at Dax, she added, "Her comm signal's weak, though. I doubt anyone but us picked it up."

"How convenient," Dax said under her breath. "Mister Helkara, are there any known navigational hazards in the vicinity of the *Tullahoma*'s transmission?"

"Several. That region is on the edge of the Black Cluster. She might have encountered a gravitational anomaly, a cosmic string . . ."

"Noted," Dax said. "Lieutenant Mirren, can we confirm the *Tullahoma*'s position and status?"

"Not at this range, Captain."

Dax threw a look at Bowers. "Your thoughts, Sam?"

"Sounds like a trap, sir. It's just far enough away that we can't verify the message without moving off station from the Breen border, and it's in a region where we'd be out of contact with Starfleet." Bowers frowned. "The perfect location for an ambush."

"Agreed," Dax said. "Mister Tharp, plot a course for the *Tullahoma*'s last known coordinates, warp nine."

"Aye, Captain," said the Bolian flight officer.

"Lieutenant Kedair, transmit a response to the *Tullahoma* and let them know we're en route. Notify me if and when they acknowledge."

Bowers and Kedair exchanged concerned glances, and Bowers sidled up to Dax's chair. "Captain, why are we taking the bait if we know it's a trap?"

"First," Dax said, "we don't *know* it's a trap, we only *suspect* it's a trap. It's possible the *Tullahoma* really is in trouble, and we're required by law to investigate and render aid. Second, even if this is a ruse by the Typhon Pact to move us out of position, we have to play along."

Cocking an eyebrow, Bowers said, "May I ask why?"

"Because if we don't respond to the *Tullahoma*'s Mayday, we'll be telling the Breen and their allies that we have a more urgent mission that compels us to remain on their border—in which case we might as well confess that we're supporting a covert operation inside their territory."

From the helm, Tharp said, "Course laid in, Captain."

"Engage, Mister Tharp."

With a single tap on his console, the Bolian pilot propelled the *Aventine* to warp speed on its new heading.

Lowering his voice, Bowers said, "What if Bashir and Douglas call for extraction while we're out of position?"

"Julian's clever, and Sarina makes *him* look slow," Dax said. "They'll think of something. Right now, the need for operational secrecy trumps the tactical risk."

Bowers grimaced. "If the Typhon Pact set this trap, that means they already suspect what we're up to. So what does it matter if we play along?"

"It's called 'plausible deniability,' Sam. We're not doing this for our benefit. We're doing it so some politician can have the upper hand when the Typhon Pact's ambassador comes looking to complain about us lurking on the Breen's border."

"And what if this isn't just about moving us out of position? What if we're being set up for an ambush by the Romulans?"

Dax smiled. "We'll burn that bridge when we come to it."

Commander Marius simmered with anger as he read General Valnor's latest report of being stonewalled by the Breen starship designer in charge of the slipstream project. *Damn the Breen and their useless paranoia,* Marius fumed. *They're wasting valuable time. If they'd shared the Starfleet designs, we might have a working prototype by now.*

It had been months since Marius and his crew on the *Dekkona* had helped extract the Breen's saboteur-spy from the Utopia Planitia Fleet Yards in the Sol system. Marius had been sorely tempted while ferrying the spy to Salavat to seize the slipstream plans on behalf of Romulus, risking imprisonment and even execution—the treaty with the Typhon Pact be damned. He still didn't understand why Praetor Tal'Aura had debased the Empire by making it acknowledge the Gorn, the Tholians, and the Kinshaya as its equals. Gorn were little better than animals, as far as Marius was concerned, the Tholians were glorified bugs with delusions of grandeur, and the Kinshaya were superstitious fools, slaves to religion and blind to reason. As for the Tzenkethi, they were the most vexing race Marius had ever encountered. He cursed whoever had invited them into the Pact.

But the Breen? Mercenaries and opportunists. Paranoid and treacherous. They didn't deserve to be called allies of the Empire, in Marius's opinion, so much as betrayers waiting for an opportunity to seize an advantage. Even more baffling to him was why the praetor and the Tal Shiar would deign to let the Breen take the lead in adapting and developing the Federation's slipstream technology when they had yet to master the incorporation of Romulan cloaking devices into their ships. Nothing he knew of the Breen so far gave Marius any confidence in their abilities.

The sound of a sensor alert gave Marius a reason to

switch off the data slate in his hand and set it aside. He leaned forward in his command chair. "Report."

Centurion Kozik, the second in command of the warbird, looked up from the tactical console and faced Marius. "The Starfleet vessel is changing course, Commander. They are heading at warp nine toward the source coordinates of the distress signal and transmitting a reply to the *Tullahoma*."

"Interesting," Marius said. "Are they taking the bait, or just playing their part?" Dismissing his rhetorical queries, he added, "Helm, set a pursuit course. Centurion, alert our battle group in the Inasa system to stand ready."

Kozik carried out the order, verified that the *Dekkona* was under way on its pursuit course, and then approached Marius's chair with a wary mien. "Commander," he said, his voice barely more than a whisper, "why have we alerted our Inasa fleet? What have you set in motion?"

"My plans will be revealed when the time is right," Marius said. "All that I require from you and from this crew is obedience."

In a sterner voice, Kozik said, "Has the Senate overturned its proclamation forbidding open combat with the Khitomer Accords powers? If so, I must have missed the announcement, Commander."

"You have missed no declarations," Marius said.

"Perhaps the Tal Shiar rescinded its order directing us to refrain from assault on the *Aventine*? If so, I should have been summoned to authenticate—"

"No new orders have been received, Kozik."

"Then what, precisely, are we doing, Commander?"

Marius steepled his fingers in front of his chest. "Showing initiative, Kozik. The Senate and the Tal Shiar seem content to be patient and wait upon the largesse of the Breen." An evil smirk tugged at his mouth as he eyed the image of the *Aventine* on the forward viewscreen. "I am not."

16

Bashir swallowed hard and pushed back against a swirl of vertigo as he looked out the open maintenance hatch at a hundred-meter drop to a dark street patrolled by armed Breen soldiers. He and Sarina were inside the secured perimeter of the military and government sector on Rasiuk's lowest level, though hardly in a position of easy access. "You're certain this is the only exit on this level?"

"Yes," Sarina said. "I checked three times. This is the only hatchway that opens on the correct side of the checkpoint."

Peeking over the edge, Bashir said, "Not that it does us much good. This ladder ends next to the gatehouse, and there are half a dozen troops who'd see us before we reached the ground." He shook his head. "Maybe we should lay low until the city's not on such high alert anymore."

"That's not an option." Sarina backed away from the open portal and started retrieving various small components from pockets on her suit. Assembling them, she continued. "Our ride home won't wait for us forever, Julian. We can't afford to bide our time and take the easy way out. We have to be bold."

"Sarina, there's *bold* and then there's *suicidal*. If we try to climb down this ladder, those soldiers will shoot us full of holes long before we reach the ground."

Snapping her device's last component into place, she smiled. "Who said we'd be using the ladder?" The item in her hand resembled a tiny harpoon gun. "We'll anchor the wire up here and fire the bolt at that building with the ledge that runs most of the way to the comm center."

"You must be joking. You don't really expect me to—"

"Stand clear."

He went silent as she embedded the anchor bolt into the stone ceiling behind her, turned, and took aim at the distant ledge. There was a soft hiss of displaced air as Sarina fired the bolt out into the perpetual night of the underground city. A few seconds later the barely visible strand of monofilament wire rushing from the anchor mount went taut. Sarina plucked the wire like a string on an instrument, clamped a miniature pulley over it, and nodded at Bashir.

"Express elevator," she said, "going down."

She tucked her knees up to her waist, and gravity did the rest. Sarina sped away, dangling from the handheld pulley as it raced down the wire toward the ledge far below. Bashir muttered curses under his breath as he found his own compact pulley among the myriad devices hidden in his disguise, attached it to the wire, and prayed that his hands didn't choose that moment to get a cramp.

Free fall left Bashir feeling as if he had deserted his stomach up on the ledge as he plunged headlong across the chasm in pursuit of Sarina. It was so dark in this part of Rasiuk that he was barely able to see the end of the zip line until he was all but on top of it and heard Sarina tell him via his helmet's transceiver, *"Brakes!"*

Bashir squeezed the handgrip with increasing pressure until he felt himself slow down. He glided the last few meters at an easy pace and dropped onto the narrow ledge beside Sarina. "That was fun," he deadpanned, detaching his minipulley from the zip line. "Just out of curiosity, have you given any thought to how we're supposed to get back up there?"

"We're not." She nodded at the checkpoint below and behind them. "Look closer. The guards are only checking identichips on people coming *into* the sector. They're not scanning anyone on the way out."

"Not manually, anyway," Bashir replied, but Sarina was already shimmying away, heading deeper into danger.

Moving in cautious sidesteps, Bashir followed her. He was thankful for two things during his long, shuffling walk along the ledge. First, his helmet's visor was equipped with a powerful night-vision mode that rendered his pitch-dark surroundings into a pale green twilight. Second, because the Breen's city was deep underground and relied on a regulated environment, there was almost no strong air movement, not even at heights such as the one he was traversing.

They arrived at the end of the ledge. Sarina kneeled, peering down at the street below. "There's enough shadow beneath us to cover our descent," she said. "As for how we get inside the comm center, I'm still working on that."

She armed her bolt thrower and sank an anchor into the

ledge. Then she dropped the bolt, which fell away, trailing an all but invisible monofilament behind it. "I'll go first," she said. "Stay here until I give you the all clear." She locked her minipulley onto the line and tumbled gracefully over the edge. In seconds she rappelled down the wall and vanished into the darkness.

It annoyed Bashir that Sarina was presuming to give him orders. *I guess she's forgotten I outrank her.*

Over his transceiver, Sarina reported, *"All clear."*

He secured his minipulley and eased himself over the edge. He descended in a classic rappelling pose, bounding off the wall at regular intervals, bending at his knees to absorb his momentum and push off again. He had to be careful not to squeeze the pulley grip too tightly, for fear of engaging the brake by accident. Then his feet touched the ground, and he detached the device from the line.

Sarina was crouched a few meters away against the wall. Bashir stole forward and squatted behind her. They were facing the front of the military comm center. Its entrance was defended by several armed Breen soldiers, and its main doors were closed and appeared to be made of thick metal.

Bashir frowned. "Don't tell me we're just going to go up and knock."

"I haven't ruled that out."

The doors opened, and three Breen officers left the building. Bashir eyed the markings on their uniforms. "The one in front is a *thot*," he said.

"That's like an admiral. Can't be many of those here."

"What if we follow them and get just close enough to read the signals from their identichips? Then we clone the identity signatures and modify our suits with insignia like theirs. We might be able to access the entire base."

Rising to her feet, Sarina said, "I like it. Good plan."

As Bashir stood up, an electronically neutered voice said from behind them, "Actually, that is a *terrible* plan."

Sarina drew her disruptor and spun around. Bashir pivoted out of her way and looked back. Her finger started to tense on the trigger when Bashir threw his hand in front of the disruptor and snapped, "Stop!"

He was looking at a Breen in civilian clothing. Slight of frame, the Breen had recoiled from Bashir and Sarina, apparently in fear of being shot. Bashir put his hand on top of Sarina's disruptor and eased it down and away from the Breen, saying in a soft voice, "He's unarmed."

"I am a she, actually," the Breen said. "My name is Chot Nar."

"I am Ket Rhun," Bashir said, resorting to his cover alias.

Sarina nodded at Nar. "Minh Sann."

"I doubt those are your real names," Nar said.

Bashir replied, "Why do you say that?"

"Because no one goes to all the trouble of having themselves zeroed just so they can go around giving out their true names," Nar said.

Sarina holstered her disruptor. "How did you know we've been zeroed?"

"That is how I found you," Nar said. "The surveillance networks have been reprogrammed—people who have been zeroed trigger null-value errors in the commerce grids and information kiosks. I thought all the fellowships had been warned. Did you come from one of the outer colonies?"

"You could say that," Sarina lied.

"I thought as much."

Bashir asked, "Why is my plan to clone the *thot*'s identichip a bad idea?"

"Because the surveillance network will trigger an alert the moment it detects two chips with the same ID signature," Nar said. She circled Bashir and Sarina and peeked in an anxious manner around the corner. "I need to get you off the streets." She beckoned them. "Follow me. I will bring you to my home. You will be safe there until I can fix your identichips."

Sarina looked at Bashir, and for a moment he thought she was going to say something. Then she turned and followed Nar. Bashir sighed and did likewise. *Well*, he mused, *at least now we don't have to sleep in a tunnel.*

The journey from Rasiuk's nadir to the neon-lit level on which Nar resided was long under even the best of circumstances, but it was even longer this evening because Nar needed to avoid the seemingly ubiquitous nodes of the city's urban surveillance network. Having gone to the risk and effort of intercepting two fellow dissidents before they tried to carry out whatever foolhardy plan had taken them to the threshold of the militia's communications center, Nar was determined not to condemn them—or herself—by permitting them to be detected and recognized.

Minor adjustments to their helmets—plucking off redundant pieces, defacing some insignia, adding a couple of random components Nar had brought along as a precaution—had made it less likely the zeroed pair would be flagged by the system's automated pattern-recognition programs. Keeping them away from active information kiosks and commerce sensors was the real challenge, however.

She timed their arrival at her building, a massive arcology that constituted most of Level Fifteen, to coincide with a pedestrian traffic spike caused by the impending shift change. Waves of citizens surged out of the arcology's many entrances, bound for their late-shift employment. "This will give us some cover," Nar said to her fugitive guests. "Stay close to me and do not speak."

"Understood," replied Rhun. They remained close at Nar's back as she led them through the arcology's main entrance hall. Despite the crushing momentum of the crowd against which she was moving, Nar stuck as close as she could to the center line of the hall, a high-ceilinged space that was wide enough for more than five hundred people to walk abreast and long enough to hold hundreds of such rows at once. At times of peak traffic volume, the vast concourse was a sea of functionally identical forms and faces, an irresistible force pressing in one direction or the other, out or in, all trudging in lockstep under the sickly green cast of naked fluorine lights.

The only breaks in the utilitarian gloom were the hundreds of commerce screens that lined the walls on either side of the hall, pummeling passersby with nonstop visual and auditory assaults of garish color and blaring noise. Nar knew that she needed to keep as many bodies as possible between the screens and Rhun and Sann, lest the zeroed duo trigger null errors right here inside Nar's home.

They piled into a spacious lift along with a score of others, leaving room to spare as the doors slid shut and the car began its ascent. Voices called out floors, and the computer acknowledged each in turn. Nar shouted, "Seventy-one," and her request was confirmed with a simple double beep from the overhead speaker.

She nodded at Rhun and Sann to accompany her when the doors opened at her floor. They followed her down long intersecting corridors to her apartment. With a wave of her hand over the biometric sensor, she unlocked the door and ushered her guests inside. Then she slipped in behind them and locked the door after it slid closed.

"Make yourselves comfortable." She gestured at the simple furnishings in her main room: a short sofa, two chairs, a low table, and a wall-mounted vid screen that she had long ago disconnected from the municipal data network. "It is not much, but it is all I can offer you for now."

Sann and Rhun stood in the middle of the main room and turned slowly as they examined their surroundings. Nar could not imagine what the duo found so interesting about her residence; aside from a few pieces of art passed down to her by her parents, it had few personal touches to set it apart from any other state-approved dwelling. It was, as with all things governed by the Confederate Congress, "within established norms." Or, as Nar put it, "aggressively average."

She retired to her bedroom and unlocked the clasp on her helmet's air seal. It released with a sensation that always made Nar think of a hand releasing a choke hold on her throat. With relief she pulled off her helmet and set it atop its stand on her dresser. Next she removed her gloves, revealing her delicate, bronze-hued fingers. Piece by piece she stripped away her government-mandated shell of identity, until she was able to turn and regard herself in the bedroom mirror. She teased her shoulder-length white hair so that a few wisps fell playfully in front of her wide, jade-colored eyes, and then she donned her favorite robe, one made of metallic red Tholian silk with a fractal pattern embroidered on its back in gold.

Rhun and Sann are being very quiet, she noticed. *I hope nothing's wrong.* She returned to the living room, where the two fugitives stood huddled in a far corner, conversing in low metallic whispers that Nar could no longer understand without her helmet to translate. "Excuse me," she said. "Forgive me for being critical, but it *is* impolite to remain masked after your host has unmasked."

The pair stood and stared at Nar for a few seconds, long enough for her to begin to feel self-conscious and then to become suspicious. "You will be safe here," she said, unsure whether she was trying to reassure her visitors or herself. "Please remove your masks and be at home."

Sann and Rhun looked at each other, and they nodded in unison. They reached up, undid the seals on their helmets, and with almost grudging slowness pulled them off. When they looked up and met Nar's gaze, her jaw fell open.

She had seen almost every species that had ever lived under the Breen banner—but until that moment she had never seen humans with her own eyes.

17

Bashir was still getting used to the idea that the lovely humanoid woman standing in front of him was the same person he and Sarina had met on the street just hours earlier, and then Nar spoke. "Excuse me. Forgive me for being critical, but it *is* impolite to remain masked after your host has unmasked."

The mission briefing hadn't addressed this circumstance. Given the intense brand of paranoia that informed so much of Breen culture, it had never occurred to the Jack Pack or to any member of SI that Bashir and Sarina might be invited to remove their disguises. Seconds passed while Bashir stood paralyzed with indecision. Then Nar continued, "You will be safe here. Please remove your masks and be at home."

Sarina whispered to Bashir over their private transceiver channel, *"We can't really refuse. Follow my lead, and let me do the talking."* Bashir nodded once in acknowledgment, and Sarina returned the gesture. Then they unfastened the seals between their helmets and suits and pulled off their snout-shaped masks.

Nar's eyes widened and her jaw fell open in a familiar expression of shock. "You . . ." Her voice trailed off, and she blinked. Then she took a step back and added, "You are *human*."

"Yes," Sarina said, holding up her hands with her palms facing Nar. "We're civilian cultural observers from the United Federation of Planets. Our mission is peaceful, and we mean you no harm." The ease and calm with which Sarina lied made Bashir uneasy, but he trusted that she knew what she was doing, so he kept silent as she continued. "We're grateful for your help and for shelter."

The white-haired woman backed away a half step. She asked in a nervous voice, "Civilians?" Sarina nodded. "Cultural observers?"

"That's right," Sarina said. "We're just here to learn about your people."

"Then why were you trying to break into the military communications center? Why did you attack civil-control officers in Merchants Circle?"

Sarina shot a quick look at Bashir, as if to remind him to stay quiet. Then she replied to Nar, "First, we didn't attack the civil-control officers, they attacked us. We defended ourselves, and we did everything we could to get innocent civilians out of the crossfire. As for the comm center, it doesn't take a genius to see that your people live under constant surveillance. We thought that if we could access the comm facility we could gauge the scope of the surveillance program."

Shaking her head, Nar said, "Then you were in the wrong place. The surveillance network is run by the Breen Intelligence Directorate, not the military."

Bashir asked, "It's a civil-government program?"

"Yes. The BID is a subdivision of the Confederate Information Bureau." An uneasy silence followed Nar's reply. Her voice and expression betrayed her suspicion as she asked, "What happens now that I have seen your faces?"

"That depends," Sarina said. "Do you have any food?"

Nar shrugged. "Some."

Sarina smiled. "Then maybe we could sit down, have a bite to eat, and you could tell us things we don't know about the Breen."

"Like what?"

Unable to contain his curiosity, Bashir said, "I would love to know more about *your* species—starting with what you call yourselves."

After considering the question for a few seconds, Nar said, "My people are the Silwaan. We were one of the founding members of the Confederacy."

Holding up his helmet, Bashir said, "I'm guessing the snouts on these things weren't put there for your benefit."

With a smile of faint amusement, Nar said, "No, that feature is included to accommodate the Fenrisal. They dwell on the far side of the Confederacy from Federation space. I do not think your people have ever encountered their kind."

Sarina set her helmet down on a low table and eased into one of the chairs. "One of the rumors I'd always heard was that Breen have no blood and need to wear refrigeration suits or else they'll evaporate."

"Whoever told you that encountered the Amoniri," Nar said.

Bashir asked, "Are they the ones with four-lobed brains that foil telepaths?"

"No," Nar said. "Those are the Paclu. They are also very strong and are one of the preeminent members of the Confederacy. They and the Amoniri dominate the military because they best meet its performance requirements."

Settling into the chair diagonally across from Sarina's, Bashir continued the gentle interrogation. "Are you saying certain occupations in Breen society are geared to favor particular species? Like a caste system?"

"No." Nar edged closer. "The Confederate Congress sets uniform standards of performance and service for all positions within the military, government, and educational sectors. These criteria are chosen to ensure optimal performance, not to engender bias. That certain species are better able to meet the demands of particular occupations is not a result of favoritism but a reflection on what was judged to be in the best interest of the commonwealth."

"Remarkable." Bashir grinned with sincere excitement. His jovial manner seemed to be drawing Nar closer, so he continued. "If it wouldn't be too impertinent to ask about the masks . . ."

Easing herself down onto the sofa opposite Sarina and Bashir, Nar replied, "What about them?"

"Well," Bashir said, "why, exactly, do your people wear them?"

"To prevent exactly the kind of discrimination you hinted at," Nar said.

Sarina said, "I don't follow you. How do the masks do that?"

"Outside the family unit, only the CIB is authorized to know the true species of individual citizens. Because we know each other only by our official names and performance records, we evaluate one another strictly on our merits. Irrelevant factors are excluded from the decision-making process when personnel are considered for promotion. No one is advanced because of species, or physical attractiveness to a superior, or age, nor is anyone denied for any such cause. Breen are judged by their works alone."

Bashir chuckled. "An entire culture predicated on blind tests." He looked at Sarina. "I'll say this for it. It certainly sounds *fair*."

"Nar," Sarina said, "how do citizens find mates to create new family units?"

Shifting uncomfortably, Nar said, "Marriages are arranged by the CIB under strict, confidential seal. Unsanctioned couplings are a criminal offense."

Intrigued, Bashir leaned forward. "How do unsanctioned couplings occur if Breen citizens never see one another's faces outside the family unit?"

"I did not say that we never see one another's faces," Nar said. "Only that we are not supposed to. The fact that I invited you both to unmask should serve as proof of that." She took a deep breath and continued. "There is a small but vibrant dissident culture that lurks in the hidden spaces of Breen cities. Agitators who yearn to live openly, to pursue relationships of choice. To be free."

Sarina asked, "Why are you telling us this?"

"Because I am one of them. I use my job within the BID to warn my friends of danger. With your help, I could provide them with something better."

Bashir arched one eyebrow. "What would that be?"

"Political asylum in the Federation."

18

Thot Keer stood in front of his superior's shuttle and was grateful that his mask concealed his growing sensation of dread. A subspace comm from one's superior usually meant bad news; a personal visit *always* did.

The spacecraft's ramp lowered and touched down on the hangar's deck with a clang and a scrape. Keer straightened his posture as he heard Thot Naaz's heavy footsteps from inside the shuttle. The steps grew louder. Naaz emerged, descended the ramp, and loomed over Keer. "I have bad news," he said.

"I presumed as much, sir." Keer gestured toward the exit to the corridor. "Shall we continue this discussion in my office?"

Naaz turned his head from side to side and belatedly appeared to take note of the several members of the ship-yard's hangar deck crew who were working near his vessel. "Yes," he said, "that would be sensible."

Keer led his guest to the corridor and then into a lift, followed by another corridor that terminated at his office. He entered first and stepped aside to let Naaz pass and, if the supervisor wished, position himself behind Keer's desk. He did. Naaz stood at the broad window that ran the length of the back wall and looked out upon the mostly dismantled prototype slipstream vessel.

"The Typhon Pact's governing board has convened a special session to discuss our reluctance to share the slipstream drive schematics," Naaz said. "The Romulan delegate insisted, and his motion was seconded by the Gorn and Tholian delegates." Turning to face Keer, he added, "This complicates matters, I fear."

"On what basis have the Romulans objected to our position?"

"Kalavak says that because they shared their cloaking device technology with all Typhon Pact member states, they deserve access to the slipstream data—in the spirit of reciprocity, you see." Naaz turned back toward the husk of the prototype suspended in the microgravity hangar below. "Most inconvenient."

Shaking with anger, Keer replied, "*Absurd* is more like it, sir. The Romulans' gift of cloaking technology is all but worthless in the short term. Their system generates chronitons that would destabilize our engine cores. If we install Romulan cloaks on our vessels, we will have to rebuild our energy distribution networks. In essence, they gave us a technology that works only on *their* ships."

Naaz replied over his shoulder, "From what you have told me about the slipstream drive, it has much the same shortcoming. So why not return the Romulans' empty gesture in kind and put this matter behind us?"

"It is not that simple, sir. Many of the Romulans' hull designs possess far more fluid lines than do any of ours. If they acquire these plans before I finish the prototype, they might be able to equip entire squadrons of their fleet in months."

"Just a moment, Keer." Naaz cocked his head at an angle that implied he was both amused and making a joke at his subordinate's expense. "Are you telling me that the real reason you are refusing to share this technology is that it would be of more use to the Romulans than it is to us?"

Keer denied the accusation with outward sweeping movements of his hands with the palms toward the floor. "Not at all, sir. I am resisting their demands for access to prevent the Confederacy from being relegated to second-class status among the nations of the Typhon Pact. Once we have integrated this technology into our own fleet, I will have no objection to sharing it with our allies."

Naaz circled around the desk and walked back to confront Keer, snout to snout. "Your patriotism is commendable, Keer. However, it might soon become irrelevant. The domo and Delegate Gren are stating our case for exemption from the Pact's information-exchange requirements, but reports that have leaked from the meeting suggest the argument is failing to sway the Tzenkethi, Tholian, or Kinshaya delegates. Unless the domo can persuade at least two of our allies to back our position, it seems likely that the vote will come soon—and go against us."

"Where does that leave us, then?"

"Facing a short deadline," Naaz said. "If you can power up a prototype as proof of concept before the board casts a binding vote, we might be able to lay claim to the technology as an exclusive state asset."

"I am close to resolving my difficulties with the

equations," Keer said. "However, I am ill equipped to act upon them with any haste. If the domo wishes to negotiate from a position of strength, I need more matériel and more personnel on-site in a matter of hours."

"I told you before, Keer, our resources—"

"Are overextended. Yes, I know. But this is the price of victory, sir. If the domo wishes to claim it, it is time to pay the cost."

19

Sam Bowers stood behind Kedair at the tactical console, anxious for any sign that the *Aventine*'s high-warp detour had not been made in vain. He looked back and forth between the console and the main viewscreen. "Anything?"

"No sign of the *Tullahoma*," Kedair reported.

Moving across the bridge toward the science station, Bowers asked Helkara, "What about debris? Are we picking up energy signatures from weapons fire?"

The wiry Zakdorn shook his head. "No, sir. Sensors are clear."

"I knew it," Bowers muttered. The *Tullahoma* had ceased transmitting its distress signal when the *Aventine* was still roughly ninety minutes away from the freighter's last reported coordinates. It was a classic ploy for luring starships away from their designated routes and patrol sectors.

He walked over to stand next to Dax's chair. The captain sat with her right leg crossed over her left at the knee and her arms folded across her chest. She looked remarkably sanguine, given the circumstances. "Captain," Bowers said in a muted voice, "there's no sign of the *Tullahoma* within sensor range. I respectfully submit that we appear to be the victims of a hoax."

"If we're lucky," Dax said. "Mister Tharp, plot a return course to the Breen border. Bring us about on the new heading and hold at full impulse."

"Aye, sir." Tharp began keying commands into the helm.

An enigmatic smile tugged at Dax's mouth. "If I'm right, this is all about to get a *lot* more interesting," she said.

Worried that he might be asking a question to which he didn't really want the answer, Bowers replied, "Right about what, Captain?"

The Red Alert klaxon wailed, and the bridge lights dimmed as crimson panels flashed on the bulkheads. Kedair announced, "Three *Mogai*-class Romulan warbirds decloaking in an attack formation—we're surrounded, Captain!"

Dax looked up at Bowers and pointed at the overhead. "About that." She looked at Kedair. "Shields to full. Who's here to greet us, Lieutenant?"

"Energy profiles match those on file for the *Terrinex*, the *Dekkona*, and the *Kytonis*," Kedair said. She looked up and added, "Also known as the wing leaders of the Romulan Star Empire's Fifth Fleet."

"I'm guessing they aren't here to answer the *Tullahoma*'s distress call." Dax uncrossed her legs and pushed herself to her feet. Striding toward the forward consoles, she said, "Charge phasers. Hail the warbirds."

"Channel open, sir," Kedair replied.

"Attention, Romulan vessels. This is Captain Ezri Dax of the *Starship Aventine*. You have ten seconds to respond and explain yourselves."

Surprised expressions were volleyed from one bridge officer to another. Stepping up behind Dax's shoulder, Bowers leaned in close and asked in a tense whisper, "What are you doing, sir?"

"Trust me."

The main viewscreen changed to show the angular cheekbones and prominent brow ridges of a Romulan man in the prime of his life. His gaze was fierce and unblinking, and there was a hint of smugness in his expression. *"Hello, Captain Dax,"* he said. *"I am Commander Marius of the warbird* Dekkona. *Your vessel is outnumbered, outgunned, and surrounded."*

"I'll give you two out of three," Dax said, flashing a cold smile at the Romulan. "You definitely outnumber us, and I can't deny we're surrounded."

Her cockiness seemed to throw Marius off. He frowned. *"You will lower your shields, surrender your vessel, and prepare to be boarded."*

"The *hell* I will."

Marius seethed. *"Let me be blunt, Captain. Surrender your vessel and the secrets of its slipstream drive, or we will take them from you by force."*

Dax replied with mocking sweetness, "Oh, I have a *choice*? How *gracious* of you, Commander." She hardened her gaze and her tone. "My answer is still *no*."

"As you wish, Captain. Your crew's blood will be on your hands." He turned away and said to someone offscreen, *"All ships, lock weapons and—"*

One of Marius's crew members interjected, *"Ships decloaking, sir!"*

The transmission from the warbird cut off, and the *Aventine*'s main viewer reverted to an image of one of the Romulan ships—with two new shapes rippling into view behind it.

Kedair furrowed her brow as she reacted to alerts on her console. "Captain, five Klingon ships decloaking: three *Qang*-class heavy cruisers and two *Negh'Var*-class battleships. They're locking weapons on the Romulan ships."

Amused, Bowers glanced at Dax. "You knew that would happen."

"Yes, I did."

"Captain," Kedair said, "Commander Marius is hailing us."

Dax walked back to her chair, sat down, crossed her legs, and set her hands palms-down on the armrests. She collected herself, mustered a wry smile, and faced the main viewscreen with her chin up. "Put him on, Lieutenant."

Marius looked annoyed. *"Well played, Captain. I salute you."*

"Give yourselves some credit," Dax said. "I couldn't have done it without you. Specifically, without your predictable nature and total gullibility. I mean, seriously—this isn't even the *first* time you guys have fallen for this." She waved her hand as if that would dismiss the matter. "Anyway, this has been a hoot and a half, but my crew and I have places to be and things to do, so we'll be going now."

"This is far from over, Captain," Marius said through clenched teeth.

"Tell it to the Klingons. They'll be sticking around awhile, just in case this lesson hasn't sunk in yet." She smiled. "Don't be a stranger, Marius. *Aventine* out." The screen switched to a view of the multivessel showdown transpiring around the *Aventine*, and Dax added with sharp urgency, "Mister Tharp, get us out of here, best possible speed."

"Aye, sir." Tharp engaged the impulse engines to navigate clear of the standoff and set a course back to the Breen border.

Bowers struggled not to sound angry as he said sotto voce to Dax, "You might have told me in advance that we had a Klingon escort fleet, Captain."

"I might have. But I didn't." She narrowed her eyes in a playful glare. "Admit it, this wouldn't have been as much fun if you'd known in advance."

"If by 'fun' you mean 'traumatic,' then yes."

Stars on the main viewer stretched into twisting ribbons of light as the ship hurtled away into warp. Dax got up from her chair and patted Bowers's arm as she passed him on her way to her ready room. "Lighten up, Sam. What's the point of this job if we can't enjoy a good ambush now and then?"

20

After waiting for what had seemed like a preposterously long time for her friend to arrive, Nar's attention deteriorated into idle thoughts, which is why the sharp buzz of her doorbell startled her even though she had been expecting it all night.

She hurried to the door, stepped behind the privacy screen, and activated the security monitor. It powered up and showed one person standing outside her door. Erring on the side of caution, Nar asked through the intercom, "Who is it?"

Her visitor replied over the translated channel, *"Chon Min."*

"Enter the pass code," Nar said. She watched her screen as Min used the keypad beside the door to key in a string of symbols they had chosen for the purpose of identifying each other and verifying that they were not being observed or coerced. The code checked out. Nar responded with an all-clear string and then unlocked the door of her apartment. It slid open, Min entered, and as soon as it closed Nar locked it behind him.

Min was pulling off his helmet as Nar came out from behind the privacy screen. The golden fur on his lupine face and neck was matted from being inside the snug, full-head mask. He lifted his snout at Nar. "Sorry I took so long getting here," he said. "I came as quickly as I was able. What seems to be—" Turning his head toward the bedroom, he sniffed twice in quick succession. "Strange scents. Not like any I know." Suspicious, he snarled at Nar and asked, "Who is here?"

"Calm down," Nar said. "My guests are outsiders, but they have come in peace. Treat them as friends, Min." Stepping between her Fenrisal compatriot and the door of her bedroom, she called out to Sarina and Bashir, "You can come out."

The two humans emerged from the darkened bedroom. Bashir went first, placing himself between Sarina and Min. There was a protective quality to his bearing that made Nar suspect the two humans might be mates as well as partners. "Min," she said, "allow me to introduce Julian Bashir and Sarina Douglas of the United Federation of Planets."

Min let slip a low growl of alarm. "Nar, have you lost your mind? Why did you bring them here? More to the point, why did you let them see me?"

"They are here as cultural observers," Nar said, "to learn about us, about our culture." She reached out and gently gripped Min's arm. "They can help us."

He yanked his arm from Nar's grasp. "They can get us all killed."

"I did not ask you here to debate this," Nar said, taking a defensive tack. "I need you to modify their identichips with better profiles. Right now they show up in the system as zeros." Adding some challenge to her tone, she asked, "Can you help them, or do I need to find someone else who can?"

The gruff engineer gave a derisive snort. "Telling more people about these two is the last thing you need." Relenting somewhat, he added, "I can do the job." He pulled off his gloves, revealing his thick but dexterous digits. Extending one paw to the humans, he said to them, "Give me your chips. I can upgrade them here."

Bashir handed over his chip and Sarina's to Min, who set them on Nar's low table and started fishing tools from under his clothes.

Sarina watched with a keen stare as Min accessed the restricted portions of the chips by means of some fine-grade tools. She said, "Thank you for your help."

"I am not doing this for you," Min said. "I owe favors to Nar."

"All the same, we're grateful," Sarina said. "Part of the reason we risked coming here was that we hoped to find people like you."

Min glowered at the humans and then focused on his work. "I will link these chips to existing cover identities prepared and active on the BID's server," he said. "Each has its own commerce history and comm log record—both above reproach."

"We'll need security clearances high enough to get us inside government buildings," Bashir said, drawing a bitter stare from Min.

Nar handed a small data tablet to Min. "The necessary protocols are on there," she said. "That should be enough to gain them one-time access."

Nostrils flaring in a subtle display of irritation, Min said, "Very well." It took him only a few more minutes to complete his modifications to the two ID chips. He passed them back to Bashir. "Install those in your helmets now."

Sarina and Bashir did as Min said. While they busied themselves with that task, Min turned his attention to the rest of their disguises. "We will need to make some adjustments to your clothing," he said. "Nothing major. Cosmetic changes, for the most part." He opened a small folding pouch made of synthetic material. Inside it were more precision tools. "I am going to add some insignia to your shoulder pads and the backs of your helmets. This will help you fit in better."

He worked quickly, stenciling new permanent marks onto the humans' suits. Reviewing his handiwork, he said to Nar, "They will need some pieces from your wardrobe to cover the more paramilitary elements of their disguises. These suits offer good protection but make them look conspicuous in a civilian environment."

"Agreed," Nar said. She repaired to her bedroom and searched her walk-in wardrobe for dark material that Min could fashion into coverings for Bashir's and Sarina's garments. By the time she returned, Min had finished his modifications to the humans' suits. Nar handed Min what she had found. "Will this do?"

"Yes." He crafted Nar's assortment of worn-out pieces into dark, torso-concealing serapes. "Much better."

Nar asked, "Will it be safe now for them to move around in public?"

"I think so," Min said. "At the least, their presence

should stop setting off null errors and triggering pattern-recognition systems."

Bashir quipped under his breath, "Well, *that's* a relief."

Taking Min aside a few paces, Nar whispered, "They need a place to stay. Somewhere safe. I want you to take them down to the warren."

"Absolutely not," Min said. Leaning closer, he added, "Do not trust them."

"They need to be watched, of course," Nar said. "But do not treat them like prisoners. They could help us set up a way out of the Confederacy, to asylum." She stroked the side of Min's face with her palm. "This could be our chance to escape."

Her confidant glared at the humans and then whispered to Nar, "Listen to me. They say they are civilians, but those chips of theirs have been modified with isolinear processors—a *Starfleet* technology." He picked up his helmet and barked over his shoulder at the humans, "Get dressed. I am taking you someplace else." While the humans put their disguises back on, Min narrowed his eyes at Nar. "This had best not be a mistake, Nar. Because if it is, we are all going to die."

Bashir and Sarina followed Min down a steep, long staircase that vanished into darkness. The paranoid part of Bashir's mind wondered if Min was taking them somewhere remote to execute them. He hoped his vocoder concealed his anxiety as he asked, "Are you sure we're going the right way?"

"Yes," Min said. "I am taking you to a haven off the

grid. A place untouched by the urban surveillance network. Only a handful of us know of this sanctuary."

Their plodding descent took several minutes and entailed half a dozen switchback turns at short landings. At the bottom of the stairs was a large, barricaded door. Beside it was a shattered light fixture mounted on the wall. Min rotated the fixture aside, revealing a button in a recess. He pressed it. Seconds later, a synthetic voice said over a hidden intercom, *"Valley."*

Min replied, "Harbor." Next came the sound of heavy bolts being retracted and the low thrum of a magnetic seal being neutralized. The door that had seemed so impregnable swung open. Leading Bashir and Sarina inside the enclosure, Min declared to the two armed Breen standing guard, "I bring new friends. Welcome them." Apparently satisfied by Min's assurance, the guards lowered their weapons and waved the trio past them.

Once the trio was clear of the entryway, the guards closed and locked the portal. Min led Bashir and Sarina around a high privacy barrier and said over his shoulder, "Welcome to the warren." As Bashir turned the corner behind Min, he was rewarded by a remarkable sight.

A multilevel complex stretched out ahead of him and Sarina. Unmasked Breen citizens of many species mingled in the wide thoroughfare. They traded goods and haggled over prices while standing in front of shops, and they socialized over drinks and plates of food while sitting together at tables along the street. Music filled the air, and the sound of many languages being spoken all at once reminded Bashir of a busy day on Deep Space 9's bustling Promenade.

"We will draw a few stares by remaining masked," Min said, "but it will be much worse if anyone sees who you are. These people risk their lives when they come here. It would be best not to frighten them any further."

"We understand," Sarina said. "We don't want to cause any trouble."

"Stay close," Min said, guiding Bashir and Sarina onto an open lift platform. "I know of an open unit on an upper level where you can stay until Nar calls for you." He closed the lift's safety gate and pulled a manual-control lever to initiate its lethargic ascent. "If you need food, I can arrange to have some delivered."

"That's very kind of you," Bashir said. "We'd appreciate that."

"Then it will be done," Min said.

The lift car climbed slowly inside its four-point metal frame, turning each level of the complex into an ephemeral tableau of Breen society's best-kept secrets. Tiny nooks run like speakeasies were packed with polyglot crowds, pungent with the fumes of alcohol-laden drinks and spicy cuisines, and aglow with warm but dim lights sheltered by sconces. Interspecies romantic assignations transpired in the slivers between structures and behind half-shaded windows. On the other sides of flimsy walls and ramshackle doors, tight clusters of aliens danced in bobbing packs beneath multicolored strobe lights, to bass-heavy dance beats that thumped like the muffled pulse of a culture.

A few levels higher, revelry gave way to somber ritual. Hundreds of Breen citizens hailing from a dozen different species gathered in a circle, each holding a lit candle and chanting softly together over a shrouded body on a bier.

The next several tiers of the complex were relatively quiet. Through one half-open window, Bashir heard a child weeping. A door ajar gave him a glimpse of an artist dabbing paint on a canvas. A lone male figure paced outside a door, ostensibly racked with indecision.

Elevated enough to take in the full scope of this hidden sector of Rasiuk, Bashir estimated that it might house as many as ten thousand persons on twenty densely packed levels. A thick haze hung in the air, a by-product of primitive cooking methods, establishments devoted to groups smoking from water-cooled pipes, and lack of access to the municipal air-purification system. He could only hope that its water supply and waste-removal infrastructure were not so overtaxed as its atmospheric scrubbers.

Min halted the lift and opened the gate. "Out." Bashir and Sarina exited the lift car, and Min closed its gate as he followed them. Bashir turned one way and then the other and saw what appeared to be a deserted level of tiny residential boxes pressed together without a hair's breadth of space between them. Walking along the open terrace, Min said, "This way."

He led them to a nondescript unit, pressed buttons marked with alien symbols on a panel beside its door, and stood aside as the portal slid open. "This is it."

It was a single room with a bed, a comm unit, a cooking nook, and a partition that Bashir presumed hid the lavatory. There wasn't a single lick of color or personality—just a drab gray box with the bare essentials. Min moved to the windows and pulled all the curtains fully closed.

"It's perfect," Bashir said. "Thank you."

Handing a small data device to Sarina, Min said, "This has the codes for your door and its intercom, and today's and tomorrow's challenge-and-response phrases for the main entrance of the warren. Guard this data with your lives."

"We will," Sarina said.

Min walked back to the door, which opened ahead of him. He paused on its threshold and turned to face Bashir and Sarina. "Remember to wait here until Nar calls for you. Do not move about the warren without your masks. And do not tell anyone who you are."

"Understood," Bashir said.

"I hope Nar's trust in you is not misplaced." Min moved to leave, then turned back to add, "Stay safe." Before either Bashir or Sarina could reply, Min hurried away, back toward the lift.

The door of their hideout slid closed and locked. Bashir removed his helmet and smiled at Sarina. "Home, sweet home."

21

Dax knew something was wrong even before Bowers said, "We have a new problem, Captain." The XO stood at the tactical console, whose readouts had monopolized his and Lieutenant Kedair's attention for most of the last half hour.

"Put it on the main screen," Dax said, expecting the worst.

"Aye, sir." Bowers relayed the data to the forward viewer. A map of the sectors surrounding the *Aventine*'s current position appeared. Dots of many colors and sizes marked the positions of nearby star systems; icons resembling different powers' national insignias indicated the whereabouts of allied and hostile starships. Dax made an approximate count of the icons massed on the opposite side of the Breen-Federation border and was dismayed to note that they appeared to have multiplied since her crew's last sensor sweep of the area.

She turned her chair toward the tactical console. "It looks as if the Typhon Pact is flexing its muscles along the border, doesn't it, Commander?"

Bowers nodded. "Yes, sir, it does. We're looking at a mixed force of Breen and Romulan warships moving in a staggered formation, shadowing our course."

Mirren looked back from ops. "Is that their oh-so-subtle way of warning us to stay on our side of the border?"

"After a fashion," Kedair said. To Dax she added, "They have more ships on the way from the El-Nahab Sector. I'm reading Gorn and Tholian signals."

Lieutenant Commander Helkara said, "Commander Marius must have pitched a fit after the trick we pulled on him and his friends." He stepped away from his station to study the map on the main screen more closely. "Could they be getting ready to come after us in force?"

"Doubtful," Dax said. "We're back within sensor range of Deep Space 3. Unless the Typhon Pact is itching to turn this cold war hot, they won't attack us out here in plain sight." She got up and walked forward to stand beside Helkara, facing the enormous map. "Kedair, show me a progression from the last three hours: the positions of the ships in the Breen fleet relative to us and the Alrakis system."

As soon as the brief sequence played out on the screen, it became apparent to Dax what was happening. "They're maneuvering to keep themselves between us and Salavat," she said. "That's not an attack fleet—it's a blockade."

Kedair and Bowers conferred in whispers for a moment. From the helm, Lieutenant Tharp said, "At slipstream velocity we might be able to sneak through."

"I don't think so," Dax said. "Their fleet is maintaining a steady distance from us. Look at these intervals, here and here. When we moved half a light-year closer to the border, they dropped back by the same distance. They're giving themselves room—which equals time to react if we try to race through."

Mirren held the sides of her console and leaned forward, her forehead creased with the effort of concentration. "There must be options," she said. "Ways to mask our energy signature, or blind their sensors for a few seconds."

Rubbing his goateed chin, Bowers wore a pensive look as he eyed the map and asked rhetorically, "I don't suppose we have time to go back to Deep Space 9 and ask to borrow the *Defiant*'s cloaking device?"

"Wouldn't matter if we did," Helkara said. "It's Romulan-made. Those warbirds would see us coming half a sector away. Plus it'd suck so much power that we couldn't go to slipstream, which would leave us too slow to get through."

"We're not going back to DS9," Dax said. "We need to stay on-station in case Bashir and Douglas call for extraction." She studied the map and frowned. "Not that we could reach them right now without getting ourselves blown up."

Kedair enlarged a section of the map with an inset box in the corner of the screen. "There's another matter to consider, Captain. This map shows only those vessels we're able to detect. Given the sensor capabilities of the ships in that blockade, their deployment pattern is far from optimal." She touched her console as she spoke, highlighting portions of the map. "There are multiple gaps in their sensor net. Some of them are relatively minor, but others are substantial."

"I know," Dax said. "They're daring us to run the blockade there." She cracked a grim smile. "Which means that's probably where the cloaked ships are."

"My thoughts exactly, Captain," Kedair said.

Bowers chimed in, "Fighting cloaks with cloaks worked

for us once. Maybe we need to hand off the extraction to the Klingons—send in a bird-of-prey."

Dax shook her head. "No, we played that card. The Romulans are watching for it now. I anticipated their ambush site yesterday and had the Klingons move in and run silent till the warbirds showed themselves. But if we try to sneak a Klingon warship into the Alrakis system, odds are it'll be detected and destroyed."

"Once again turning a cold war into a shooting war," Bowers said. He thought for a moment. "What if we don't ask the Klingons to break through but just smoke out the cloaked warbirds? They wouldn't have to uncloak or even cross the border. If they get close enough to force the blockade to shift its deployment, it might open a gap that either we or a Klingon ship could exploit."

"I see what you're saying," Dax replied. "Force them to pick their battle: the one they can see or the one they can't—and either way, they lose." She nodded. "It would take a lot of cloaked ships, but it's worth a try." She turned toward the tactical console. "Kedair, where's the nearest Klingon battle group?"

"Refueling at Starbase 514," Kedair said.

Returning to her chair, Dax said, "It never hurts to ask, but we'll have to go through channels for this. Hail Starfleet Command. I have major groveling to do."

22

Bashir held the curtains of one window half a centimeter apart and peeked through at unfamiliar aliens of the Breen Confederacy as they passed by on the promenade outside. Foot traffic on this level was sparse, but in just a half hour he had seen individuals from two races he had never before encountered.

"You should stay away from the windows," Sarina said. "Someone might see you. I'd rather not lose the one safe haven we've managed to find."

He let the curtains fall together and walked back to join Sarina, who was sprawled on the low bed at the far end of the room. "Fine. I'd hate to make the natives restless." Sitting down on the edge of the bed, he continued, "So, we're 'cultural observers,' are we? That's a clever story. Not that Min was buying it."

"Min strikes me as a chronic paranoid," Sarina said. "Even if we'd prepared that cover story in advance, he wouldn't have bought it."

"You admit you spun that lie out of thin air."

Sarina shrugged. "It had to be done, so I did it." She rolled her head toward him. "Besides, it's not as if we could risk telling these people the truth about us."

"Why not? They're dissidents. You saw how eager Nar was to help us."

"Once I told her we were civilians," Sarina said. "I doubt she'd have been as helpful if she knew we were Starfleet Intelligence operatives."

Reclining beside her, Bashir replied, "I think she would have."

"Don't be so sure. Just because she and Min are dissidents, that doesn't make them *traitors*. Sheltering peaceful observers is one thing. Aiding and abetting a pair of spies on a mission to sabotage a military program is something entirely different. The bottom line is that it's better for them if they don't know why we're really here. If they end up compromised because of us, they can't divulge what they don't know."

He flashed a teasing smile. "How thoughtful of you. But how do you know they aren't listening in on us right now?"

"Because while you were busy peeping out the windows, I was sweeping the room for surveillance devices." Returning his chiding look with her own disarming grin, she added, "Occupational hazard."

He rolled onto his side to face her across the pillows. "Alone at last."

"And it took you only six years to get me here." Putting on a mock frown, Sabrina added, "My mother warned me about fast boys like you."

"Did she?"

"Actually, it was Lauren," she said, reminding Bashir of her sexually predatory ex-peer in the Jack Pack. "She always said those boys were the most fun and encouraged me to seek them out whenever I could."

He rolled his eyes, chortled once, and nodded. "That sounds like Lauren." Then he looked into Sarina's eyes, only centimeters away from his, and they fell silent for several seconds. A hundred jumbled thoughts flew through his mind, but he said nothing and thought he might let the moment pass unremarked.

Sarina said, "You're thinking something. I can see it in your eyes."

"This isn't the time or place to talk about it."

"Sure it is. One or both of us might not make it off this rock alive, Julian. If you have something on your mind, share it. We might not get another chance."

Part of him was resisting saying what he wanted to say, what needed to be said. Then Sarina reached out and caressed his cheek, and he touched her flaxen hair, and the words he had held prisoner for so long broke free in a mad rush.

"I missed you so much after you left. You needed space, so I didn't call and didn't write. But I wanted to, more times than I could count. You were the woman I'd waited my whole life to meet, the one I'd spent my life searching for. And then, there you were. At my side. In my arms." Memories of her bittersweet departure from Deep Space 9 brought tears to his eyes. "I understand why you had to go away, why you had to leave me behind. I let you go because I thought that's what was best for you. But watching you go, I felt like my heart was being cut out."

A lonely tear escaped from the corner of his eye. As Sarina brushed it away with the back of her hand, Bashir saw that she was crying, too.

"I didn't understand then what I meant to you," she whispered. "Or what you meant to me. I couldn't. But if I had . . . I don't think I could have left." Her lips grazed his, and her breath was warm and close. She met his teary-eyed gaze with her own. "I don't want to leave you again. Ever."

He pulled her close, and they kissed. At once passionate and tender, hungry yet giving, it was the most natural connection Bashir had ever felt with another being. There was no awkwardness, no hesitation or uncertainty.

Their hands found each other's bodies, stripped away layer after layer of clothing, all with easy grace and languid movements. His fingertips traced the elegant line of her jaw, the perfect slope of her nose, the delicate curve of her chin. She kissed the side of his neck and pulled her fingernails down his back, leaving warm scratch trails from his shoulders to the last of his ribs.

One moment bled into another with the hazy quality of a dream. They rolled together, and then he was on top of her. She wrapped her arms around his neck and her legs over his hips. Their rhythm increased in vigor, and Bashir lost himself in her, in the moment, in the riptide of his desires. Perspiration glistened between her breasts, and he was mesmerized by the beauty of her profile as her head lolled to one side and the muscles of her face tensed with exquisite agonies.

As he surrendered to his own release, he knew that he felt as Sarina did: he never wanted to leave her again. Ever.

No one had stopped Chot Nar on her way inside the Breen Intelligence Directorate, and that much at least still seemed right with her world. It had been a few hours since she had reached her task pod, and in seclusion she had set herself to work on parallel jobs: routine data analysis ran on one side of her holomatrix while on the other she put the finishing touches on the humans' new identichip profiles.

It should be easy to pass them off as Silwaan like me, Nar figured. That would enable them to purchase food or beverages appropriate to their biology without triggering any alerts in the network. Though they had come prepared with a fair amount of hard currency, Nar knew they would raise fewer suspicions if they conducted their transactions with credit lines linked to their ID profiles. To that end, she created a pair of well-funded accounts for their new aliases. It still amazed her that a culture as paranoid as the Breen's had allowed its commercial infrastructure to become so vulnerable to virtual fraud. *We have spent so much effort on hiding our identities from one another that money must have come to seem like a trivial concern,* she reasoned as the two credit accounts were confirmed as active.

As a test of her work, she ran an offline analysis of the new profiles, to see if either one would appear suspect during normal contact with the automated network. Neither generated any alerts during her isolated trial run, and she was satisfied that they would more than pass inspection if needed. She uploaded the files to the public servers and then deleted the copies from her local drive. Next she initiated a secure-erasure protocol to make certain the deleted documents would be unrecoverable. While her machine labored on that operation, she accessed the logs of multiple servers and routers in the Breen surveillance network and either deleted or altered the file-transmission records to conceal the origin and creation dates of the new identichip profiles. Working backward from her first actions to her last, she wiped out the evidence of her cover-up, including the cover-up itself.

Her final act of sabotage was to upload a self-erasing program into the secure backup servers at the BID, to ensure that her peers and superiors could not use them to reconstruct the data expunged from the public system.

That will do, she decided. She opened an encrypted channel and keyed in the code for the remote comm deck at the hideout in the warren. The call signal buzzed a few times before Nar's message was received. A small image popped into the lower left corner of her holomatrix. Looking back at her over the connection was a Breen mask whose altered markings she recognized as Bashir's.

"*Yes?*" he said, his true voice rendered into machine noise by his vocoder.

"This is Nar. The work we spoke of is done."

Bashir nodded. "*Thank you. What should we do now?*"

"Do you still need access to the BID for your research?"

"*Yes, as long as it doesn't put you in danger.*"

His sentiment almost made her laugh. "We are quite past that."

"*We also need access to that comm center,*" Bashir said.

Nar wondered if perhaps Min had been right when he'd warned her not to trust the humans. "Why do you need that? I already told you that the BID controls the surveillance of the civilian population."

"*I know, but we have reason to suspect the BID is sharing*

its data with the military, and vice versa. We need to be sure. It's a mission imperative."

Though his request made her uneasy, she was not ready to lose her faith in him. "If you really need to go inside the comm center, you can," she said. "I gave you both high-level government clearances. Your chips will identify you as senior officials in the Confederate Information Bureau. Unless someone sees you commit a crime, no one on Salavat should have the authority to hold you."

"Excellent," Bashir said. *"Thank you again."*

"There's more," Nar said. "Your ID chips are linked to credit accounts. You should use those to pay for things. It will leave traces, but it will also seem more normal. Certain purchases are flagged for investigation when paid for in cash."

Bashir cocked his head at an angle that expressed wariness. *"What kind of purchases, exactly?"*

"Intercity and interstellar transport. Weapons. Controlled pharmaceuticals. Private vehicles. Large quantities of industrial chemicals."

"Understood. We don't plan on buying any of those—at least, not as far as I know. But I'll keep that in mind for future reference."

"Good. Your new alias is Hesh Gron. Sarina's is Hesh Rin."

"Noted. Anything else?"

"Your new ID chips alone will not be enough to get you inside government and military buildings. You will need special credentials. I have prepared them for you. Can you and Sarina meet me here on Level Forty-five to get them?"

"Yes. How soon do you want to meet?"

"Be here in one hour. Wait by the kiosk between Erkot and Arawn sectors, in the third crossroads from city center."

"We'll see you there," Bashir said. *"And Nar—thank you."*

Suppressing the impulse toward sentiment, Nar said, "Do not be late," and closed the channel. The inset screen vanished from her holomatrix.

An alert on her console snared her attention. Ever mindful of the risk that she might be detected by someone else within the BID as a subversive element, Nar had created a number of applications to monitor her incoming and outgoing data packets for signs of monitoring and interference. Several of those warnings were sounding off at once. She checked the logs and quickly perused the reports. Internal channels at the BID were listening in on her communications and lurking behind her holomatrix interface.

They know, she realized. A sinking sensation left her feeling sick and hollow. Her peers and supervisors had been spying on her for at least the past few minutes—maybe longer. Nar had no way of knowing for certain just how much they had heard and seen or how much they knew. The only thing of which she could be certain was that she had just unwittingly invited Sarina and Bashir into a trap.

23

After a night alone with Sarina, Bashir felt more than a bit overwhelmed by the madding crush of the crowded streets of Rasiuk. They had made their way there from the warren without incident, and Bashir had noticed a few shopkeepers adopting postures more subservient than usual when they saw the kinds of advertisements that his and Sarina's presence triggered.

Nar wasn't kidding when she said she'd turned us into VIPs, he thought. Resolving not to abuse the protection and privilege with which he and Sarina had been blessed, Bashir pressed on at her side toward the third crossroads, which was a short distance ahead but obscured by the sheer mass of people filling it. When they were still twenty meters or so from the intersection, it became possible to see the public-information kiosk in its center.

Sarina poked Bashir. "There she is, at the far terminal, facing us."

"I see her." Though Nar resembled every other Breen in sight, Sarina had reprogrammed the HUDs of their helmets to recognize Nar and Min by the signals from their identichips, highlighting them in the duo's visors. Bashir forged ahead, leading with his shoulder so he could blade through the knots of people congesting the streets in every direction.

Sidestepping toward Nar, he was surprised when she turned away from him and started wending her way through the gray sea of pedestrians. Bashir and Sarina walked faster and risked elbowing and bustling a few people to catch up to Nar.

As soon as they were within arm's reach of her, Nar said without looking back, "Walk behind me and say nothing." She led them onto a sidewalk where the foot traffic was moving more briskly, and they walked quickly to keep up with her. "The two of you should be free and clear to move, but I have been compromised." They followed her around a turn onto another equally jam-packed boulevard. "I had your credentials delivered by confidential courier to deposit boxes under your new names, at the Bank of Ferenginar branch on Level Thirty-seven, Padlon Sector, Commerce Row. Good luck." Nar changed direction without warning and cut across the street. The last thing she said that Bashir heard over the white noise of the crowd was, "Do not try to follow me."

Bashir and Sarina continued walking in the same direction they had been, and neither risked looking back. They were a block away when they heard sirens and a commotion that quelled the hubbub of the street, but the interlude passed in less than a minute, and then urban clamor rushed like water to fill the sonic void.

A dark mood turned Bashir silent and melancholy. Nar had trusted him and Sarina, and it grieved him to think Nar would come to harm because of them, but there was nothing he could do now to help her. Nothing except go forward.

It wasn't until he and Sarina reached the Bank of Ferenginar that he realized neither of them had really been leading the other; he and Sarina both seemed to have grown accustomed to the layout of Rasiuk and had become adept at reading street signs and building markers in their native markings. They were greeted in the bank's ludicrously gilt lobby by a husky Ferengi man wearing garish clothes and an assortment of gaudy latinum rings, pendants, and chains. Pressing his wrists together in front of him, he bowed slightly to Bashir and Sarina as he said, "Welcome to the Bank of Ferenginar. My name is Lag, senior accounts supervisor. How may I serve you?"

"Safe-deposit boxes," Sarina said. "Hesh Rin."

"Hesh Gron," Bashir said, figuring the less he said, the better.

Lag bowed. "Of course." He straightened to reveal a scanning device in his hand. "If I might be permitted to scan your ID chips to verify your identities . . ."

Sarina said, "Proceed." She and Bashir stood still while Lag scanned them.

"Excellent," Lag said. "Please follow me to the deposit room."

The stout Ferengi led Bashir and Sarina past the bank's offices to a private room with a table and some chairs. "Please wait here while we retrieve—" He paused as two young Ferengi clerks in far simpler garb rushed in holding deposit boxes, which they set on the table. "Here they are," Lag said. Backing toward the door, he continued, "Your boxes are coded to open on contact with your ID chip. Take as long as you like. Press the bell when you're ready to leave."

The Ferengi backpedaled out the door, which slid closed behind him and locked with a resonant magnetic hum.

As promised, the lids of the two lockboxes sprang open as soon as Bashir and Sarina touched them. Inside each box was a security card marked with Breen symbols for the Confederate Information Bureau. They tucked their cards into hidden pockets of their disguises.

"There's no way of knowing how long it'll take the Breen to make Nar talk," Sarina said. "But if we hurry, we should be able to get in and out of that military comm center before they know we were there."

A pang of guilt gnawed at Bashir. "Hang on. We need to warn the people of the warren. If the interrogators break Nar, all those people are in danger."

"That's not our mission, Julian. We came here to find the hidden shipyard, destroy the slipstream prototype, and sabotage any copies of the plans—not get mixed up in the Breen's internal politics."

"Well, I'm sorry, but I can't be so blasé about it. Those people sheltered us, and I think we owe them at least a fair warning that their lives are in peril."

"Not to be a bitch about this, but—no, *we don't*."

"How can you say that? After the risks Nar and Min took for us, how can you just turn your back on them? Is this some kind of latent elitism of the genetically enhanced rearing its ugly head?"

"No, Julian, it's common sense. Nar's not a field agent.

She isn't trained to resist interrogation, and we have no way of knowing how resilient her species is under stress. Now that they have her, it's only a matter of time before they make her talk. Maybe she'll betray us first, maybe the warren. If I had to bet, I'd say she'll sell us out *long* before she betrays them. Which means we have a hell of a lot less time to finish our mission and get out of here than we did before."

Bashir shook his head in angry refusal of Sarina's argument. "I can't believe what I'm hearing. You really think we have no obligation to the dissidents?"

"An *obligation*? No. But if we find what we need at the comm center and have a chance to warn the dissidents before we move on, I'd be fine with that."

After a grim chortle, Bashir replied, "How noble of you."

"No one ever said intelligence work was noble. Just necessary." She slammed shut the lid of her deposit box. "Time's wasting. Let's go." As Sarina marched to the door, Bashir closed his own deposit box and followed her.

Sarina pressed the door signal, and Lag opened the door a moment afterward. He shadowed Bashir and Sarina to the bank's front entrance, pestering them with obsequious expressions of gratitude every step of the way. It took all of Bashir's willpower not to swat the bothersome Ferengi. As he and Sarina left the bank and melted back into the crowd, Bashir could only hope they would be swift enough to spare ten thousand freethinkers from a bitter fate.

24

Nanietta Bacco stood back from the table as a troop of chefs and servers swarmed around it, setting out the last of the items to leave the kitchen and making certain that every possible detail was as close as possible to perfect. Her chief of staff, Esperanza Piñiero, stood a few meters away, one hand pressed to her ear while she listened for an updated report from the Palais de la Concorde's event scheduler.

"He's on his way, Madam President," Piñiero said. She turned to the white-suited staff of the Roth Dining Room and shooed them away. "Clear out, people! On the double, let's go!" As the workers scurried back into the kitchen, Piñiero looked over the assortment of Klingon delicacies that adorned the only table in the cavernous room. It was like an oasis of *gagh* and *pipius* claws in the midst of a granite-tiled ocean of gray. "A lot of effort for one man."

Bacco sighed. "I'd hate history to say we failed for lack of effort."

Poking at something that might have been *bregit* lung, Piñiero said, "You'd rather it said we failed because the Klingon ambassador gorged himself to death?"

"Don't be silly, Esperanza. He won't touch any of this."

"Then why put it out?"

"How long have you worked in politics? This is all about the gesture."

"If you insist. But I get the feeling we'll be seeing a lot of Klingon dishes on the commissary's menu for the rest of the week." Piñiero backed away toward the president's private entrance, which was hidden behind a ceiling-to-floor tapestry along the dining room's back wall. "He's ten seconds out. Good luck."

"Thanks."

The chief of staff nodded, withdrew at a quick step, and vanished behind the heavy scarlet curtain.

The main doors at the far end of the dining room swung inward, and Ambassador K'mtok strode inside unescorted. "Madam President!" he bellowed, his rich baritone booming and echoing in the emptiness around them. "We really must stop meeting like this." Bacco put on a taut smile as the hulking diplomat crossed the great hall to join her at its lone table. "Normally, I'd resent being sent for this early in the day"—he picked up a *pipius* claw—"but I never could resist the charms of a woman who was willing to cook for me."

"Are you done acting like a jackass, Your Excellency?"

He flashed a sawtooth grin. "Yes, Madam President."

"Good." She picked up a decanter of bloodwine and filled the stein beside K'mtok's place setting. "Have a seat. Let's talk."

He sat down, lifted the metal mug, and downed a long draught of the tart alcoholic beverage. Bacco tossed a few *pipius* claws onto her plate and sat down.

K'mtok sleeved dribbled wine from his chin. "So? Talk."

"Don't play dumb," Bacco said. "You know why you're here. Has Martok agreed to my request for Klingon military aid in the Alrakis system?"

"No." To Bacco's surprise, K'mtok scooped up a fistful of *gagh* and shoved the wriggling worms into his mouth. He chewed behind a smile of satisfaction.

In a tenor that was firm but still calm, Bacco said, "I need more than a one-word answer, Ambassador. Why has our call for reinforcements been denied?"

Still chewing, K'mtok said, "Are you kidding? The last fleet we sent there never came home." He held up his hand to stave off Bacco's brewing protest. After he swallowed, he continued. "The truth is that our military is as over-stretched as yours—perhaps more, since most of our empire was built and retained by force."

"I understand that, but you have an entire battle group refueling at Starbase 514, less than a day away from—"

"They've been recalled," K'mtok said. "On the chancellor's orders."

She shoved aside her plate. "Recalled? For what purpose?"

"To deal with growing threats to our border colonies. Membership in the Typhon Pact has made the Gorn and the Kinshaya bold enough to dare taking what belongs to the Klingon Empire. I did not think I would ever see such a day . . . but we live in uncertain times, Madam President."

"Indeed, we do, Your Excellency. However, some risks need to be taken, even in perilous days such as these. And the matter on which we require your aid is one of the utmost secrecy and importance."

K'mtok nodded and waved a half-devoured *pipius* claw. "Yes, yes, your two spies stranded on Salavat. We know all about it."

Feigning incomprehension, Bacco said, "I'm sorry, Mister Ambassador, but I don't have any idea what you're—"

"We *know.*" K'mtok met Bacco's stare with a challenging look. "And if we have this intel, it's almost certain the Typhon Pact has it."

Bacco leaned forward. "How did you find out about Salavat?"

Matching the president's pose, K'mtok said, "Can you keep a secret?"

His question drew a pained smile from Bacco. "Yes, I can—and so can you, which is why you won't tell me."

"You're quick, Madam President. I've always liked that about you." He pushed aside his plate, sleeved bits of food from his mouth, and stood. "Please accept Chancellor Martok's regrets and my apologies, Madam President." Lowering his chin, he made a respectful half bow. "By your leave."

"Thank you for coming, Your Excellency. "

He nodded, backed up five steps, then turned smartly and walked at a leisurely pace out of the dining room. As the great doors closed after him, Bacco heard the private executive entrance open. Piñiero emerged from behind the curtain and walked toward the president, who left the table and met Piñiero halfway.

Grimacing at the sight of Bacco's expression, Piñiero

said, "I'm guessing the Klingons refused to help us extract Bashir and Douglas."

"What gave it away?" snapped Bacco. "Ambassador K'mtok just informed me that there's a leak in our intelligence service. Get on the horn and tell Admiral Nechayev and Jas Abrik I want them both in my office five minutes ago."

"Yes, ma'am." She proffered a padd to Bacco. "There are some other emergent situations I'll need to brief you on when you get—"

"No time, Esperanza. Sum them up while we walk."

"Yes, ma'am. Starfleet reports there have been new attacks by Tzenkethi harriers along our shared border—looks like they're itching for another fight."

Bacco shook her head. "The only true universal constant: the Tzenkethi are jerks." She waved it off. "What else?"

Piñiero tapped on the padd, switching to a new page of information. "We're hearing rumbles of discontent from the planetary government on Andor, and they're trying to play the secession card again."

"Tell them, 'Nice try, but I'm not buying it.' Next?"

Another tap on the padd. "The Tholians are harassing interstellar shipping to and from the Cardassian Union. The best part? They're saying it's actually all *our* fault, because we forced them to do it."

"That's not news, that's just the Tholians being Tholians."

They passed through the executive entrance and strolled side by side down the corridor to the turbolift to Bacco's fifteenth-floor office. As they entered the lift, the president let out a long, demoralized sigh. "How long until I stand for reelection?"

"Two years, three months, and nine days, Madam President."

"Is there any way to rig it so I lose next time?"

"I'll try, but I regret to inform you that your approval ratings are excellent."

"Do what you can."

25

In spite of Nar's preparations and Sarina's assurances, Bashir still felt queasy with anxiety as he and Sarina approached the checkpoint for the government complex on Level Fifty-six. He was certain the guards—or, to be more precise, their automated screening devices—would see through his and Sarina's disguises. If that happened, it would be too late to flee; the checkpoint was situated in the midst of an entire platoon of heavily armed Breen soldiers.

His fear of exposure persisted even after the guards ushered him and Sarina through the checkpoint with speed and deference. Once their credentials had been scanned and verified, no one dared ask them any questions. All that the soldiers seemed to care about was moving them along to their destination as quickly as possible. As the duo walked away from the soldiers, Sarina confided to Bashir over their private comm channel, *"One down, one to go."*

If he hadn't known better, he might have thought she was having fun.

They continued on until they arrived at the military comm center. Muttering over the encrypted channel, Bashir said, "Now for the real test of these identities."

He stepped ahead of Sarina and paused to let the comm

center's guards examine his identichip and access card. Bashir expected the soldier in charge to at least ask what business a member of the civilian government had inside a military facility—a query for which he and Sarina had rehearsed some hard-to-debunk replies—but instead the broad-shouldered guard handed back Bashir's access card without a word and motioned for him to pass and enter. Sarina received the same perfunctory once-over before being permitted to pass.

Neither of the two spies said anything until they were inside the building and away from the guards' post. As they passed through the library-quiet, gray granite lobby of the comm center, Bashir asked, "Where do we go?"

"Look for a directory," Sarina said, still relying on the private channel between their helmets to keep their conversation safe from eavesdroppers.

Bashir nodded at an interactive panel along a nearby wall. At a glance, he said, "It's touch activated. Probably as a biometric security precaution, so it can scan our ID chips."

Sarina started tapping on different Breen symbols, and the panel responded with floor plans, directions, and supplemental information regarding which personnel were in command of which areas. It wasn't until Bashir had finished skimming the high points of the intel that he realized he had done so without the need for his visor's translation interface. While he was marveling at his new grasp of written Breen, Sarina pointed at an isolated section of one floor plan. *"That's what we're looking for, on the twenty-third floor."*

Following the line implied by her pointed finger, Bashir

eyed the schematic. "Auxiliary systems control? Why make *that* our target?"

"Because auxiliary systems tend to be less defended and less staffed than primary facilities, and they often have override capabilities, which can be useful if something goes wrong." She blanked the information screen. *"There's a lift back there, in the corridor on the right. Let's go."*

A handful of Breen officers stared at Bashir and Sarina as they crossed the lobby to the bank of lifts, but no one spoke to them or impeded their passage. Although it was impossible to see any faces, Bashir had come to recognize certain tics of Breen body language; the postures of the military personnel who observed him and Sarina seemed to be reacting with equal parts fear and resentment. *I guess there's some friction between the government and the military,* Bashir speculated as he and Sarina entered an elevator car, whose controls were laid out in a vertical, diamond-shaped configuration.

"This is your show," Bashir said. "Take it away."

She pressed one of the buttons. The doors slid shut, and the elevator ascended with a soft purr and a barely noticeable sensation of movement. Seconds later the doors opened, revealing a corridor whose walls, floor, and ceiling all were composed of polished black granite. Sparse lighting contributed to a gloomy ambience. Sarina led Bashir out of the elevator. *"C'mon,"* she said.

They stole down the corridor, passing several doors marked only with Breen numerals. Even though they stepped lightly, their footfalls sounded loud and sharp and echoed off the hard surfaces. "I hope we don't need to sneak up on anyone," Bashir said to Sarina, only half joking. She let his halfhearted attempt at humor pass without comment and pressed on around a corner to the end of the corridor.

Pointing at the door directly ahead of them, at the terminus of the dead-end passage, Sarina said, *"That's it."* Facing Bashir, she added, *"I'll try and fast-talk whoever's inside into giving us access to the system, but I don't know whether our cover personas give us the authority to get away with that."*

"And if they don't? What then?"

She shrugged. *"I'll make something up."*

"You're not exactly filling me with confidence right now."

"Just stay close and watch our backs." Sarina walked to the door of the auxiliary systems control room. She stared at the sensor pad beside the door. *"Pretty simple interface. Doesn't look like it uses an access code, just a biometric identification."* Looking back at Bashir, she asked rhetorically, *"Feeling lucky?"*

"Ask me again in ten seconds."

Sarina pressed her hand against the door's sensor pad.

The door slid open, and she walked in without hesitation.

A lone technician sat with his back to the door, surrounded by towering banks of computers and a 270-degree wraparound holographic master-control interface. He dispelled the holomatrix with a sweep of his hand as he stood and turned to confront Sarina and Bashir. "Who are you? This is a restricted area!"

"I am Hesh Rin." Sarina gestured at Bashir. "This is Hesh Gron. We have been sent by the Confederate Information Bureau to demand your cooperation."

"I need to see confirmation of those orders before you access my task pod."

The technician's demand was met by a moment of silence.

Sarina's hand shot forward and struck a knifing blow into the Breen's throat. He made a gagging sound and staggered backward as Sarina launched a jumping snap kick. Her heel slammed into the soldier's chin, which jerked back with a sickening wet snap. His body went limp and collapsed on the floor.

Pointing at a long access panel along the bottom of the wall behind the task pod, Sarina said, "Open that up and put the body in there. Make sure you disable his identichip transponder. The longer it takes his people to find him, the better."

Bashir stood in mute shock, staring at the body while Sarina logged into the task pod's interface and began searching through the Breen Militia's information network. While switching between screens of data, she glanced at Bashir. Her tone was urgent and uncompromising. "Julian, you have to hide the body. For all we know, identichips might alert the system if their wearer dies."

"Right," Bashir said, still struggling to accept his role as an accessory to murder. As he accessed the dead soldier's identichip and neutralized its transceiver, he rationalized his actions to himself. *I'm a Starfleet officer on a military operation. This man was a uniformed member of a hostile military, a valid combatant.* None of his excuses felt convincing. He kept coming back to his Hippocratic oath, his sacred pledge as a physician: First, do no harm. Telling himself that Sarina had done the bloody deed did little to help Bashir distance himself from the taking of a sentient life.

He was still looking for a lie that he could live with as he stuffed the corpse into a maintenance crawlspace and then closed the hatch, hiding it from view.

From the task pod, Sarina said, "I have something." She waited until Bashir joined her before she continued. "A lot of encrypted files and communiqués, all tagged for a special research division in the starship-design bureau here on Salavat. I'll bet that's the slipstream project." Working the holographic interface, she explained, "I'm downloading the data to a portable unit that we can analyze once we're safely out of here."

"And *after* we've warned the dissidents in the warren," Bashir said.

The insistent note in his voice made Sarina pause before she replied, "Yes, of course." She disconnected a portable data device from the task pod's console, stepped away from the holographic interface, and headed for the door. "Let's go."

26

Nar awoke to darkness and the rough kiss of coarse fabric on her face. She tried to reach up and pull away whatever had been draped over her head, only to find her hands restrained behind her. Struggling to move, she quickly took stock of her predicament. The last thing she remembered was a fleeting glimpse of black-armored enforcers from the BID closing in on her as she parted ways from the two humans. Then had come a jolt of electricity, a white flash of pain, and oblivion.

It became clear to her that she was seated. Her feet were shackled into place. Inside the close confines of the hood, her breathing sounded loud, and each desperate gulp of air tasted hotter and more rank than the one before.

Then she heard the mechanical scratch-speak of a vocoder, followed after a half-second delay by its common-tongue translation in a synthetic masculine voice from an overhead speaker: "Hello, Chot Nar."

The hood was yanked off her head. A single blinding light assaulted her vision. She squeezed her eyes shut, but when she tried to turn her head she found it restrained by panels on either side. Even with her eyelids closed, the searing light was painful in its intensity. "Please give me my mask."

"Traitors do not deserve to wear the face of the Breen."

"I am no traitor. Why have you brought me here?"

"You are here to answer questions. And there is no point denying what we already know. You are a dissident and a malcontent."

Lurking behind the light, barely a penumbra at the edge of shadow, was her questioner: a BID senior inquisitor. Nar asked, "Who are you?"

"My identity is not important," said the inquisitor. "Yours is."

Nar tried to shut out the overpowering shame of having been forcibly unmasked by a stranger. To remove one's mask before another was an intimate act reserved for family and friends. Even in a semipublic setting such as the warren, the unanimity of exposure served to put everyone mutually at ease. In front of an inquisitor doubly hidden—behind his mask and a curtain of darkness—Nar felt more vulnerable than she ever had before. "I am no one of consequence," Nar said.

She heard footsteps. The inquisitor was circling her.

"You give yourself too little credit. You are a data analyst in the BID. This occupation gives you access to the urban surveillance network and a wide assortment of intelligence resources." His footfalls grew louder as he drew closer behind her. "You consort regularly with Chon Min, a known agitator and suspected thief. He has made several visits to your home—including one last night, at your invitation. Why did you ask him to come to your residence?"

"I do not remember," Nar said.

"You are lying. This behavior is expected, but it will

soon be dealt with." The inquisitor paced in front of Nar and stopped. Judging from his height and bulk, she guessed he was probably a Paclu under the all-black suit. Leaning over to thrust the snout of his mask into Nar's face, he said, "You have covered your tracks well, Nar. Or should I call you by your native Silwaan appellation—Deshinar Tibbonel, is it?" Nar scowled, and the inquisitor cocked his head at a rakish angle, ostensibly amused by her reaction. "We might or might not be able to recover the data you deleted from your task pod's local drive, Deshinar. But even if that proves impossible, I guarantee you will tell me all that I want to know—and much more. Because I know you so very well. I know what you like and dislike, what pleases you and what frightens you . . ."

She spat at him. As the wad of her saliva dribbled down the snout of his obsidian mask, Nar said, "You know *nothing* about me."

"On the contrary. I know every detail of your life—including how, where, and when it is going to end."

27

Most of the Breen enforcers wore brown uniforms; their supervisors wore gray. The seemingly endless line of prisoners they marched out of the building that concealed the entrance to the dissidents' warren wore black hoods instead of helmets. Passersby on the street turned away and averted their gaze from the spectacle, as if the very thought of a citizen unmasked in public was too shocking to bear. No one looked down from the windows that faced the street as the prisoners were herded into a staggered procession of transport vehicles and carted away without fanfare or comment.

Bashir and Sarina observed the mass arrest from a few intersections away, hidden behind a corner and a pyramid of empty metal canisters awaiting removal. Adjusting his visor's holographic magnification, Bashir asked, "Do you see Min?"

"No," Sarina said. "I'm not sure how I could. There are so many people coming out of there, and they're all in hoods. How would I recognize him?" She frowned. "I can't believe they didn't have alternative routes out of the warren."

"Maybe they did," Bashir said. "But if Nar revealed

all of them, it wouldn't matter how many there were—the BID would've rushed all of them."

Up the street, a prisoner broke away from his captor and started running, despite being hooded and having his hands tied behind his back. He had taken all of five awkward strides before he stumbled over a curb. As he fell, a barrage of disruptor fire converged upon him. He was dead by the time his smoldering body struck the ground. A pair of brown-suited guards retrieved the body and dragged it away to a transport set apart from the others for the purpose of carting corpses.

"My God," Bashir said, "it's a damned pogrom." Guilt twisted in his gut, filling him with a cold, nauseating sensation. "If only we'd warned them sooner—"

"We'd have been caught up in it," Sarina said. "Whom would we have warned, Julian? Nobody in there knew us or trusted us. And how would we have explained what we knew? If they'd found out who we are, do you think they'd have believed us?" She shook her head. "I hate this as much as you do, but you have to put aside your empathy for these people and accept that there was nothing you could have done to stop this." She tugged on his arm. "We should go."

He resisted her pull. "Go? Go where?"

"Away from here, for a start." She gestured at the brown-suited soldiers. "They might be setting up a dragnet for people who visit the warren but weren't there at the time of the raid. We can't risk getting swept up in that."

It galled him to turn his back on tragedy and injustice, but he knew she was right. "Fine," he said. "But we've lost our hideout, and we can't go back to Nar's apartment, so where do we go from here?"

"We could head for the maintenance tunnels," Sarina said. "I just need someplace private where I can study the data we took from the comm center."

Bashir backed away from the corner. "Good enough. I think I saw an access point one sector over. Let's go." He and Sarina retreated out the far end of the alleyway onto a busy street and let the crowd swallow them up.

As they separated to weave around a slow-moving civilian, he heard Sarina's voice over the secure transceiver channel inside his helmet. *"I'm going to fall back a few paces in case anyone is looking for us walking together."*

He switched off his vocoder and replied over the private channel, "Good thinking. If you lose sight of me, let me know and I'll slow down."

"Don't worry about it. I've got you pinpointed in my HUD."

Bashir used a control pad on his forearm to set his HUD to monitor Sarina's position. It added a real-time update along the bottom of his display that let him know she was remaining approximately six meters behind him. Despite this assurance, he soon felt alone in the throng of masked faces. It made him think of the masquerade balls once popular in Earth's ancient royal courts, minus the variety and imagination.

A side street led away from the city's center, and Bashir noted several familiar landmarks that confirmed he was heading in the direction of the maintenance tunnel access hatch. When he reached the narrow passage that led to the hatch, he saw a locked gate that barred access to the alley. Opening his channel to Sarina, he said, "I don't remember that being there, do you?"

"It wasn't there," Sarina said. *"I'm positive. Look how shiny its bolts are. That gate was just put in."* She caught up to Bashir and looked around, as if worried they were being watched or followed. *"They must be closing off access to the maintenance tunnels. I could try to pick the lock, but knowing the Breen, they probably have one or more hidden cameras watching each gate."*

Bashir nodded. "So if we break in, we'll be telling them where we are." He pondered their predicament for a few seconds and then began thinking aloud. "When Nar created these identities for us, she said they had access to generous credit lines. She also created false credit histories for them." Reacting to a flash of inspiration, he beckoned for Sarina to follow him. "Come on." He led her to a nearby information kiosk. Manipulating its controls with an ease that he found both exciting and unsettling, he let the kiosk read his identichip, and then he called up his credit profile. In many ways, the interface resembled those used by the Ferengi businesses on Deep Space 9. Bashir wondered if the Ferengi, who had a long history of trade with the Breen, had been involved in developing the Confederacy's credit and financial networks. Perusing the details of his account's most recent transactions, Bashir found what he had hoped would be there. "Look at that," he said. "We're staying at a visitors' lodge on Level Ten."

Sarina leaned forward and looked past Bashir's shoulder. *"Makes sense,"* she said. *"If we're visitors from offworld here on government business, we'd need a place to stay. That was good thinking on Nar's part."* She elbowed Bashir playfully. *"And you didn't do too bad yourself."*

"Kind of you to say." Bashir logged off from the kiosk. "Let's go check into our hotel room and have a look at those data files."

28

Thot Keer was surrounded by authority figures. His supervisor, Thot Naaz, sat beside him in his office. They were facing the holomatrix, which was divided into a split screen showing two real-time subspace feeds. On one side was the visage of Thot Gren, the Confederacy's delegate to the Typhon Pact's board of governors; on the other was Domo Brex, the appointed leader of the Confederacy. Never before had Keer been in such immediate proximity to so much political power. He found it distinctly unsettling and hoped never to be in such a position again.

Gren said, *"I have invoked an obscure point of order to force the board to accept a prolonged recess from deliberations. However, this tactic cannot be used indefinitely. We have at most three days before we are compelled to resume."*

"That is enough time," Keer said. "I have finished revising the slipstream equations, and I am certain they are correct. Now that the computations are verified, all that remains is construction and deployment."

Naaz leaned forward to draw the attention of Gren and Brex. "We can overcome those hurdles, sirs, but doing so will entail pressing many new workers into service, and we need a sizable influx of new materials, parts, and fuel."

Gren jabbed a finger accusatorily, as if he could reach through the screen and poke Keer and Naaz. *"A waste of men and money. All we ever get from you two is promises, never results. Your project is late, over budget, and now a political liability. By any reasonable standard, your operation is a failure."*

Keer felt his hearts racing, but he kept his posture relaxed and his voice at a level volume as he replied, "It will become a failure only if it is abandoned before yielding a success. With all respect, Domo, I know that the Confederacy has invested heavily in this project, and that additional investment might seem like a waste, but the only truly wasteful act would be to let our research and labors come to naught when we are so close to bringing them to fruition."

Before the domo or the delegate could respond, Naaz added, "There is another factor to consider, sirs. If the Romulans develop and implement this technology before we do, we will lose not only political influence within the Typhon Pact but also the ability to project military force throughout local space."

"Thank you, Thot Naaz," said Delegate Gren, *"but the domo and I are well aware of the potential consequences associated with the collapse of this project. However, you seem unaware of the risks to which you expose us by continuing to pursue a failing course. If we defy a majority vote by the board of governors that directs us to share our research, we will face stiff economic sanctions under the terms of the Pact's charter. We might even find ourselves subject to expulsion from the Pact—which would leave us exposed before three great powers."*

"If you really want to feel exposed," Naaz said, "let the Romulans master this technology without us. They already wield power disproportionate to their numbers because of the advantages provided by cloaking technology. If they acquire slipstream propulsion before we do, the Typhon Pact will cease to be a coalition and begin an inexorable slide toward becoming a monopolar entity."

Gren replied, *"Your political analysis is foolish and simplistic."*

"Is it?" A harsh buzz of anger was audible through Naaz's vocoder. "Then why are you working so hard to do the Romulans' dirty work for them? Are you already adapting to a life beneath their banner instead of celebrating our own?"

"Choose your words with care, Naaz," Gren said, his threat implicit.

Domo Brex said, *"This has been presented as a simple matter of logistics and economics. For the time being, let us treat it as such. Thot Keer, answer the following questions with specific details and hard numbers. How many workers do you require to complete your slipstream prototype in less than three days?"*

"Seven hundred twenty-eight, Domo. My written request specifies the exact numbers of personnel required within each technical specialty."

Brex picked up a data tablet and perused it. *"Are all the requisite personnel currently on Salavat and available for immediate employment?"*

"Yes, sir. We also have space to board them here at the shipyard, and our provisions are more than sufficient to support such a workforce."

"*Good,*" Brex said. "*I assume, then, that the chief impediment to your operation is money. Or, to be more precise, the acute lack thereof.*"

"Yes, sir. That is correct." Keer checked his figures with a glance at his own data tablet. "To hire the crew and work them all in double shifts for three days will cost an additional three hundred thirty-four million *sakto*."

"*What about the costs of additional supplies, parts, and fuel?*"

"My current estimate of the total matériel cost is six point four billion."

The domo was silent for a moment. "*A steep request.*"

Naaz replied, "Consider it an investment in our future, Domo."

Gren shot back, "*A gambler would call it doubling down.*"

Eager to stave off another volley of pointless insults and posturing between Naaz and Gren, Keer said, "I can have the slipstream prototype powered up and ready for preliminary testing in fifty-two hours, Domo."

"*If I grant your request for funding and personnel,*" the Domo replied.

"Yes, sir. *If* you grant my request."

Everyone was silent while the domo considered the matter. Then he lifted his head in a proud gesture. "*Requests approved. Get it done. Gren, do whatever is necessary and legal to stall the board of governors. Naaz, anything that money cannot buy for Keer's project, I authorize you to commandeer. Anyone who refuses to be hired, I give you permission to kidnap and press into service.*"

"It will be done, Domo," Naaz said, bowing his head.

The domo leaned forward, making his face appear huge and distorted in the holomatrix. *"May fortune smile on you, Keer. The Confederacy is risking much to support you in this. If you fail, I assure you, the repercussions will be severe."*

"I understand, Domo."

The subspace channel was terminated, and the holomatrix above Keer's desk seemed to evaporate, leaving him and Naaz alone.

Naaz stood, took a few steps toward the door, turned, and said, "Keer, I just want you to know that no matter what happens in the next three days, if you lead this project to disgrace, I intend to see that you bear the blame alone."

"Of course, sir," Keer replied. "But how can I fail when I have such bold leadership as yours to inspire me?" The supervisor stood flummoxed by the jab of sarcasm, then turned and stormed out of Keer's office muttering vulgar epithets and low curses. Keer stood and looked out his window at the prototype vessel in the microgravity hangar.

Under his mask, he smiled.

Time to go to work.

29

Sequestered in the privacy and luxury of his alter ego's rented accommodations, and sitting by while Sarina decoded the data stolen from the Breen Militia, Bashir found himself cursed with an overabundance of time to reflect on the day's bloody events. His conscience nagged at him to say something about the killing of the Breen communications technician, but he resisted for fear of driving a wedge between him and the woman he loved and couldn't bear to lose.

He watched her work. Her hands were quick and nimble, manipulating the interface panel of the device she'd liberated from the comm center. Seated on the end of the bed with her helmet and gloves off but otherwise still in her Breen disguise, she cut a strange figure, in Bashir's opinion—fragile yet aggressive, a human beauty encased in an alien culture's primary symbol of ugly conformity.

Catching his reflection in a mirror on the other side of the room, Bashir thought he looked more like a boy playing dress-up, trying on clothes two sizes too large for his frame.

"I think I've cracked the encryption," she said, interrupting his mental digression. "With a little luck, we should have a decrypted file in a minute or so."

Bashir decided that if he didn't speak his mind at that moment, he might not be able to muster the will to do so again. "There's something we need to talk about," he said.

Sarina set aside her work and met Bashir's troubled gaze with a placid look. "Okay, then let's talk about it."

"At the comm center," he said, "when the technician didn't buy our cover story . . ." He hesitated to see what she might say, but she remained silent. Despite his reluctance to play the role of her accuser, he continued. "You killed that man."

She nodded. "Yes, I did."

"You didn't have to. I saw how skilled you are in martial arts. You could have knocked him unconscious."

"I could have," Sarina said, "but you're wrong when you say I didn't have to kill him. I know it's not the choice you would have made, but it was the right one."

"By what reasoning?"

"Because it's true." She got up and walked toward him as she continued. "If I had just knocked him out and left him there, even bound and gagged, sooner or later he would get loose and summon help." She squeezed his upper arm. "Then he'd tell others about us, about what happened. Then our covers would be blown."

He pulled free of her grip. "Our covers are already as good as blown when they find his body."

"Which, if we're lucky, won't be for several more hours. And even then, we'll be only two of hundreds of possible suspects."

"Until they check the activity logs for his computer," Bashir said. "When they see what data was accessed the last time that station was used, they'll know what we're looking for—and they'll know what information we've acquired."

Exasperated, Sarina flung her arms toward the ceiling and paced away from Bashir. "Yes, we're playing a cat-and-mouse game—I *know* that, Julian. The choice I had to make was whether to give us an hour to analyze the data and take action, or to give us several hours." She returned and gently pressed her palms to his face. "I'm sorry that man had to die, but it's *done*. You need to accept it, because he might not be the last person we have to kill to complete this mission."

Bashir didn't know what bothered him more—the prospect of spilling more blood in a fashion that felt more like murder than like war, or the fact that Sarina's argument was eminently logical and her prediction likely correct.

Before he could respond, the data device on the bed made a series of chirping noises. Sarina picked it up, studied its display, and said, "We've got it. Still no specific location for the shipyard, but most of these messages are between the comm center and a factory that provides most of the machined parts to the shipyard. Based on some of their manifests, it looks as if they're definitely working on a slipstream drive."

He moved to stand beside Sarina and read over her shoulder. "Does it say where the factory is? Is it here in Rasiuk?"

She shook her head. "No, we didn't get *that* lucky. It's nearly two thousand kilometers away on the other side of the planet, in a city called Utyrak."

Bashir nodded. "I saw that name on a public-transit

map in one of the kiosks. High-speed maglev trains provide underground express service between the major cities on Salavat. We could be there in less than seven hours."

"Helmets on," Sarina said as she got up. Bashir lowered his helmet into place. Sarina donned her mask and gloves, walked to a companel on a wall, and activated it with a touch. Navigating its menus with speed and precision, she seemed as comfortable with the Breen interface as would a native. Then she switched off the panel. "Done. We have two tickets for the next express to Utyrak waiting for us at the maglev terminal. If we move quickly, we'll just make it."

As he followed his fleet-footed partner down the hotel corridor, he joked over their private comm channel, "Seems a shame to leave so soon. I mean, this is one of the most popular lodging halls in Rasiuk, and we've only just checked in."

Sarina replied in a teasing lilt, *"We didn't come all the way to the ass end of space just to see the inside of a hotel room."*

"Sounds like something my mother used to say to me when I was a boy."

"A word of advice, Julian: Never compare your lover to your mother."

30

Bowers rubbed his eyelids, which felt as if their insides were coated with sand that made his eyes itch. "We've been staring at star charts for hours," he said. "I need a break. And a cup of coffee. And a shower. And a few hours of sleep, to be honest."

"I'll second that request," said Kedair, "if just to see something other than the inside of this room for a few minutes."

Captain Dax leaned against the edge of the conference room's long table and kept her attention on the bulkhead companel in front of her. "Requests denied. There has to be a way through this blockade, and we're going to find it." Running the fingers of her right hand through her short, dark hair, she added, "I admit it's a tight net, but it's our job to rip a hole in it. So focus, people."

Kedair let out a sigh. "If all we had to do was find a weakness for the Klingons to exploit while cloaked, that might be possible. But now that we know they aren't sending anybody, this is just an exercise in futility."

"I don't have time to listen to excuses for why we can't succeed," Dax said. "I need to hear ideas for how we can make this happen. Bashir and Douglas are counting on us to pull them out on little more than a few minutes' notice. I don't care whether we sneak through or shoot through, as long as we *get* through."

"Well, I can foresee a few challenges," Bowers said. "For starters, we don't even know if Bashir and Douglas are still alive. If they get killed or captured, we won't have any way of knowing. And if they don't accomplish their mission before the Breen launch that prototype, their condition becomes a moot point."

Kedair asked, "Why would it be a moot point?"

"Because," Dax said, "according to the mission profile, if the Breen launch their prototype, the op is officially a failure, and we're to leave the sector immediately—to preserve plausible deniability for the Federation."

The security chief shook her head. "That's just great."

"I don't like it any more than you do," Dax said. "But for now, let's assume the operation succeeds, and either Bashir or Douglas sends the extraction signal."

Bowers folded his arms. "Okay, let's start there. Since we don't know when that's going to happen, we need a tactic for breaking the blockade that's not time sensitive. It has to be something we can trigger with no notice, that will produce a rapid enough change in the blockade's deployment that we'll be able to respond to the extraction beacon before it's too late, and that will buy us enough time to get back out of Breen space after we recover Bashir and Douglas." Raising his eyebrows in a show of incredulity, he asked Dax, "Does that about sum it up?"

"Yeah, I'd say that hits the high points," the captain

said. She covered her mouth with her fist as she yawned. "The floor is open to suggestions."

Kedair got up, circled the table, and studied the star chart on the companel up close. Bowers could tell from the intense expression on the Takaran woman's dark green, delicately scaled face that she was deep in thought. Using both hands, Kedair began manipulating the companel display, enlarging a single subsector located inside Breen space but still within range of the *Aventine*'s sensors. She pointed at an icon. "This is a Breen subspace comm buoy." Looking over her shoulder at Bowers, she asked, "Did the ship captured by Special Ops have access codes for the Breen communication network?"

"Probably," Bowers said. "Not that anyone saw fit to share them with us."

Dax added, "That sort of intel gets parceled out on a need-to-know basis."

"Well, I need to know," Kedair said. "Can we ask Starfleet Command to send us those access protocols on the double? I have an idea."

Bowers felt his energy level perk up with a flush of excitement. "I bet I know what you're thinking," he said. "A fake distress signal."

"Why not?" Kedair shrugged. "If it was good enough for them to try it on us, I see no reason not to return the favor." To the captain, she added, "If we hack into their comm relay, we can use it to generate a message that will be indistinguishable from an authentic planetary distress signal."

The captain looked skeptical. "Are you sure you have the skills to pull off that kind of a complex electronic forgery?"

"No," Kedair said, "but I'm positive that Mirren and Helkara do."

Dax nodded. "All right." Then she asked, "What kind of emergency would be big enough to lure more than one or two ships away from the blockade?"

Bowers smiled. "How about a Klingon attack against multiple worlds?"

"Maybe," Dax said, "but would that really be credible?"

He pointed at the map. "The Klingon fleet at Starbase 514 is scheduled to ship out in less than two hours. That's our plausible threat."

"Except that they've been recalled to Klingon space," Dax said.

Kedair shot a sly glance at Bowers, then said to Dax, "True, but the Breen don't know that. If the Klingon fleet cloaks as soon as it leaves the starbase . . ."

A gleam of comprehension lit up Dax's face. "Then for all the Breen know, the Klingons could be *anywhere*." She smiled. "It might work. I'll contact Starfleet Command and ask for the codes to the Breen comm relay. Sam, contact Starbase 514 and tell the Klingons what we need them to do. Lonnoc, wake up Mirren and Helkara. I want them ready to hack that relay the second we get the codes."

Kedair nodded in acknowledgment and made a quick exit. Bowers was right behind her, but he paused on the door's threshold and looked back at Dax. "After I talk to the Klingon fleet commander, then can I get a shower and some rack time?"

"Sure," Dax said. She checked the ship's chrono and grinned. "But sleep fast. Your shift starts in three hours."

31

After disembarking from the maglev train at the Utyrak terminal, Bashir had expected to find himself and Sarina in a city similar to the one they had left hours earlier. Instead, they followed the crowd of arriving passengers out one of several large archways that lined one wall of the terminal and found themselves on a long pier studded with broad docks, on the shore of a black subterranean lake that stretched away into unfathomable darkness.

Berthed at each dock were a variety of small waterships. Some were mere skiffs, barely large enough to hold a trio of passengers in front of their poleman. Others were like small yachts. A few were ferries capable of transporting up to a hundred persons. Breen civilians haggled with boatmen for passage across the lake, and hard currency changed hands quickly as people were ushered into vessels.

"We should hurry up and find a ride," Bashir said to Sarina as they made their way down the nearest dock, "because I don't see any other way out of here."

Sarina pointed at the pilot of a small skiff tied at the end of the dock. "Let's see if we can hire him. The fewer people we interact with the better, so I'd like to avoid those big ferries if we can."

"Sounds good. Do you want to haggle, or should I?"

"Depends. How comfortable do you feel using Breen idioms?"

"Okay," Bashir said, falling back half a step, "you do it."

He let Sarina do the talking as they approached the pilot. At first, Bashir noticed nothing special about the content of Sarina's conversation. Then he realized that important cues were being conveyed by shifts in posture, a tilt of the head, and subtle hand gestures. After a few seconds, Bashir caught on. One's posture and the angle of one's head could imply authority or subservience, confidence or humility. Verbal exchanges specified such details as distance, destination, and cost, while the hand gestures were a means of adding or diminishing emphasis, deflecting inquiry, or making ironic side comments.

Sarina paid the skiff pilot a few coins of Typhon Pact currency. Then the pilot stepped into his craft and beckoned Bashir and Sarina to follow him. Bashir boarded first. The flat-bottomed boat wobbled under his feet. He turned to help Sarina, but she climbed in with no apparent difficulty. As they sat down, the pilot untied the skiff from the dock, lifted his pole from its resting place against the bow, and pushed off into the great darkness beyond the docks.

All around the skiff, dozens of small vessels made their way across the lake. Light spilled from the hoverboat ferries and shimmered on the rippling waters. There was a faint sound of engines, and a handful of boats moved quickly enough to cut shallow wakes as they sped away from the rest of the flotilla.

Leaning close to Bashir, Sarina said in a low voice, "The

pilot tells me it's not usually this busy. Something big is happening in Utyrak, and people are coming in from all over Salavat to get work."

His curiosity piqued, Bashir asked, "Does he know what kind of work?"

"Shipbuilding," Sarina said. "A government contract."

"Interesting," Bashir said, leaving unspoken what they both already knew.

The skiff followed the other boats through a starboard turn. As one of the ferries navigated the turn ahead of them, residual illumination from the larger vessel enabled Bashir to see the corner of the massive, sheer cliff beside which they had been maintaining a parallel course. As the skiff completed the turn, Bashir and Sarina beheld a new and impressive vista.

Ahead of them, a city rose from the black water and reached up to the dark granite ceiling hundreds of meters overhead. The major structures of the city were shaped like wide hourglasses and looked as if they had been carved from the bedrock. Delicate bridges linked adjacent towers, and dozens of meters above the surface of the lake, causeways held up with wires traced curving paths around the bases of the majestic stone pillars. Small craft traversed the waterways of the sunless city, whose great towers flickered with a hundred hues of light. It was austere but lovely, and Bashir found it hard not to compare the Breen's peculiar underground metropolis to such Earth cities as Venice, Amsterdam, and Bruges.

The pilot guided the skiff toward the nearest hourglass-shaped tower. Only as it loomed above Bashir did he truly appreciate its size. According to the HUD in Bashir's helmet, the tower was more than three hundred meters tall, and its base at the waterline and its apex where it met the vast cavern's ceiling both were approximately three hundred meters in diameter. At its center, the tower—which up close resembled a fortress—tapered to roughly fifty meters.

In the vast reaches of open space between the dozens of towers, tiny hovercraft darted to and fro, their dark hulls hidden by the perpetual night but revealed by the light-amplifying filter of Bashir's mask. In the distance, he saw the end of the great cavern. Several far-off towers spat plumes of fire and smoke from their foundations, making the local air hazier than in Rasiuk.

The skiff landed with a loud scraping of metal hull over rough-hewn stone. Bashir let Sarina thank the pilot for the ride, and then they went ashore, where they found themselves amid a crowd of hundreds of Breen citizens who, like them, had just arrived by boat.

Sarina activated their private channel. *"Plenty of manpower here. This must be the place."* She pulled Bashir through the crowd toward a nearby kiosk similar to the ones they had learned to use in Rasiuk. Reviewing its options and manipulating its interface with ease, Sarina muttered, *"C'mon, where is it . . . ?"*

Bashir whispered in reply, "Where's what?"

"The shipyard," Sarina said, still poking at the kiosk's screen.

Bashir looked out across the cavern and considered the infrastructure that would be necessary to support a city in that environment. Then he imagined the needs of an experimental shipyard attempting to create a slipstream-capable starship and tried to picture where in Utyrak it might be.

He reached over and turned off the kiosk. "Stop. We were wrong."

Sarina sounded annoyed. *"What're you talking about?"*

"Look around," Bashir said. "There's nowhere to hide a shipyard in this city. We know they make slipstream *parts* here, but they must be sending them someplace else for assembly. Which means we have to find out where that *someplace else* is."

32

Nar was long past the point of tears or of crying out. Her pain was too deep now, too pervasive. It was all she had left; the inquisitor had taken everything else.

"You have told us much, Deshinar," the inquisitor said. "But I remain certain that you have concealed something from us. Something important."

She said nothing. There was no point in lying, nothing to be gained from denying the obvious. The inquisitor's tools measured her brain waves, her pulse, and the galvanic responses of her skin, rendering all her deceptions transparent. Her early attempts at disinformation had cost her the fingers of her left hand; her initial refusal to give up the location of the warren had cost her the digits of her right hand. A token gesture of defiance had led to hours of simulated drowning.

The inquisitor jabbed her with a neural truncheon, overloading her synapses with pure agony. For seconds that felt like forever, all Nar knew was suffering beyond measure, pain that defined her existence. Then it ceased, leaving her with the banal miseries of flesh and bone. Bloody froth spilled over her cracked lower lip. Dull aches and knifing pains filled her torso.

"Who were the two people you helped? You covered their tracks well, but we found enough to know you sheltered them in your home. Are they dissidents like your friend Chon Min?" The inquisitor circled Nar while waiting for her to reply, but she said nothing. Silence was the safest tactic because it was neither the truth nor a lie—it gave the inquisitor nothing to confirm or refute.

Standing behind Nar, the inquisitor leaned close to her and said, "Chon Min does not have to die. Tell me who the newcomers are, and I will spare Min's life."

"I do not believe you," Nar said. Even in her broken state, she was neither so desperate nor so foolish as to accept an inquisitor's word. Anything he offered, any promise he made, could be revoked as easily as it was given. Only the most naïve prisoners fell for such blatantly insincere ruses.

The neural truncheon slammed against Nar's lower back. All-consuming fire raged up her spine and burned away her sense of self, time, and place. White heat left her burning from the inside out. She felt herself scream but heard nothing except the piercing screech that had usurped her auditory nerves.

Torment gave way to emptiness. All she wanted was to give in to gravity, fall to the floor, and sink into the cold comfort of the grave, but she was bound to the chair, propped up for the inquisitor's convenience.

"Their names," said the inquisitor. "Tell them to me."

It took a great effort on Nar's part just to speak. "They told me their names were Ket Rhun and Minh Sann and that they'd come from an outer colony."

The inquisitor stepped in front of Nar. "Much better. Who are they?"

"Knowing their names will do you no good. They were zeroed."

Technically, she had spoken the truth. The humans had identified themselves to her with those aliases and background stories, and they had been zeroed. Direct lies were easy for the inquisitor to uncover; Nar decided to see whether lies of omission were any more difficult for the BID investigator to detect.

"Zeroed? Did they cause the null-value errors in the surveillance matrix?"

Averting her eyes from the inquisitor's mask, Nar said, "Yes. That was how I found them. Then I wrote a code patch to cancel out the errors."

Slapping the truncheon against his open palm, the inquisitor asked, "Was that before or after you sheltered them inside your residence?"

"After," Nar said.

"Then you saw them unmasked," he said. "What species are they?"

Nar said nothing, even though she knew it would only stoke the inquisitor's curiosity. Then he looked away, and Nar guessed that he was listening to a private transmission through his helmet or an earpiece. When he looked back at Nar, he waved the business end of the truncheon in her face. "You lied to me about writing a code patch. You hold a level-six rating as a software engineer—hardly sufficient to have created the perfect zeroing filter. What did you really create for Rhun and Sann? New identities?" He leaned closer. "I shall interpret your silence as a confirmation. Under what names are they traveling?"

"Bosh and Saar," Nar said, spicing her lie with grains of truth, fragments of the humans' real names. "I gave them fortunes and ranks worthy of envy."

"No doubt," said the inquisitor. "Tell me what species they are."

He tolerated her angry silence for several seconds before thrusting the truncheon into her abdomen. Absolute suffering erased his question from Nar's mind, along with every memory and feeling she'd ever known.

She returned to herself feeling only half formed, as if her hold on her mortal body was being pried loose. Distanced from its physical torments, she felt as if she had become a mere spectator to her life's final moments, an empty vessel that could no longer be touched by the inquisitor's brutal hand.

He locked a gloved hand around Nar's throat. "What species are they?"

"Human," she said, realizing only too late that her body was answering questions as if it had a will of its own. She struggled to retake the reins of her mind as the inquisitor hurled away his truncheon and grabbed Nar with both hands.

"What are humans dressed as Breen doing on Salavat?"

"Spies," Nar's body said, against her wishes. "Said they were cultural observers, but Starfleet made their tools." *Must regain control*, she raged.

"Where are they going? Are Bosh and Saar their real aliases?"

Resisting a desire to sink into unconsciousness, Nar said, "Those are their new identities: Thot Bosh and Thot Saar." She coughed. "Destination unknown."

The inquisitor let go of Nar and detached a communication device from the belt of his uniform. "Issue a general alert to all stations on Salavat: We have two human spies on the planet's surface. Secure all sites and information networks, and put out warrants for Thot Bosh and Thot Saar. Check all transit records for their movements within Rasiuk, and cross-reference with intercity transit logs." He put away the comm device and returned to Nar's side. "Thank you, Deshinar. You have been most helpful."

Nar said nothing in reply. As the inquisitor left the room, Nar submerged into the embrace of her final slumber, taking solace in the knowledge that her last lie about Bashir and Sarina's aliases, though minor, would permit her to go into the darkness with one tiny shred of her dignity intact.

33

Scaling the lower half of the hourglass-shaped rock tower had been relatively easy. Despite its steep angle, the tower's exterior had been rife with fissures and protrusions, affording Bashir and Sarina no shortage of purchase.

Ascending the tower's upper half was proving far more perilous. Dangling by his fingertips from the inverted slope, Bashir was certain this was the most arduous physical challenge he had ever faced. Even with assistance from his suit's myoelectric enhancements, which amplified the strength of his grip as well as the power of his limbs, Bashir's body was quaking from the effort of the free climb.

Giving up was not an option; neither was going back down. It would be just as difficult—maybe even more so—to retrace his path to the lower slope as to continue upward toward the nearest opening, and there were no such entrances on the tower's lower half, which lay dozens of meters below his feet.

Sarina was a few meters ahead of Bashir. Despite having less upper-body strength, she seemed to be having an easier time coping with the inverted climb. Bashir surmised that Sarina's slimmer physique and lower mass made her suit's strength-enhancing technology proportionally more effective than his own. Looking down at the rocky slope far beneath him, he winced as his subconscious reminded him, *The bigger they are, the harder they fall.*

He was relieved when Sarina pulled herself over the edge of an opening in the tower's rocky façade. Over his helmet's transceiver he heard her say, *"All clear."*

"Copy that." It took him half a minute more to reach the ledge. Sarina grasped his forearm and helped him up and over, then eased him down onto the floor of a deck that led to two corridors, one at each end. Back on level ground, Bashir felt depleted. All he wanted to do was lie still and breathe.

Pushing him up to a sitting position, Sarina said, "We have to keep moving."

If he'd had more strength, he might have argued the point. Instead he let her pull him back to his feet, and he plodded along behind her, summoning whatever stamina he could coax from his body to keep his footfalls as light and quiet as hers.

The inside of the tower was as sleek and modern as its exterior had seemed rough and primitive. Sarina led Bashir down a corridor past what appeared to be executive offices and communal work areas, all of them dim and unoccupied. Several cubicles contained computer terminals. Gesturing at one, Bashir said, "We're surrounded by unsecured workstations. Why don't we log on to one?"

"Because they probably won't have the access level we need." Sarina paused at a corner, peeked around it, then beckoned Bashir forward. Pointing ahead, she said, "That's what we're looking for, I think."

He looked over her shoulder at a locked office suite. "Good point."

They skulked forward to the suite's semitransparent double doors. Sarina checked them and said, "Locked, with multiple alarms. I can bypass them, but it'll take me a few minutes. Watch our backs in case this place has roaming guards."

Bashir returned to the corner and cast occasional peeks back the way they had come, vigilant for any sign of patrolling security. Minutes later, Sarina said, "We're in. Let's go." He rejoined her and slipped inside the executive suite.

The office was spacious and as luxurious as any Bashir had ever seen in the Federation. Whoever worked in it seemed to have a taste for well-crafted furniture, flowering plants, and abstract art that was half painting, half sculpture. Sarina and Bashir walked behind the desk, and she activated the computer terminal. Right away its holographic display came alive with a wild flurry of data. "Don't worry," Sarina said. "That's just me using my suit's HUD to hack this terminal." The crazy hash of symbols in the holomatrix slowed and stabilized, and then it showed a collection of simple icons and Breen ideograms. "There we go," Sarina said.

Leaning closer, Bashir asked, "What are we looking at?"

"Classified shipping manifests. This tower houses a factory for precision computer parts. Looks like they're making components for a chroniton integrator."

"One of the key elements in a slipstream drive," Bashir said. "Where do the parts go after they leave here?"

Sarina called up a new screen of data. She recoiled

slightly from the display. "This doesn't look right." She pointed out a specific line of information. "According to this, everything this factory makes gets sent to another facility here in Utyrak." Looking up at Bashir, she added, "It all goes right to the waste-processing and recycling plant."

"That has to be a mistake," Bashir said. "Who would go to all the trouble and expense of creating precision parts just to send them for recycling?" As Bashir put together pieces of the puzzle in his imagination, a notion occurred to him. "The skiff pilot said this whole city is like one big government project, right? Is it possible they share a common information network?"

Sarina considered the question and then began keying commands into the computer. "I get it—you want me to hack the recycling plant from here."

"Exactly. At the very least it'll save us some walking."

"Good thinking. Let me see if I can find— Hang on, I've got something. Daily shipping reports from each division are compiled for all the executives. Here's yesterday's report from the recycling plant." She looked back at Bashir. "Does anything about that look odd to you?"

Bashir had to concentrate to translate the Breen written symbols. Once he did, however, he understood what Sarina was implying. "They're shipping a lot of toxic waste for remote disposal."

"Millions of metric tons in the past month," Sarina said. "I don't see many industries in this directory whose operations would generate toxic waste, do you?"

"No, I don't. But I do see a lot of production plants sending massive amounts of material for recycling—and almost the exact same amount of total material leaving the recycling plant for a disposal protocol."

"Wherever that ship is dumping its payload is the hidden shipyard," Sarina said. "The scow doesn't have warp drive, so it has to be somewhere local."

"Do the manifests specify where the disposal site is?"

"No," Sarina said. "I'd bet that info's kept on a need-to-know basis."

"Well, I can tell you one person who'd definitely need to know," Bashir said. "The pilot of the garbage scow leaving the recycling plant in forty minutes."

Sarina logged off the network, shut down the terminal, and stood up. "Let's go hitch a ride to the shipyard."

"And how are we supposed to get inside the recycling plant?"

"Easy," she said. "We'll just walk in."

Half an hour later, Bashir and Sarina entered the recycling plant on the other side of Utyrak. Just as she had said, they were walking in. What she had neglected to mention was that they were doing so underwater.

Most of the so-called waste delivered to the facility arrived via the city's waterways in long, flat-bottomed barges that cruised inside the recycling tower through a wide passage cut into one side of its broad base. The barges' contents were unloaded by massive machines whose powerful vibrations kept the water between the plant's internal quays agitated and murky—providing much-needed cover for Bashir and Sarina as they strolled along the sludge-covered bottom.

The numerous enhancements Starfleet Intelligence had made to Bashir's and Sarina's helmet visors were the only things that spared Bashir from being blind and lost in the cloudy, polluted water. Passive sensors updated his HUD with such basic data as his current depth, remaining air supply, and direction. Light amplifiers and filters helped him pierce the opaque waters up to a point and provided him with virtual wireframes of objects beyond his visible range. Noting a shape emerging from the gloom, he said, "Ladder at eleven o'clock, in the corner."

"I see it," Sarina replied over the transceiver. *"Let's hope it comes up someplace dark and out of the way."* She reached the ladder first and started climbing, and Bashir stayed a few rungs below her. Near the surface, she slowed and looked around. *"Clear,"* she said and climbed out of the water.

Bashir broke the surface and scrambled onto a concrete ledge beside Sarina. They were at the end of the tower's outer bay, near a lock separating it from a massive interior harbor. In its center, a cargo ship that had been converted into a garbage scow stood on an open circular elevator platform. "Am I imagining this," he said to Sarina, "or is the inside of this tower almost entirely hollow?"

"That's what it looks like," she said. "At least the lower half, anyway. The upper half might house offices or storage spaces, but I'd guess at least a quarter of its volume is needed to power the lift platform beneath that ship." She nodded at the scow. "We have less than ten minutes to find a way onto that ship. There's no telling how long it'll be until the next one."

A bell rang, its clanging loud and bright and echoing in the yawning space. Overhead, a spinning light flashed. Looking back the way he and Sarina had come, Bashir saw a barge motoring toward the lock. "Back in the water," he said, stepping off the ledge and sinking into the murk. Sarina submerged beside him as he activated his transceiver to tell her, "We can slip inside the main bay when they lower the lock for the barge."

"Good thinking," Sarina said. She stayed close at his side as they edged toward the lock. As Bashir had predicted, it retracted downward, kicking up more silt and sludge. The barge rumbled overhead. Its motor's vibrations were so intense that Bashir imagined his internal organs shaking against one another. Pushing forward against the wall of water while his feet slipped over greasy mud, Bashir stumbled over the edge of the lock. Sarina took his hand to steady herself, and then they were over the barrier and inside the tower's main bay.

"It'll take too long to walk this underwater," Bashir said.

Sarina pulled him toward another ladder to their left. *"You're right."*

This time Bashir climbed up first and used his HUD to scope the area for warm bodies, electronic surveillance, or light sources. "No company," he said as he broke the surface, "but it's a bit bright up here. We'd better keep moving."

As soon as he was on the ledge he started walking toward the nearest patch of shadow, which was in a corridor more than a dozen meters away. Sarina remained close behind him, and as they stepped back into the shelter of half-light, she huddled against him. "I see six causeways leading out to the platform," she said, nodding at the scow. "Four for cargo, two for personnel."

Weighing their options, Bashir said, "The personnel bridges have security checkpoints, and there aren't many people using them. Too risky, I think." He pointed at the nearest crossing. "All the cargo goes over sealed inside garbage pods. That looks like our best bet. We can move one of those empty pods into the queue over there, then climb in and ride it across."

"Nice idea—in theory," Sarina said. "But if the system's that heavily automated, it probably uses computer-tracked inventory for loading and offloading. Putting an unscheduled pod into the system might send up a red flag. Or worse, get you dumped into a real recycling furnace. Judging from the flame jets on the outside of this place, they must be running at least a few for appearance's sake."

"Inserting a pod on this side of the inventory control scanner will at least get us to the platform," Bashir said. "We have six minutes. If you have a better idea, this would be the time to share it."

"Okay, let's go hijack a trash pod." They jogged in crouching poses to the cargo access portal. Sarina checked its control panel. "It's not locked."

"This pod's empty," Bashir said, guiding the light-weight metal shell over a track of rolling bars that led to the access portal. He opened the panel on its side and gestured for Sarina to step inside. "Your chariot awaits."

"You first," she said. "I'll have an easier time working

the override on this control panel. Get in and hold the door open for me."

Bashir stooped and tucked himself inside the pod. He steadied himself with one hand and held open the pod's hatch with the other. Sarina guided the pod into the pneumatic tube that would propel it across the open expanse of black water to the scow's launch platform.

She had just started entering commands into the access panel when the deep, angry buzz of an alarm resounded throughout the entire facility, followed by a masculine Breen voice: *"Attention, all personnel. This is a security control alert from the Breen Intelligence Directorate. Human spies have infiltrated Salavat. All communication and public-transit systems are locked down. Remain where you are and cease all operations until your identichip credentials have been verified by Confederate security officers. This is not a drill. Attention, all personnel: This is a security control alert . . ."*

As the message repeated, Bashir struggled to mask his growing dread. "That's not good," he said.

"No, it's not." Sarina punched in a final command on the cargo console, said "Have a nice trip," and then reached over to shut the pod's hatch from the outside.

He held the door open. "What're you doing? Get in!"

"Julian, they're locking everything down. This pod'll get you most of the way to the platform. I'll make a distraction and buy you time to reach the ship."

"No! We're not splitting up! I'm not leaving you here!"

She punched him in his mask's snout and knocked him back inside the pod. "No time to talk," she said, adding as the hatch closed, "Don't let me down." The door closed with a leaden thunk, and Bashir was pinned to the back of the pod by its sudden acceleration. His memory echoed with the sound of the closing airlock door that had riven him from Sarina six years earlier as he hurtled away, once again forced to go on without her . . . alone.

Julian will be all right, Sarina told herself. *He has every advantage, even if he doesn't seem to realize it yet*. Watching his trash pod shoot away inside the pressurized tube mounted under the causeway, she reassured herself one more time that she hadn't just done something terrible. *He'll be fine*.

She made some rapid-fire mental calculations. Based on the pressure inside the tube, her best estimation of Julian's mass, and the distance to the scow's platform, she deduced that it would take his pod sixteen point nine seconds to make the crossing. Keeping track of the elapsing seconds in her mind, she walked away from the access portal. When her countdown reached arrival minus four seconds, the hiss of pressurized air inside the tube went silent and she knew that Julian had been halted nearly a dozen meters shy of the platform. She had no idea how he would reach the scow; she knew only that it was her duty to provide a compelling distraction that would buy him the time he needed.

Ducking down a side passage, she saw two armed Breen soldiers walking toward her. One lifted his neural truncheon and pointed it at Sarina. "Stop!" he said in a commanding tone. "We need to verify your credentials."

There were more footsteps drawing closer behind her.

Retreating would not have been an option in any event, because it would only lead her pursuers back toward the access hatch through which she had sent Julian. For his sake, she needed to press on and bring with her as many of the base's personnel as possible.

Sarina halted and waited for the soldiers to reach her. They were broadly built and stood a head taller than she did. Confronting her at point-blank range, the one with the truncheon waved it in her face. "Identify yourself," he said.

"Hesh Rin, Confederate Information Bureau," Sarina said, figuring that if her cover was blown she was as good as discovered, and if it wasn't, it soon would be, anyway. Striking a defiant pose, she added, "Identify *yourselves*."

The two soldiers seemed taken aback, stunned at having their demand parroted back to them. They looked at each other in apparent confusion.

Sarina struck with her left palm and drove the tip of the first soldier's neural truncheon into his chest. There was a sharp crackle and a flash of light as the Breen guard's body was racked by spasms. As he began to collapse, she slammed her right palm into the snout of the second soldier's mask. He staggered backward. Sarina yanked the truncheon from the first soldier's hands, leaped on top of the second man, and drove the end of the truncheon into his throat. A single jolt was enough to stun the man into unconsciousness.

Behind her, another vocoder voice squawked, "Stop that person!"

She looked back. A trio of armed guards charged toward her while drawing handheld weapons. Sarina plucked a disruptor from the belt of the second soldier

she'd felled, fired at her pursuers to slow them down, and
then started running.

Her only objectives were to keep moving away from Julian and to draw as much attention as she could. Ducking
through a maze of large machines, she fired at anything
that looked like it might explode, vent toxic fumes, or spill
something hazardous. Smoke, vapor, and flames erupted in
her wake. She led a growing cluster of Breen soldiers on a
winding chase through a sublevel crowded with pipes, up a
ladder to a series of linked catwalks above a huge smelting
furnace, and into a sprawling cargo warehouse, where she
sent a load lifter careening into a mountain of stacked shipping containers with one well-placed disruptor blast into
its front axle. For a moment she entertained the possibility
that she might even be so lucky as to evade the swarming
Breen security forces and make a clean escape.

Then she rounded a corner to find a skirmish line of
Breen troops waiting for her, weapons leveled and ready, in
the main aisle of the warehouse.

A mad clatter of footsteps came to an abrupt halt behind her. She was surrounded, outnumbered, and outgunned. A silence heavy with anticipation fell between her
and the Breen who held her in their sights. Sarina didn't
know whether they planned to kill her or stun her as a prelude to arrest.

Wincing at a flash of weapons fire, she realized she
would have her answer only when—or if—she woke up
again.

34

The pod lurched to a stop and slammed Bashir against its forward-facing side. He had been counting the seconds since Sarina had launched him across the causeway. *I can't be at the platform yet*, he realized. *It would've taken another four seconds to cross the full distance.* Assembling the available facts into a plausible scenario, he concluded that the security lockdown had halted his pod short of the scow.

He opened the pod's hatch with caution. All he saw was the transparent shell of the transfer tube, the water beneath it, and, overhead, its linkages to the causeway. A brief but deep vibration was followed by a sensation of gradual backward motion. At first Bashir thought the pod was being pulled back the way it had come. Then he realized the tube and the causeway above it were moving. There wasn't enough clearance between the pod and the tube's wall for him to look forward, but in the distance he observed the launch platform's other bridges retracting.

Bashir drew his disruptor, stood back as far as possible from the pod's hatchway, and fired a full-power shot at the tube's wall. The energy pulse flashed against the transparent metal barrier but inflicted no damage beyond a minor discoloration. *So much for that idea*, Bashir decided.

Then he noticed that the shot had slagged the edges of
the pod's hatchway. He pressed his back against the pod's
rear wall and fired his weapon at the forward bulkhead.
The front of the pod disintegrated into slag and fragments
that scattered away inside the empty circular tube. Bashir
leaped out of the pod and sprinted down the tube toward
the slowly receding launch platform. Charging against the
motion of the tube felt a bit surreal to Bashir—it was like
something out of a dream, taking two steps forward and
one step back, running just to stand still.

He stumbled to a halt at the open end of the tube. The
platform was more than fifty meters away and growing
more distant with each second. Bashir holstered his disruptor and drew his bolt thrower from the other side of his belt.
Rather than secure the zip line inside the tube, he left its
anchor bolt inside the device as he aimed at the launch pad.

As he settled upon a target, the platform started rising.
You've got to be kidding, he thought, adjusting his aim. *I'm
going backward and it's going up, so now I have to hit a moving target? It's a far cry from beating Miles at darts . . .*

Knowing he would get only one shot, he calculated
the multiple variables of relative motion, increasing range,
and shifting trajectory, exhaled to steady his hands, and
squeezed the trigger. The bolt shot out and sailed on a high,
gentle arc toward the ascending platform. If not for Bashir's
enhanced eyesight, he might have lost track of the tiny
metal bolt in flight. Instead, he followed it all the way to its
mark, where it sank deep and stuck fast.

Half a second later the monofilament line jerked taut
and pulled Bashir out of the tube. He swung through the

air as he was pulled simultaneously forward, toward the center of the cavernous space, and up, toward the underside of the launch pad. Gritting his teeth, Bashir gripped the bolt thrower with both hands and hung on. Its tiny motor whirred as it winched him steadily upward.

By the time he reached the superstructure beneath the platform, it had risen more than a hundred meters above the water and was close to entering the shaft in the center of the tower. He detached the bolt thrower's cable from its anchor in the metal beam, retracted the slack in the line, and tucked the device back into his suit. Clambering inside the dense network of beams and pipes packed into the base of the launch pad, he pulled himself from one handhold to another, leaped across gaps with no margin for error, and fought his way upward to a ladder that led to a locked hatch. One shot from his disruptor blasted out the lock. With effort he slid the heavy panel open and climbed up onto the pad.

Everything was as dark as night. Bashir switched on his visor's night-vision mode, which revealed his surroundings in a crisp, high-contrast green twilight. He was under the Breen scow's aft port thruster. The pad was less than a hundred meters from the top of the tower, which was veiled behind a blinding wash of daylight. Within seconds the ship—and Bashir—would be exposed. *Can't stay here*, he told himself. *When those engines kick in, I'll get fried.* Looking around, he saw no means of infiltrating the ship. He knew better than to try to climb up through the landing gear bays; at a glance he saw that they had been designed to leave no empty space when retracted. If he tried to stow away inside one of them, he would be crushed. Cutting through the hull would set off alarms for certain. *No open ports, no emergency hatches on the ventral hull.* He grimaced in frustration. *This thing's tight as a drum.*

The top of the shaft was only seconds away. Bashir made a fast inventory of the systems of his modified environment suit. He looked no farther than the standard-issue features before finding what he needed: full vacuum support and magnetic clamps built into the boots and gloves, for deep-space extravehicular repair work.

He looked over the ship from bow to stern and assessed its aerodynamic profile, noting stress points, likely airflow during atmospheric operations, and what areas of the hull were least visible from the likely vantage points of the Breen ground crew and control tower. Then he made his best guess, picked a spot between two bulges on the ship's port side, activated his suit's magnetic clamps, and scaled the ship. As the ship's dorsal hull breached the top of the lift shaft, Bashir pushed himself as far back into the gap on the hull as he was able. Looking down at his torso and legs in full daylight, he was relieved to find that his armor was roughly the same color as the Breen scow's hull.

The ship's engines powered up with a piercing shriek that felt like a knife through Bashir's skull, and then a thunderclap shook him to his core as the vessel began its ascent into the dreary, tin-colored sky. A moment of powerful acceleration and hammering wind shear threatened to rip him loose from the hull until the ship's exterior inertial dampers engaged. Even with that protection, it was a battle to hold himself in place, to resist the brutal impact of wind and the merciless pull of delta-v as the ship soared into a banking turn.

Dozens of kilometers below, the gradual curve of Salavat rolled past, its details vanishing as the scow continued to climb. As the haze of atmosphere faded to reveal the cold beauty of space, Bashir wondered for the first time how long and wild a ride he had just hitched . . .

. . . and whether he would ever see Sarina alive again.

35

Consciousness returned as the heavy, dark hood was lifted from Sarina's head in one rough pull. Her blond hair fell in a crazy mess over her face as she squinted against the glare of a white-hot spotlight aimed into her eyes. She tried to turn her head only to find her range of motion limited by metal restraints on either side.

A quick look down confirmed that she wasn't imagining the chill of cold air across her bare limbs and torso. Her Breen armor and mask had been removed and heaped on the floor in front of her, and she had been stripped to her undergarments. Her arms and legs were stippled with gooseflesh, and her feet felt as cold as ice from resting on a bare concrete floor.

She heard a door open and close behind her. Slow footsteps. On the other side of the spotlight, a shadow moved across a canvas of deeper darkness.

Then came a synthetic male voice speaking in monotonal English, its every syllable cobbled from harsh scratches of metallic noise—the hallmark of words translated by a Breen vocoder. "We have taken away your costume, human," he said. "For an outworlder to wear the garments of a Breen—never mind the insignia of a *hesh* of the Confederate government—is a disgrace." He circled behind her. "What is your name? And do not waste my time with your Breen aliases. I know already that you are neither Hesh Rin nor Minh Sann."

"Alice," she lied, picturing herself well and truly down the rabbit hole. "Which I guess makes you the Mad Hatter."

"I am your inquisitor." His iron voice betrayed no emotion. "That is all you need to know." He paced around her with a predator's slow deliberation. She could almost sense him taking her measure, assessing her weaknesses from a safe distance, searching her eyes for the faintest glimmers of fear or prevarication. "I must admit, however," he continued, "that I enjoy questioning outworlders. Interrogating someone whose background is unknown to me, whose personal history is not a matter of public record in the Confederate database . . . the challenge it presents is exhilarating, like that of an artist facing a blank canvas."

Sarina smirked as the Breen stepped back into her field of vision. "Is that what I am to you? A work of art in the making? Am I to be your *masterpiece*?"

The inquisitor stopped and faced her directly. A faint spill of reflected light revealed the details of his mask's snout. "You taunt me? Interesting. Your defiance is refreshing. All I got from your accomplice Nar was silence—that is, until I broke her. Then she gave me everything I wanted." He resumed his slow orbit of Sarina. "Would you like to know how long she resisted? Or what it took to break her?"

"Not especially, no," Sarina said. "I'd much rather find out what it's gonna take to break you." Her challenge seemed to go unnoticed; the inquisitor continued his steady pace without missing a step.

"It amuses me that you think yourself capable of testing my limits," he said. "You act as if oblivious of your peril, but your obvious intelligence makes such a charade hard to believe. I assure you, any delusions you might possess about escaping and revenging yourself upon me are merely that—*delusions*. I hold your fate in my hands, so do not test my patience."

She let out a snort of derision. "Who're you kidding? You expect me to believe that *you* hold the power of life and death over *me*? I strongly doubt that. You seem like a smart man yourself, so I'm guessing you understand what a high-profile prisoner I am. And if you know *that*, then it's a good bet your superiors know it, too. Which means if you kill me, they'll have your head on a spike."

"I do not have to kill you to change the shape of your existence," he said. "My superiors will forgive my exuberance if I deliver you to them in a somewhat *maimed* condition. Their concern is for your survival—not for your well-being."

"Touché," Sarina said. Then she added, in stilted but grammatical Breen Standard, "*Puhun hitaasti, koska et niytü ëlykøs. Olyn vierosta olet Fenrisal?*"

Her condescending query caught the inquisitor off guard. He paused in his circling and seemed to take a reflexive half step back from her. "Impressive. You speak our tongue without a vocoder. Can you also read our written language?"

Rolling her eyes, she replied, "Probably better than you do."

"Doubtful," the inquisitor said. "But I respect your spirit. It will make your eventual surrender all the more satisfying to me—professionally speaking."

"I notice you ducked my question," Sarina said. "Are you a Fenrisal? With a build like yours, I can tell you're no Silwaan. And your body language is all wrong for an Amoniri. I guess you could be a Paclu . . ."

The inquisitor rubbed his gloved palms together. Then he extended one arm, and some unseen figure in the darkness behind him passed a neural truncheon forward into his hand. Batting its half-meter-long shaft against his open palm, the inquisitor stepped out of the shadows and loomed over Sarina.

"You seem to be very knowledgeable about my people," he said. "Now let us see what you can tell me about yours."

36

Bashir watched the gray surface of Salavat drift by hundreds of kilometers below. He remained stuck fast to the hull of the Breen scow with his suit operating at its lowest power setting, his comms off, and his visor at maximum screen to shield his eyes from the unfiltered white glare of the star Alrakis. The ship had made two orbits of the planet, and Bashir expected it to begin its descent at any moment.

Envisioning the next few minutes of his mission, Bashir foresaw two serious complications: first, not getting torn off the ship's hull as it reentered the planet's atmosphere at several multiples of the speed of sound; second, detaching himself from the ship after it landed at the hidden shipyard and getting back to cover before being seen by the Breen ground crew.

He suppressed his rising tide of anxiety and took stock of his physical condition. His limbs trembled; holding on to the Breen ship during its liftoff had been exhausting. *I'm probably starting to dehydrate*, he realized. *And I should eat one of my ration bars as soon as I can, to keep my strength up.*

Looking back down at the planet, he thought of Sarina. *I never should have left her*, he castigated himself. He pushed back against his guilt. *You had no choice. She didn't give you one. If you'd stayed, her sacrifice would've been for nothing.* For a moment, he felt ashamed. He was a commissioned Starfleet officer; he knew his first duty was to complete the mission and that he and Sarina were considered expendable. She had been able to accept that and do what was necessary—so why did he find it so difficult? Why did she need to force him to do what was right?

Vibrations in the hull alerted Bashir that the ship's impulse engines were engaged. He checked his hold and braced himself as the ship began to accelerate. Studying the ship's exterior, he noted the Breen vessel didn't seem to be equipped with ablative plating, which suggested that it relied on navigational shields to protect itself during atmospheric entry maneuvers. *Good,* Bashir told himself. *Whatever protects the hull should protect me, too.*

He waited several seconds to see the curve of Salavat flatten into a horizon. It didn't happen. Twisting at the waist and craning his neck, he looked up and back. *Are we making an inverted approach?* All he saw were more stars and darkness. When he looked back down, Salavat was visible again, most of it in darkness, a thin crescent radiant with reflected sunlight—and it was also very small. *No, not small,* Bashir corrected himself. *Far away—and getting farther away by the second. We must be moving at full impulse.*

Clinging like a barnacle to a ship speeding off into deep space, Bashir felt more vulnerable than ever. His suit still had several hours of air, but would it be enough? If the scow's destination was on the next planet, it might be, but if its destination was the edge of the system, Bashir knew that would mean trouble. At full impulse it would take the ship more than twenty-five hours to reach the system's outer comet ring. *If this ship doesn't reach someplace habitable before I run out of air*, Bashir realized, *I'll have two choices—find a way inside the ship without getting detected, or abort my mission, let go, drift away, and activate my extraction beacon.* The first option seemed all but impossible, and the second option was unacceptable; for Bashir, quitting after Sarina had given herself up to the Breen would feel like a betrayal.

During the next several minutes, Salavat receded. It shrank to a bright but tiny pinpoint barely distinguishable from the billions of stars around it. Bashir waited to see another planet loom large ahead of the scow, but the vista surrounding him remained static and placid.

All right, he reasoned, *either Starfleet was wrong about the shipyard being hidden on Salavat, or Sarina and I were wrong about this scow being used to smuggle parts and personnel to it. Or maybe we were all wrong, Sarina and I have wasted our time, and I'm hitching a ride to a toxic-waste dumping site. But if this scow is going to the shipyard, that would put it somewhere in the Alrakis system. So how did Starfleet fail to detect an orbital shipyard?*

The question nagged at him and fueled his imagination. *Maybe it's cloaked*, he thought. *But hiding something that big that would kick up tetryons, tachyons, and about half a dozen other exotic high-energy particles. And it's not as if the Breen are known for cloaking technology.* He ruled that out, but still the mystery tantalized him. *So, what are the Breen known for?* That query sparked his memory of the destruction of Deep Space 9's first *Starship Defiant* by the Breen during the closing days of the Dominion War.

Energy-dampening weapons, Bashir recalled. *If they can cripple energy-distribution systems, maybe they can also hide their own energy emissions. If that's true, then as long as their shipyard doesn't look like one, they could put it almost anywhere. Unless someone knew exactly what to look for . . . it would be as good as invisible.*

Bashir conjured a map of the Alrakis system in his mind's eye and made an educated guess, based on Salavat's position and the scow's departure trajectory, as to which way he and his ride were headed. The system's outermost planets were gas giants with many small satellites, but Bashir doubted that any of them were the scow's destination. Even with its energy signature masked, the shipyard would still have been detected by visual scans if it were in the open. No, Bashir concluded, there was only one place the Breen could have hidden it:

The Alrakis system's asteroid belt.

His best estimate placed the shipyard approximately an hour ahead of the scow at full impulse. Until he saw it, there would be no point in trying to devise any further strategies; he would simply have to hang on and, when an opportunity presented itself, improvise.

He hoped that Sarina was in a position to do the same.

Sarina screamed as the inquisitor stabbed his neural truncheon into her back for what felt like the hundredth time. She had thought the pain was something to which she could adapt, or develop a resistance, or learn to block out, but she saw now that she had been wrong. The agony only grew worse with each injury.

Another burning jolt forced a primal cry from her, and she went limp as the horrific stimulus was withdrawn. Before then, she had known everything about the Breen's infamous neural truncheons except what it felt like to be struck by one. It was worse than she could ever have imagined. The suffering it inflicted was so consumptive that it left her drained. Her existence had been reduced to a binary state: hideous torture or an aching void, with nothing in between.

Sagging in the chair, she imagined how she must look to the inquisitor. Weak. Helpless. Broken. *Perfect*, she gloated behind her slack expression.

The Breen interrogator leaned close to her and asked in his machine-noise vocoder voice, "Are you ready to answer my questions yet?"

"Anything," she said, straining to push out more than a whisper.

"Tell me about your partner. The one named *Bashir*."

She was trembling—not as a deception, but for real. Looking away from the inquisitor's mask, she asked, "What do you want to know?"

"Start with where he is." The inquisitor grabbed Sarina's chin and forced her to look at him. "Did you and Bashir split up inside the recycling plant?"

"He was never there," Sarina said, using lies to goad the inquisitor into telling her what the Breen knew. "When we left Rasiuk, I went to Utyrak and he went to Tanhevit. The plan was to rendezvous in Pohodok two days from now."

Fiery blades of pain shot down her spine as the inquisitor pressed the tip of the truncheon against Sarina's neck.

When the pain stopped and the echoes of her screams faded, the inquisitor leaned close. "I do not believe you."

"Well, then we're both in for a very long day, because it's the truth."

"Why were you in Rasiuk?"

She hesitated just long enough to draw a small breath. "We came to make contact with the dissident cells in the warren. Nar was our contact."

"The dissidents have little influence and few resources," the inquisitor said. "Why would Starfleet risk two intelligence operatives to contact them?"

"Because they were our ticket into your society," Sarina said. "The plan is to infiltrate your outer colonies first by sending agents posing as cultural observers to establish relationships with the dissidents. Once we win their trust, they'll help us put operatives onto the Confederacy's core worlds." She forced a small smile onto her ragged, bloody lips. "And I have to tell you, the fact that your entire society walks around wearing masks makes all of this a *hell* of a lot easier."

"It must appear so to an outworlder," the inquisitor said. "I think that if your people had penetrated deeper into our society, you would find its reality is much more complex and difficult to navigate without detection."

Sarina broadened her smile into a grin. "*If . . . ?*"

Her taunt seemed to have no effect on the Breen interrogator. He circled her in slow steps. "Where is Bashir now?"

"I told you. He's in Tanhevit, contacting dissident cells there."

The inquisitor was behind her. "How would he find them?"

"Nar gave us contact information."

"Unlikely. I questioned her at length. She made no mention of other cells."

Sarina let out a derisive huff. "Maybe we were more persuasive than you."

"I doubt that very much." Passing in front of her, he continued. "If your mission is to contact dissident cells, why did you come to Utyrak? This is a one-industry city with an itinerant population. Certainly, you don't expect me to believe there is a thriving dissident culture here?"

She masked her lies with a bit of truth. "Of course not. I was here to sabotage the recycling plant as payback for the attack on the warren."

"Why target the recycling plant? Why not one of the factories?"

"Disabling municipal infrastructure does the most damage with the least effort," Sarina said. She knew that she was putting the inquisitor in an untenable position. His line of questioning had telegraphed his desire to ask her about the mission to find the hidden shipyard, but obviously he was under orders not to reveal or confirm its existence. Because he couldn't refer to it directly, it was going to be very difficult for him to impeach the veracity of her answers.

Just as she wondered how he would adjust his verbal strategy, the inquisitor jabbed the truncheon into Sarina's rib cage. It forced her to scream so fiercely that she was left breathless, gasping, her diaphragm racked with spasms from the ongoing neuroelectric shock. Her vision purpled, and she started to gag on her tongue. When the torment ended, saliva spilled from her contorted mouth and tears streamed from behind her squeezed-shut eyelids. She wanted to surrender herself to heaving sobs of fury, but her lungs refused to fill with air.

The inquisitor sounded unmoved by Sarina's miseries. "Where did you get your armor and mask?" He kicked the helmet off her piled Breen disguise.

Fighting for air and a voice, Sarina said, "I told you. Starfleet made it."

"Another lie," the inquisitor said. "Starfleet *modified* it. That much is clear. Many of the tools hidden within it are of Starfleet or Klingon manufacture. But the armor itself is genuine. Nanomarkers in its fiber matrix confirm it was made by the Breen Militia for paramilitary use. So, I will ask you again: Where did you get it?"

"Starfleet gave it to me."

"Where, when, and how did Starfleet acquire it? Has the Federation captured a Breen vessel? If so, which one?" He turned and extended a hand toward the darkness. Someone lurking in the shadows handed him a data tablet, which he looked at before continuing. "Was it the *Sitkoskir*? By any chance is that how you came to be in our company? By posing as Ket Rhun and Minh Sann?" He waited a few seconds, handed the tablet back to his subordinate, and said, "I will interpret your silence as a confirmation of my suspicions."

"I've never heard of any ship called *Sitkoskir*," Sarina said.

"Then how did you reach Salavat?"

Blinding, jaw-clenching pain ripped through Sarina as the truncheon was jammed up into her armpit. Magenta spots swam in her vision as the pain abated. Her lungs felt as if they were full of fluid. Deep, wet coughs made her chest ache.

The inquisitor sounded as serene and patient as he had when he had first come in. "Perhaps you know of the *Sitkoskir*, maybe you do not." He held the top of the neural truncheon in front of Sarina's face. "We will know soon enough."

37

The asteroids looked much closer than Bashir would have liked. He told himself that they were farther away than they appeared to be, that judging distances in space, without the benefit of intermediate objects to provide parallax or the subtle cue of atmospheric haze, was very difficult. But each ragged hunk of icy rock that drifted past the scow seemed closer than the last, and all he could do was hope that Breen pilots didn't tolerate scrapes and near misses.

Vibrations traveled through the ship's hull as its thrusters fired, filling the space beneath the scow with the warm glow of fiery exhaust. The starscape ahead of Bashir seemed to roll gently on two axes as the ship pivoted around a crater-pocked gray mountain in space. Its surface rose to meet the ship and blocked Bashir's view of the heavens. Watching the rocky details of the asteroid's surface resolve in ever greater detail, he wondered if the scow was going to land.

An X-shaped fissure appeared on the asteroid's surface. It sharpened and spread into four triangles retreating from one another. The gap between them widened to reveal a dark space on the other side, and Bashir realized he was watching an enormous set of camouflaged hangar doors slide open. He strained to see what lay beyond them, but his eyes were unable to pierce the darkness.

This is why my visor has a night-vision filter, he remembered, activating his mask's light-amplification mode. As it powered up, an enormous form took shape inside the hangar. Its flattened profile and long, fluid lines resembled those of the *Aventine* and its sister ships in the *Vesta* class. Upon closer inspection, it reminded Bashir of a sand shark. Though most of its exterior had been hulled, he saw through a few holes that most of the vessel's interior was still empty. *That must be the prototype*, he concluded. *Not much more than a spaceframe with a stardrive and some impulse coils.*

The doors had retracted fully into the walls of the asteroid, but the scow held its position and made no move to enter the hangar. Examining the cavernous spacedock, Bashir noted there was no place for the scow to dock. The work traffic surrounding the prototype was so dense that Bashir doubted the scow could even pull inside to offload its cargo and personnel.

They must be beaming everything over, he figured. *Which makes sense. It'll take less time than moving it all manually. But then why open the hangar doors?*

On a hunch, he adjusted his visor's sensor frequency to scan for ambient energy readings. The ship to which he clung gave off a brilliant halo of random particles, and the hangar—which had looked pitch-dark to his naked eyes—gave off an intense aura, but only through the open doors. The rest of the asteroid around it appeared inert, just a worthless hunk of rock drifting in the void.

There's the energy-dampening technology at work, Bashir

thought. Now he understood why the doors were open: to provide a narrow window for transport, one that would be temporary and angled away from the Federation's listening posts. With the cargo ship and other asteroids obstructing the view, it was no wonder that the hidden shipyard had evaded detection. *This changes the plan*, he concluded. *If they're using transporters to move their cargo, this ship isn't going to land. So how am I supposed to infiltrate the shipyard?*

The scow's maneuvering thrusters fired, sending a mild quake through the hull. On the asteroid's surface, the tips of the four triangular hangar doors emerged and started creeping back toward one another.

There was no longer any time to plan, only time to act. Bashir turned off his suit's magnetic clamps and pushed himself away from the cargo ship and toward the hangar doors with as much force as he could muster. He drifted through the vacuum in a slow, awkward tumble. Behind him, the cargo ship negotiated its way clear of the big asteroid and its smaller neighbors. Ahead of him, the space between the hangar doors shrank all too rapidly. He checked the readings in his visor's holographic HUD, which confirmed his distance and speed. *I'm not going to make it*, he realized. *I'll either get crushed or stranded on the surface.*

Calling upon his zero-*g* training, Bashir stabilized his tumble and faced himself away from the hangar doors. He drew the bolt-throwing gun from its pouch on his suit and loaded a bolt without a cable attached. Using his visor's HUD to help guide his aim, he fired the bolt on as close to a straight line away from the hangar doors as he could manage. He felt the recoil of the bolt leaving the gun and knew it meant that he'd added a tiny kick of speed to himself. *I just hope it's enough*, he thought, noting that he had only one anchor bolt left.

Floating backward, drifting blind toward his destination, he loaded the last bolt into the thrower and attached a cable to it. Setting the device for an inertia-free launch—a trick that made him glad he'd taken a few minutes back on the *Aventine* to memorize the bolt thrower's standard operating manual—he took a deep breath and held it as he waited to see whether he was about to make an unscheduled drop-in or an unceremonious crash down.

The tips of all four hangar doors were close enough that, if he'd wanted, he could have reached out and grazed one of them with his fingertips as he passed through the gap in their center. As soon as he was inside the pitch-dark hangar, he pointed the bolt thrower at a faraway rocky wall on his right. Aiming at a spot just beneath a long promontory, Bashir fired and waited for the line to stop feeding out. A second later, it did. He activated the winch and hung on as he was towed at high speed through the microgravity environment. Braking the winch just before he hit the wall, he tucked under the metal walkway and looked back to see if anyone had spotted him.

Work on the prototype continued, and no one seemed to pay any attention to Bashir's side of the hangar. He began to think of how many ways his jury-rigged plan might have backfired, but he stopped himself. *You're in. Stop thinking about what might've gone wrong and focus on what has to happen next.*

He felt a gentle tremor in the rocky wall as the hangar doors made contact with one another. Then four banks of work lamps snapped on, floodlighting the prototype starship hovering fewer than a hundred meters away from Bashir. Hull-assembly teams swarmed over the experimental vessel, and two armies of robotic arms—one on each side of the ship—constructed its slipstream nacelles.

Bashir used a compact plasma drill to cut a two-millimeter hole in the walkway above him and pushed through it a tiny remote transmitter that relayed images and sounds to his helmet. Up on the promontory, a cluster of workers passed over his position. They were headed to a hatch that he guessed led to the facility's interior.

His next move was a gamble, but he saw no other option.

As the workers gathered at the hatch, he climbed up onto the walkway behind them. He picked up a bundle of optronic cables, affected an air of weary boredom, and sidled up behind the group. As he'd hoped, they ignored him. The one at the front of the group unlocked the hatch with a security code that Bashir took the opportunity to memorize. Then they filed inside, with Bashir at their backs—and one step closer to completing his mission.

Limp in the interrogation chair and drooling bloody spittle, Sarina found it easy to feign unconsciousness. The difficult part was going to be not actually *losing* consciousness. Every part of her body that she could still feel throbbed and burned from the neural truncheon's electrical shocks, and the dark comfort of oblivion was tempting. She felt herself starting to slip into its numbing embrace.

No, she commanded herself. *Focus. Stay in the moment.*

A few meters away, she heard the inquisitor talking at a low volume to whoever had been lurking behind the spotlights during her torture session. "For a first session, this has been quite productive," the inquisitor said. "However, I still have doubts about her story. It sounds to me like equal parts truth and lies, but separating the one from the other will be no easy task."

A voice Sarina had not heard before said, "We could use a psychoactive drug to coax the truth from her."

"No," the inquisitor said. "We lack reliable information about human neurochemistry. One mistake with a narco-synthetic and we might kill her—and she is far too valuable an asset to risk such an outcome."

"How then shall we proceed?"

"Take her out of the chair and let her rest. When she regains consciousness, we can resume our standard interrogation protocols."

Footsteps. Sarina recognized the timing of the stride as the inquisitor's. A door opened with a muffled swish.

The underling said, "Where will you be when she awakens, sir?"

When the inquisitor spoke again, there was a slight echo of open space behind his voice. "My office," he said. "Hail me on Channel Twenty-three."

"Understood, sir." More steps, and the door closed with a soft hiss. The underling said to someone else, "Help me undo her straps."

The two Breen stood on either side of Sarina's chair and loosened the restraints on her head, arms, torso, and legs. One stood back, taking up what Sarina supposed was a covering position, while the other finished releasing the restraints that had kept her immobilized during her hours of questioning. She knew what to expect next. The Breen military's standard procedure for detaining prisoners of war was to suspend them upside down from their ankles.

As the Breen soldier undid the last of Sarina's restraints and folded her forward over her legs, he said to his compatriot, "Help me put her on the hook."

"Do your own job," said the other Breen. "I will do mine."

"I think you can put away your disruptor, Gesh," said the first soldier. "I doubt the human poses any threat in her sleep."

The second Breen's vocoder crackled with a noise that suggested it was hiding a sigh of disgust and resignation. "As you wish."

Each Breen grabbed one of Sarina's legs. Together, they dragged her forward out of her chair and, with grunts of effort, hoisted her toward the ceiling.

Every part of Sarina's body—every muscle, bone, and joint—throbbed and ached and burned with deep pain. She felt as if her limbs each weighed a hundred kilograms. All she wanted was to pass out.

Instead, she willed herself into action.

She opened her eyes, plucked the disruptors from the Breen's holsters, and fired the weapons into their guts. They crumpled into fetal curls, and she rolled free to a kneeling position, pistols ready, facing the door.

All was quiet. She checked the fallen men's throats for

pulses. Both were alive. As a precaution, Sarina took prisoner restraints from their belt packs and bound them at their wrists and ankles.

She gathered the pieces of her disguise from the floor and checked to make certain they hadn't been damaged. Everything was intact. Listening for any sign of trouble, Sarina put her disguise back on and holstered her stolen disruptors. She retrieved a medkit from one of her suit's pockets and dosed herself with a pain-relief shot from a hypospray. Within moments, her suffering eased to a level she could master.

One of the guards stirred. Using her palm, she struck the man at the back of his head just hard enough to nudge him back into unconsciousness.

A quick systems check confirmed that her vocoder was functional. She grabbed the inquisitor's neural truncheon. It was heavier than she'd expected but well balanced. *This will do nicely*, she decided. She stepped over to a comm panel, hailed Channel Twenty-three, and said, "Sir, the human woman is awake."

The inquisitor replied over the comm, *"Good. I will be there directly."*

"Understood, sir." She closed the channel and slapped the truncheon into her gloved hand. *And I'll be here waiting for you.*

38

With every step Bashir took, he expected to be found out, exposed, captured, and shot on sight. Turning each corner, he imagined himself being met by a line of Breen soldiers with disruptors aimed and set to kill. Instead, he worked his way through fast-moving knots of workers and supervisors, clusters of people arguing over break schedules and blueprints, lines of technicians laden with tools. Every room of the shipyard's administrative facility seemed to be packed with people.

More astonishing to Bashir was that, even after walking through most of the base's four lowest levels in search of turbolifts on which he could discreetly hitch rides upward to the command level, he had yet to see a closed door or be challenged once for his credentials. *They're all so busy, no one has time to check identichips*, he noted as a pack of fast-talking Breen wearing tool sashes detoured around him. *If the people in charge are pushing the crew this hard, they must be on a short deadline. And judging from the mood around here, it must be getting close.*

He ducked down a short passageway to avoid running into a supervisor wearing a *thot*'s rank insignia. At the end of the passage he saw a ladder that led up through a hole in the ceiling. Though he anticipated finding nothing but a sealed-tight hatch, he peeked up the ladder—and saw part of a lit room at its apex.

Looks like an invitation to me, he told himself and started climbing. Based on the ceiling heights inside the base, he estimated that this vertical shaft was bypassing at least three levels. At the top of the ladder he emerged into another passage like the one he'd left. He hurried to an intersection with the main corridor at its far end. Quick looks in each direction confirmed that this level was not as busy as the others. Bashir heard no footsteps and saw no workers.

Restricted access, peace and quiet . . . this has all the marks of a command level, he concluded. He stepped lightly as he made his way down the corridor. Stolen glances into each office revealed Breen military officers hunched inside task pods, each one's attention fixed on a large, complicated holomatrix. The grinding-gears scratch of vocoder voices talking over one another made it difficult for him to eavesdrop on particular conversations. He wondered how the Breen ever learned to pick out one another's voices from such a cacophony.

Still cautious, he paused at the next corner and peered around it. At the end of a long hallway he saw a door marked with a symbol he now understood meant "authorized personnel only." Two armed Breen guards stood sentry on either side of it. He increased the magnification of his visor's HUD so he could read the smaller symbols above a biometric security panel beside the door. Translating the ideograms with ease, he knew he had reached his destination: the shipyard's master operations center. He exhaled. *Nothing left to do now but walk up and knock.*

He hesitated. His mission parameters specified the destruction of the slipstream prototype as well as the corruption of the Typhon Pact's copies of its schematics. Only now, on the verge of his assignment's endgame, did Bashir understand that his actions would wipe out more than a spacedock and a test bed starship. He thought of the hundreds of workers he had seen on the base's lower levels, the multitude of technicians and engineers and construction specialists, many of whom were probably civilians. If he obeyed his orders, most—if not all—of those people were about to die. *No*, he chastised himself, *don't let yourself off the hook* that *easily. They're all about to be* killed. *By* you.

Bashir felt sick. The part of him that was a Starfleet officer, sworn to obey the orders of his superiors and defend the Federation, knew that he had to go forward. It was why he had come here. Sarina had sacrificed herself to make this possible. But the part of Bashir that was a doctor was revulsed by the notion of committing murder in the name of the state. Taking lives in open combat during wartime, as he had been forced to do during the Dominion War, was one thing; blowing up a shipyard despite knowing that it would result in massive civilian collateral damage was another.

These aren't innocents, he assured himself. *They're willing members of the Breen war effort, helping build a warship based on plans stolen from a Starfleet shipyard where their agent didn't hesitate to kill our citizens.*

He hardened his heart. The Federation's clash with the Typhon Pact might be a cold war, but there was no longer any mistaking that it *was* a war.

Remembering Sarina's warning a day earlier about the need to use lethal force when operational security was on the line, Bashir set his disruptor to kill.

The guards at the end of the hallway seemed to ignore him as he stepped around the corner. When he continued walking toward them, they tensed and raised their rifles to ready positions. Bashir didn't wait to be challenged. He called out to them. "Attention," he said. "My name is Hesh Gron, and I am here on behalf of the Confederate Information Bureau. Identify yourselves."

As he'd hoped, the guards seemed confused by his demand. The one on the left said, "Chon Trem." Half a second later, his partner added, "Chon Lok."

Continuing to advance, Bashir said, "Two human spies have been detected on Salavat." He stopped in front of them at less than arm's length. "Have either of you seen anything unusual in the past three hours?"

Trem and Lok looked at each other, as if hoping to coordinate their answers by telepathy. In that fleeting moment of hesitation, Bashir drew his disruptor and snapped off two shots at point-blank range. Both guards collapsed at his feet. He grabbed Trem's wrist and lifted the dead man's hand to the biometric sensor pad beside the door. Pressing it against the pad, Bashir hoped he was right in his hunch that the guards would have access to the compartment they were assigned to defend. As the man's hand made contact, the pad changed color from pale lime to bright magenta, and the door to the Master Ops Center slid open.

Bashir strode inside, not knowing what to expect. He found himself in an octagonal, two-level working space with one side devoted to situation monitors. It was manned by half a dozen Breen engineers, who all looked up as Bashir entered—and froze when they saw the disruptor in his hand and the two slain guards on the floor behind him.

He didn't wait for any of them to speak, to ask him what was happening or what he wanted or who he was. He took aim and opened fire. Less than three seconds later it was over, and all six Breen were dead.

Bashir holstered his disruptor, pulled the dead guards inside the ops center, shut the door, and engaged the security override to prevent it from being opened from the outside. Satisfied with his precautions, he walked to the master control panel. Everything he would need to put an end to the Breen's slipstream project was at his fingertips. He took off his gloves, laced his fingers together, and flexed his hands away from his body until his knuckles cracked.

Then he went to work.

"Be careful with that!" Thot Keer shouted at the engineers connecting the final component of the slipstream prototype's navigational system. "If you damage it, I promise you will be flushed out an airlock without your masks."

The workers appeared to take his warning to heart. Their foreman halted the assembly to run spot checks of all safety protocols and connection points. Satisfied that the chroniton integrator would be installed in one piece, Keer moved on to check the work of the next crew down the line.

Almost done, he thought. It was a struggle to contain his excitement. *The final components are either in place or going in now. We should be ready to power up in less than an hour.* He marveled at his good fortune. Despite being burdened with impossible deadlines, unreasonable superiors, short supplies, an inadequate budget, and a legion of doltish malcontents masquerading as a starship construction workforce, he had succeeded in adapting the Federation's revolutionary slipstream drive to a modified Breen spaceframe—and he had done it ahead of the governing board's ridiculous and arbitrary deadline.

Some days Keer felt that being an engineer was a form of masochism. Today it felt like being a giant among the masses. It had the sweet taste of victory.

He paused on the central catwalk, which was suspended above the ship's barely covered keel. Looking up, he watched an assembly crew lower the last of the prototype's hull plates into position. As soon as it dropped into place, sparks rained down from its seams as it was welded to the spaceframe. *And now we are one step closer to the end,* Keer exulted as he moved on down the line.

Even though they were technically ahead of schedule, Keer still had the anxiety of racing the clock. He moved from station to station, ordering adjustments great and small, aware that even one mistake could undo all his accomplishments. *It takes a million stones to build a castle,* went a saying from his homeworld, *but it takes only one out of place to bring down a kingdom.* The old homily had never felt more true to Keer than it did at that moment, as he stood in the midst of naked beams and loosely bundled cables, exposed fuel pods and bare engine coils. Gazing upon the inner machinery of a starship's propulsion systems without the obstructions of decks and bulkheads made Keer feel as if he were a stage magician revealing his tricks for all to see. *Smoke and mirrors . . . quantum slipstream and sensors that can look into the future—are they really so different?*

The engine core foreman, Tul Jath, approached him. "Sir, the reactor is assembled and ready. Standing by for your order to engage main power."

Keer nodded. "Very good." He looked around at the metal miracle he and his men had wrought. "It seems wrong to let our bird leave its nest without a name." He turned toward Jath. "Any suggestions?"

Jath backed up half a step and bowed his head with humble respect. "I would not presume to claim such an honor, sir. That privilege should be yours."

"Not that it will matter," Keer said. "Once the militia takes control of the prototype, they will name it whatever they wish. Still . . ." Pressing his hand against one of the support beams, Keer felt a swell of pride and affection for his creation that had been so long in the making. *I promised myself I would not indulge in maudlin sentimentality. But perhaps I can be forgiven this one time.*

"*Marjat,*" he said. "For its maiden voyage, I anoint this vessel . . . *Marjat.*"

Jath seemed confused. "Is that a name of significance?"

"None that need concern you," Keer said, feeling no compulsion to explain himself to his subordinates. His personal history was none of their business—and who other than him would really care that he had named this ship for his beloved daughter, taken from him so many years ago during the plague on Resinoor Prime? *It is enough that* I *know*, he decided. To Jath, he said, "Bring the mains online."

"Yes, sir," Jath said and passed the word down the line. Engineers and mechanics translated the order into action, and Keer watched with pride as the scores of personnel inside the *Marjat* executed their steps in his painstakingly choreographed start-up protocol for the prototype. They might have only one chance to get it right before time ran out. Keer had done everything he could to make certain their first attempt was successful.

He activated the comm circuit inside his helmet. "Keer to ops. Prepare to initiate final diagnostics and systems check on my order. Confirm." The day's communications had been rife with delays, but Keer had not yet acquired any patience for them. After a few seconds he added, "Keer to ops! Respond!"

There was no answer. He wondered if his helmet comm had malfunctioned. As a test, he patched into the internal network and said, "Keer to Jath."

Jath answered over the comm, *"Go ahead, sir."*

"Can you raise the Ops Center on comm?"

"Hang on, sir." Several seconds passed before Jath added, *"Negative."*

Something was wrong. Keer was certain of it. He pushed through a group of mechanics who were running cables to an auxiliary control panel and shouldered his way up to the master console. "Move," he said to the technicians working there. He keyed commands into the panel's holo-matrix and ran a firmware check on the comm lines and relays to the shipyard's Ops Center. Everything was still active. He patched his helmet comm through the *Marjat's* master console. "Keer to ops."

Again, no response. Dread washed through him and left him hollow. *Stay calm*, he told himself. *Send a runner up to ops, confirm that this is only a comm malfunction. If you panic and sound an alert for no reason, work on the ship will stop and the deadline will be missed. That cannot be allowed to happen.*

It was the prudent course of action, but his conscience and his training as an engineer urged him in a different direction. *If there is a real emergency, and I wait too long to sound the alarm, there might be an accident. The* Marjat *could be damaged. My workers might die. And everything I have worked for . . . will be lost.*

Then someone else made the decision for him: an alarm sounded.

"Report!" Keer shouted over the klaxon.

Jath ran up to him in a panic. "Reactor malfunction! Breach imminent!"

Keer pointed at the master console. "All readings are nominal."

"Not on the ship, sir," Jath said. "Inside the base. *Its* main reactor."

"Evacuate the base and bring the mains online." Walking away from the ship's main console, Keer added, "We have to get the *Marjat* out of here!"

Jath called out, "Where are you going, sir?"

"Ops," Keer said, still on the move. "I need to open the hangar doors and upload the final schematics in case we fail to escape."

"How long should we wait for you, sir?"

"Until the doors open. If I am not aboard by then, leave without me."

Core-breach warnings flashed on every holomatrix display in the Ops Center. Bashir glanced at the readings from inside the matter/antimatter reactor, noted the rate at which its magnetic containment fields were collapsing, and was satisfied with his handiwork. If his estimate was correct—and he was reasonably certain that it was— then the Breen crew would have barely enough time to abandon this facility but not nearly enough time to halt the impending disaster.

I have enough blood on my conscience, he reasoned. *I won't kill if I don't have to. As long as the prototype is destroyed, that's what matters.*

There was one last task he had to complete, and he was grateful that someone at Starfleet Intelligence had already done most of the work for him: he had to sabotage the Typhon Pact's copies of the slipstream design schematics. Among the various bits of equipment SI had concealed inside his suit was an optolythic data rod configured and programmed to interface with Breen computer systems. Once connected, it was supposed to do the rest automatically—delete the primary copies of the file, corrupt all the backup copies with dangerously inaccurate data, and upload a stealth virus into the Breen mainframe that would lurk and similarly corrupt any new slipstream-related data it encountered. According to his mission-briefing packet, all he had to do now that he was inside the Operations

Center was find a compatible data port and insert the device.

Standing in the middle of the octagonal room, Bashir was at a loss. He hadn't seen even a single port on any of the center's consoles that looked remotely compatible with the data rod. *This could be a problem*, he admitted to himself. He circled the room's upper level in fast strides, his eyes searching the walls for data ports but finding only glassy-smooth touchscreen panels and metallic shells over data cores. Holding up the data rod, he eyed it with dismay. *Is it possible the SI techs got this thing wrong? Could it be obsolete?* Looking around, he considered the possibility that the *base* was obsolete. The data rod had been made to work with the newest systems on a Breen warship; who knew how old this facility was?

Bashir couldn't give up, not yet. *If I don't get this data into the system, the Breen'll just start over somewhere else.* Desperation made his thoughts race almost too quickly to process. *Think! Where else would a Breen patch into one of these consoles?* He had a moment of insight: *What if a console's touchscreen broke?*

He ran to the nearest console and lay down on the floor beside it. Probing with his fingers along a groove in a panel, he found a small recessed lever and pulled it. The panel lifted away from the console and then shifted aside on hinged supports, revealing an intricate-looking spaghetti junction of cables. Bashir traced the paths of the cables to a circuit board—on which he saw a data port that looked to be the right size and shape for the optolythic rod in his hand. He took a deep breath and inserted the rod into the port.

A screech emanated from the holomatrix above him. He got up and saw a wild flurry of Breen mathematical notation hashing across the display. Images of the prototype ship Bashir had seen in the hangar were subtly modified as he watched, and a symbol that he knew meant "Warning: permanent deletion" appeared repeatedly. As quickly as the blizzard of data traffic had appeared, it vanished. An update appeared in the holographic HUD of Bashir's visor: "All data updated—purging storage media."

Inside the console, the optolythic rod exploded with a delicate sound, like the shattering of a tiny icicle. The console went dark. Bashir shut its access panel.

On the wall of displays behind him, the core-breach countdown continued. Escape pods were leaving the base en masse through a network of disguised ejection shafts. *I'd better make sure the prototype doesn't follow them*, Bashir decided. He drew his disruptor and shot apart all the consoles. *That ought to slow down anyone looking to open the hangar doors.* He looked up.

"Computer, do you accept voice commands?"

A voice like shredding steel replied from an overhead speaker in the center of the room, *"Affirmative, Hesh."*

"Computer, where is this room's voice-command input sensor?"

"It is part of the overhead speaker assembly, Hesh."

"Thank you." He drew his disruptor and shot the speaker into slag. He walked toward the door. *Time to go.* He stopped to the right of the door, released the security override, and unlocked the exit. The door sprang open.

Two Breen soldiers rushed in carrying disruptor rifles.

Bashir shot the first one in the side of the head. The slain commando fell onto the man behind him, preventing him from bringing his weapon to bear on Bashir, who calmly shot the second man in the chest. Both soldiers collapsed in a heap. Bashir poked his head around the corner and saw no other reinforcements. He listened. There was the faintest sound of masked breathing outside to the right of the door, directly behind him. He angled his disruptor pistol around the corner and fired three blind shots. He was rewarded by crackling sounds of impact, groans of agony, and the solid thump of a body landing like dead weight. Sure that the other side of the passageway was clear, Bashir left the Ops Center and, as a precaution, fired a head shot into the third commando as he passed his body.

The mission had gone according to plan, more or less. All that remained now for Bashir was to escape the base alive, get clear of its energy-dampening field, and signal the *Aventine* for extraction. He could think of about a thousand ways those three objectives might go fatally wrong, but he chose not to. There was no more time to look back, and it was too late now to wallow in regret.

It was time to go home.

39

Sarina walked close behind the inquisitor and pressed the muzzle of her disruptor pistol against his lower back. She had subdued him with three jolts of his neural truncheon when he had returned to the interrogation room, disarmed him, disabled his helmet's built-in transceiver, and marched him out as her hostage. No one had tried to stop them, and the dim lighting in the corridors of this branch of the Breen Intelligence Directorate had helped keep her weapon from being seen.

As they approached the next intersection, she said, "Which way?"

"Turn right," the inquisitor said. "There is a cargo lift at the end of that passage. It leads up to the flight deck." Glancing over his shoulder at Sarina, he added, "It will do you no good. The flight deck is for security patrols only."

"Face forward," Sarina said, "and don't speak unless you're saying something helpful." She prodded him to walk faster as they turned the corner. Another Breen was at the far end of the corridor and walking toward them. Sarina said to her hostage, "Stay quiet and you'll both live. Try to call for help and you'll both die." The inquisitor acquiesced to her warning with silence. They passed the other Breen without incident and reached the cargo lift portal. "Open it," she said.

The inquisitor pressed his hand to a control pad that lit up on contact. From the other side of the doors, Sarina heard the low hum of machinery. The doors opened, and Sarina nudged the inquisitor inside the lift. When the doors slid shut, she slammed the bottom of her pistol grip across the back of the inquisitor's head. He collapsed to the floor, apparently unconscious. Sarina struck him again to make sure he was down and bound him using restraints taken from the guards she'd stunned in the interrogation room. As she tucked the inquisitor into a corner beside the doors, a falling whine heralded the lift's arrival at its uppermost level. Reasoning that darkness would be to her advantage in more ways than one, she used her disruptor to shoot out the lift's overhead light.

Kneeling in a shadowy corner as the lift's doors parted, Sarina scouted the path ahead. Before her sprawled a hangar wide open to the icy gray surface of Salavat. Bitter winds gusted in from outside, driving thin drifts of snow over the hangar's threshold. Sleek patrol fighters were parked in rows on the painted concrete floor. Teams of mechanics and support personnel moved from one aircraft to another checking fuel levels and ammunition load outs. Pilots mingled in a ready room on the far side of the hangar, seated in orderly rank and file as a senior officer droned through a briefing while pointing at a map.

She darted out of the lift, took cover for a few moments behind a stack of empty ammunition crates, then skulked to another hiding spot between two parked load lifters. Crouching as low as she was able, she eavesdropped on a group of passing technicians. "We need to get back on schedule," said the one leading the pack. "Are we sure these six wings are all flight ready?"

"Yes, sir," said a mechanic in the middle of the huddle. "*Nezca* Squadron has passed preflight. We should start work on *Ulco* Squadron."

The ground crew's conversation continued as they moved out of earshot. Sarina noted the markings on the nearest fighters and saw the ideogram for *Nezca* emblazoned on their aft tailfins and forward fuselages. All of them sat in launch-ready positions with their cockpit canopies open.

She looked past the load lifter on her right and saw more stacked crates. The random jumbles of Breen alphanumeric symbols stenciled on the crates meant nothing to Sarina, but she recognized the large warning icon for high explosives.

I would've preferred a silent exit and a subtle escape, she thought as she sabotaged her disruptor to cause a feedback loop inside its prefire chamber, *but this will have to do*. A diode on the top of the weapon flashed red, indicating that the disruptor had begun a slow buildup to an overload detonation. Sarina ducked around the load lifter, tossed her overloading disruptor through a gap into the middle of the massive stack of crated munitions, and walked away toward the nearest parked fighter as she silently counted down from ninety seconds.

No one seemed to notice her until she climbed inside one of the fighter's cockpits and started pulling down the canopy.

"Halt!" squawked a metallic voice. "Get out of that ship!"

She locked the canopy in place, strapped herself into the pilot's seat, and pressed the Engine Start button on the fighter's console. The cockpit's wraparound display flared to life, and the spacecraft's engines shrieked for half a second before letting out a majestic roar that shook Sarina to her bones.

On the edges of her vision, she noted dozens of Breen rushing toward her aircraft. More than a few members of her welcoming committee carried rifles.

A voice crackled over her ship's comm. *"Shut down your engines and surrender Interceptor Ten immediately. This is your only warning."*

In her head, Sarina's countdown continued: *Thirty . . . twenty-nine . . .*

She gripped the yoke and settled her feet on the thrust and braking pedals. Many of the instruments' functions seemed intuitive—level, altimeter, speed, sensors—but some she could only guess at. *They probably don't leave the manual in the cockpit*, she figured, *not that I have time to read it.* She tapped the thrust pedal. The ship inched forward. A pull on the yoke lifted the nose. *Good enough.* She pushed the pedal to the deck.

Her interceptor shot forward. It was only by the grace of her enhanced reflexes that she avoided slamming into the hangar's ceiling on her way out into the atmosphere of Salavat. The high-velocity launch pinned her to her seat, and she struggled to halt the fighter's wild rolling and yawing.

Her countdown progressed through single digits.

Eight . . . seven . . . six . . .

She gained control of the interceptor and leveled out her flight.

Five . . . four . . .

Over the comm, the same voice as before screeched, *"Set down your vessel immediately, or you will be shot down!"*

She steered into a climbing turn, stomped on the thruster, and raced toward orbit. *Three . . . two . . . one.* Far below on the planet's surface, a brief flare of crimson confirmed that the Breen had not found her overloading disruptor in time.

The gray mist of the atmosphere melted away as Sarina continued her ascent. For a moment she considered breaking orbit and triggering her extraction signal. She pushed the thought aside. *No,* she resolved. *Not after what Julian did for me. I owe him everything. I can't just leave him here— I need to find him.*

As for how she was supposed to do that . . . she had no idea.

Multiple green dots appeared on one of the cockpit's sensor displays. After a few seconds of translating the symbols on the screen, Sarina deduced that the dots represented a squadron of interceptors scrambled from some other BID facility, likely with orders to destroy her on sight.

She tested the various tactical controls around her. A toggle on the top of the yoke armed either the forward disruptor cannon or the four missiles mounted under the interceptor's wings. The trigger was on the far side of the yoke.

It took her a moment to find the energizer for the

shields, which hardly seemed up to the challenge of a dogfight against a superior force. *Retreat might be my only option*, she realized. *Unfortunately, this thing isn't built to exceed quarter impulse. Which means I can forget about outrunning whatever warships might get called in as backup if I make a run for it.*

On the sensor display, the six blips closed in, and they seemed to be gaining speed. Despite having only the most rudimentary flight training, Sarina was about to find herself in a dogfight against experienced pilots. *Improvisation is fine for learning how to sing*, she fretted, *but for zero-gravity combat? Not so much.*

The engines roared as she stepped on the thrust pedal and tugged the yoke to flip her craft's nose up and over to face her oncoming attackers.

Julian, she prayed, *wherever you are . . . I hope you're having better luck than I am right now.*

40

Thot Keer arrived at the Ops Center to find the door open, its consoles blasted apart and belching smoke, and its floor littered with murdered personnel. He was overcome with sorrow and fury. *They were just engineers and technicians*, he raged. *Why kill them? What sort of monster could do this?* He could almost understand why an enemy would kill the armed security personnel—but had it really been necessary to murder unarmed civilian workers?

Waving his hands to cut a path through the room's blanket of black smoke, he worked his way past the carnage to inspect the various consoles. He was unable to find even one intact. "Computer," he said, "acknowledge Thot Keer." There was no response. He was about to repeat his request when he looked up and saw that whoever had killed the ops team had also shot out the voice interface.

Of course, Keer thought with bitter cynicism. *The saboteur was thorough enough to murder noncombatant civilians. Naturally, he shot the transceiver.* Keer walked back to the upper level, found the auxiliary systems access panel, and pried it loose. Behind it, the backup console and secondary voice-input node were intact.

He keyed in his authorization code. "Computer, acknowledge Thot Keer."

"Acknowledged," the computer voice said from the backup console.

"Emergency override *toshbek* seven five nine," Keer said.

"Override accepted. Awaiting instructions."

"Access memory core," Keer said. "Locate all design files related to the slipstream adaptation project."

"No files found," the computer said.

Horror clouded Keer's thoughts. "No," he mumbled, voicing his denial. "They must be there. All my work, my notes . . ." He keyed commands into the backup console and waited with mounting anxiety. It told him the same thing that the synthetic voice had: his folder of annotated schematics had been deleted.

He entered more commands. *You're not that good, my little saboteur. You may have found the master copies, but you must have missed*—under his mask, he smiled with smug satisfaction—*the backup copies. You missed those. Not so clever after all, eh?* He restored his files from the backups and marked them for emergency burst transmission. "Computer, send my design files to the central databank at the Confederate Information Bureau. Update all files with my most recent annotations."

"Acknowledged. Initiating burst transmission. . . . Transmission complete."

Keer exhaled with profound relief. Whatever happened next, his work had been preserved and was safe offworld. His labors would not have been in vain.

"Open the outer doors of the main hangar," he said.

The computer replied, *"Confirmed. Opening outer bay doors."*

"Initiate shutdown protocol *liska* for the base's main reactor."

"Error. Unable to comply. Core containment failure imminent. Damage to control systems near main core is preventing completion of shutdown protocol."

Keer knew better than to push a losing position. He sprinted through the door and kept running as he opened a channel through his helmet's transceiver. "Keer to Tul Jath, respond!"

"This is Jath," the foreman said. *"Go ahead, sir!"*

"I opened the hangar doors from ops," Keer said, moving at a full run. "Can you confirm the doors are opening?"

"Affirmative, sir."

"Then get going," Keer said. "Get my ship to safety!"

"It will take five minutes for the doors to open wide enough to maneuver the prototype out of the hangar. You have that long to get back on board."

A deep rumbling shook the base. Overhead lights flared white-hot as power surges ripped through the base's energy-distribution network. Smoke snaked from behind wall panels, followed seconds later by licks of flame, and Keer knew that plasma fires would soon spread throughout the command facility.

"On my way," Keer said as he ducked down a passage to an emergency ladderway, which suddenly seemed preferable to trusting the turbolifts. "But do not wait for me one second longer than you have to," he added, dodging around a jet of fire that spat from a splintering wall panel. "Get *Marjat* to safety. That is an order."

• • •

Everywhere that Bashir looked in search of an exit he found only missed chances. Entire corridors were lined with empty spaces from which escape pods had been launched, sent hurtling away through seemingly endless tubes tunneled through the asteroid. He considered trying to crawl through one to get outside—until a thunderous sound rocked the base, and one tunnel after another imploded and filled with rubble and jagged slabs of stone.

He lagged a few paces behind a cluster of base personnel who shared his predicament. They, too, were trapped and looking for a way out, unaware that the man responsible for their plight was standing in their midst. Scurrying through the smoky darkness, they radiated panic and confusion. They had worked their way down through the base one level at a time, their collective anxiety growing as their options dwindled. Following them into the lowest level, which was made up of cargo bays that ringed three sides of the main hangar, Bashir feared that they—and he—would find no cause for hope, only a final dead end to their flight.

The first workers to enter the bay let out an ear-splitting wail of electronic noise from their vocoders. Bashir presumed it was the Breen's equivalent of a victory whoop. When he at last joined them, he saw the cause of their celebration.

The triangular outer doors of the main hangar were creeping open.

Around him, the celebration degenerated almost immediately into chaotic violence. Breen workers were fighting one another with tools and fists in order to lay claim to one of a handful of small zero-*g* work vehicles, and Bashir understood why: if the outer doors were open, then these tiny worker-bee spacecraft were the survivors' best chance of making it out of the base in time.

He set his hand on the grip of his disruptor and prepared to shoot his way through the free-for-all to the nearest work vehicle. Then he caught a flash of golden light out of the corner of his eye: the prototype was warming up its aft thrusters and preparing for its own getaway. If the prototype escaped, his mission would be an unequivocal failure; all the lives he had taken would have been ended for nothing, and Sarina's sacrifice in Utyrak would have been in vain. That wasn't an outcome that Bashir was prepared to accept. *Change of plan*, he decided.

Hovering on the edge of the riot engulfing the cargo bay ahead of him, Bashir searched the shelves of tools and equipment, taking stock of their contents and imagining alternative uses for them. Then he saw what he was looking for: a panel on the wall marked with the Breen symbols for emergency equipment. He ran to the panel, pulled it open, and retrieved a compact fire-suppressant canister. It was heavy and solid in his hands. He nodded. *This will do*.

Bashir charged toward the nearest work vehicle. The last Breen standing from the mass struggle to claim the craft was opening its side hatch. As the Breen started to pull himself inside the spacecraft, Bashir hefted the fire extinguisher over his shoulder and swung it forward, striking the Breen in the back of the neck. The Breen fell forward, twitched for a few seconds, then fell backward, away from the vehicle. He landed in a limp heap on the floor.

Watching his victim collapse with the traumatic blunt-force injury he had inflicted filled Bashir with an urge to vomit.

None of the few Breen still standing in the cargo bay seemed to notice or care what Bashir had done; they were too busy stealing the other work vehicles in desperate attempts to save themselves.

Choking back his remorse, Bashir lobbed the fire extinguisher inside the vehicle, climbed in after it, and closed the hatch behind himself. *Have to hurry*, he told himself as the prototype starship's main thruster burned ever more brightly. *I can't let that ship get away.*

He pushed the Power On button and started flipping switches, surprised at how similar the Breen vehicle's primary controls were to those used by Starfleet. The console in front of him lit up, and he skipped any pretense of a pre-flight check, choosing instead to guide the ship into motion without delay. A few Breen tried to throw themselves at his craft, perhaps hoping to hijack it, only to be knocked aside by the brutal collision with something far more massive than themselves.

There was a faint crackling of energy across the craft's front windshield as it passed through the pressurized cargo bay's invisible force field and entered the airless microgravity environment of the main hangar.

A small cloud of similar spacecraft raced toward the small but widening gap in the hangar's outer doors. Bashir turned in the opposite direction and flew toward the slipstream prototype. This kind of piloting had never been Bashir's forte. His flying was fast and sloppy, almost careless, but it didn't matter—there wasn't much for him to run into.

Within seconds he was at the rear wall of the hangar, behind the prototype's aft main thruster. Heat alarms started to sound on his console. Squinting against the engine glare, he silenced the buzzing alarm, engaged the spacecraft's manual override, and programmed the vehicle for a collision course—starting at the end of a fifteen-second delay.

He grabbed the fire extinguisher, opened the craft's starboard hatch, and jumped out. The momentum of his leap shifted the spacecraft by half a centimeter before its nav thrusters kicked in to stabilize it, enabling Bashir to launch himself clear by several meters. Even through his vacuum-rated Breen armor he felt the scorching heat of the prototype's main thrusters, and he was grateful that he had parked his craft a few degrees starboard of dead center behind the engine.

Angling the extinguisher's nozzle with care, he released a short spray of foam and compressed gas. A rapidly widening cone of foam appeared and then evaporated in the prototype's engine wash as the extinguisher's emissions propelled Bashir away from the starship. *Now a course correction.* He halted his drifting with a few spurts of the extinguisher. Relying on his visor's HUD to help him choose his angles, he unleashed a steady stream of fire suppressant. It lacked a jetpack's sensation of velocity, but he could tell he was steadily gaining speed as the extinguisher's spray pushed him through the hangar.

Thanks to the vacuum environment, there was no sound from the explosion as his abandoned work craft flew into the prototype's main thruster—just a bright and, to Bashir, satisfying flash of light followed by a spreading cloud of debris.

As he passed between the half-open doors of the hangar bay, Bashir hoped his final spanner in the works would be enough to doom the prototype to a fiery end. For a few seconds he was surrounded by walls of metal and machinery, and then he was back in deep space, floating away from the asteroid.

He adjusted his visor's filter, confirmed he was clear of the base's energy-dampening field, and turned so he could see a constellation that he knew lay in the direction of home and rescue. Breathing a sigh of relief, he triggered his emergency recall beacon. *Cue the cavalry.*

41

Dax stepped out of the turbolift in such a hurry to reach the bridge that she nearly clipped the doors as they sighed open. "Report," she said, moving toward her command chair. "Do we have a lock on the recall beacons?"

Lieutenant Kedair replied, "Yes, sir. It's in the asteroid belt between the fifth and sixth planets of the Alrakis system. But it's only *one* beacon, Captain."

Casting an anxious glance back at Kedair, Dax asked, "Which one?"

"Doctor Bashir's. We're continuing to monitor Lieutenant Douglas's frequency, just in case."

"Good," Dax said. "Mister Tharp, plot a course to Doctor Bashir's recall beacon, maximum slipstream velocity." She looked at her first officer. "Mister Bowers, sound Red Alert and get ready to cross into Breen space."

Bowers nodded, stepped over to an aft console, and opened a shipwide channel. His voice reverberated from the overhead speakers as he spoke. "Attention, this is the XO. Red Alert, all hands to battle stations. This is *not* an exercise. Repeat, this is *not* an exercise. Bridge out." The alert klaxon whooped twice as the overhead lights on the bridge dimmed to their combat setting.

"Mister Helkara," Dax said, "spring the trap."

The Zakdorn second officer looked up from the science console to face Dax. "Aye, sir." Then he exchanged nods with Lieutenant Mirren at ops. "Ready to hack the Breen comnet, on your mark."

Mirren worked her console. "Message packets standing by for transmission. Initiate breach in three . . . two . . . one . . . *mark*." Flurries of data scrolled across her and Helkara's consoles as they worked. "Uploading the batch of messages to the Breen comnet, Captain. It'll take about fifteen seconds for them to move through the rest of the nodes in this sector."

Helkara added, "Once all the nodes are primed, the virus should self-activate and begin sending phony planetary distress signals."

Moving to stand behind Kedair, Bowers said to her, "Pipe in those distress signals as soon as we pick them up. I want to hear what the Breen hear."

"Aye, sir," Kedair said. "Looks like it's starting a few seconds early."

Kedair tapped her console, and from the overhead speaker Dax heard the machine-speak of the first message, low and muffled beneath its stilted translation. *"All allied vessels, this is a Priority Alert! Ocram III is under attack by Klingon forces! Repeat, Ocram III——"* A harsh blast of static ended the message.

"I'm reading dozens more transmissions like that one, Captain," Kedair said. "Most of the Breen's border colonies on the far side of this sector are under siege by Klingon forces." She smiled. "At least, that's what I've *heard . . .*"

"Don't believe everything you hear," Dax said.

Bowers joined Helkara at the science console. "The Breen's comnet is starting to fail," the first officer said. "It should look to the blockade fleet like part of a full-scale attack on the Breen's civil infrastructure."

"Well done, everyone," Dax said. "If our intel on Breen and Romulan ships is still up to date, all those systems reporting attacks should be just outside their maximum sensor range—which means that if they want to investigate, they'll have to break formation and abandon the blockade between us and the Alrakis system."

Returning to Dax's side, Bowers said, "This is a hell of a gamble, Captain. If that fleet doesn't take the bait, we're in big trouble. After pulling this gag on us just a couple of days ago, I don't see the Romulans falling for it."

Kedair looked up and said, "We don't need the whole fleet to buy this ruse—just the Breen ships. They're most of the blockade. If we can lure them off-station, that'll create more than enough gaps for us to exploit."

"Never underestimate the power of paranoia, Sam," Dax said. "The Breen are known for having hair triggers and for responding in force to invaders."

"Assuming they believe this invasion is real," Bowers said.

"Imagine you're one of those Breen starship commanders," Dax said. "After spending days playing cat and mouse on the border with a Federation starship, you've just received word of a massive Klingon assault on all the worlds you've left undefended. Your local communications network has been disrupted, which means you can't get any real-time orders from your central command or civilian authorities. . . . It probably looks to them as if we were sent here to lure them out of position as a prelude to the Klingons' attack. Even if they think it's a trick, they can't take the chance of ignoring what might be a real invasion. If they abandon the blockade and lose track of one Starfleet ship, that's bad, but if they fail to respond to a multiplanet invasion, that's grounds for summary execution."

From tactical, Kedair said, "Captain, we're picking up a lot of encrypted comm chatter between the ships in the blockade." She shook her head. "No idea what they're saying, but it seems like a very busy conversation."

"No doubt," Dax said. To Bowers, she added, "I'll bet you the Breen ships in the blockade warp away in the next three minutes."

"No bet," Bowers said. "But even if they do, we'll still have to deal with the Romulans, and there's no telling how many of them there are. We're reading up to three warbirds out there, but who knows how many might be lurking under cloak?"

Kedair replied, "By my best estimate, at least two and no more than five."

Cocking one eyebrow, Bowers said, "And that's based upon . . . ?"

"My analysis of standard Romulan fleet deployment strategies, cross-referenced with their known ships on active duty in this sector and recent Starfleet activity reports that pinpoint the locations of forty-one of them."

"That sounds very thorough, Lieutenant."

"Yes, sir, it is."

"Carry on, then," Bowers said, cracking an amused half smile.

Dax leaned forward in her chair. She watched the stars on the main viewer and imagined Julian floating somewhere out in all that darkness, perhaps injured or worse, waiting for her to come and bring him home. "Stand ready, everyone," she said to her crew, projecting a degree of confidence she didn't feel. "The moment the road is open, we're going in."

Sarina remained steady and calm as her pursuers entered optimal weapons range. Their sensor profile had remained consistent throughout their approach; there were six of them moving in a close formation for zero-*g* combat, divided into three pairs, each with an obvious leader and wingman.

Because of their distance and the lack of direct illumination on the night side of a gas giant, where Sarina had chosen to make her stand, she was unable to see them directly and doubted that would change. At such ranges and velocities, unaided visual contact was all but unheard of.

Enough time had passed that she figured the incoming ships must already have locked weapons. She wondered whether they would attempt to hail her and demand her surrender before they—

Bright green flashes of energized plasma raced past Sarina's ship, too far away to pose a serious threat but close enough to cause her breath to catch in her chest. *So much for buying time with a surrender parley*, she realized.

Several more volleys of emerald-hued plasma shot by

her interceptor as it drifted, dark and completely powered down, relying only on its passive sensors, which were powered by an emergency battery. After a brief pause, several more plasma bolts blurred past and vanished into deep space. Alone in the darkness, Sarina smiled. *Looks like their sensors are accurate enough to track my fighter's transponder but not quite good enough to hit it.*

Thanks to an online diagnostic manual Sarina had accessed, she had learned that the fighter's transponder was accessible through a panel beneath the cockpit's forward console. Without deactivating or damaging it, she had removed the fist-sized component; after depressurizing the cockpit, she'd opened the fighter's canopy and hurled the transponder into space as an all but invisible decoy and then shut down her interceptor's nonessential systems.

Even in a best-case scenario, she expected this ploy would gain her no more than fifteen to twenty seconds' grace before the incoming pilots deduced what she had done and switched to active-scan targeting to compensate. She had no intention of giving them that much time to act.

She restarted her ship's main power, armed her weapons, locked, and fired.

Viridescent beams shot from the forward gun of Sarina's vessel, and the targeting scanner in front of her registered two direct hits, yielding two kills.

Positive she had wrung all she could from her advantage of surprise, she stepped on the thruster pedal and charged ahead at the Breen patrol, which split up and broke off into separate evasive patterns, presumably to buy its pilots time to acquire a true sensor lock on Sarina's ship.

She picked the closer pair of ships and tried to slip into a pursuit course, but the second pair adjusted course and forced Sarina back into a defensive mode. Turning tail and going full evasive was not the situation Sarina wanted. Outnumbered four to one, she knew her chances of survival would be slim.

A new salvo of shots streaked past her ship from behind, and a few nicked her vessel's wings and grazed its tailfin. Patching in a reserve booster, she rolled away in a hard turn that left her head spinning and her stomach heaving.

Get it together, she told herself, and she pushed through the handicap of her nausea and vertigo. An alert shrilled from her console and a red light flashed on her cockpit's flight display: someone behind her had locked weapons on her ship.

She fired her engines in full reverse and keyed her nav thrusters to put her above her attacker, who was now several hundred kilometers in front of her. Despite being so woozy that she could barely see, she engaged her targeting sensor and heard the chirrup of a lock-on. Struggling to regain her equilibrium, she fired.

A triple beep from the ship's console confirmed the kill. Sarina pressed her foot down on the interceptor's thrust pedal and pulled away from the conflagration.

Her pulse pounded in her temples, and her internal organs felt as if they had been put through a blender. Before that moment, she had understood the stresses of high-*g* maneuvers on humanoid bodies only in an abstract sense. Now she grasped it in an all-too-visceral manner.

As Sarina shook her head to clear the spots from her

vision so she could select a new target—or maybe pick an escape vector—an alert flashed on her helmet's HUD: it was the activation of Bashir's recall beacon. Sarina felt a swell of hope. Regardless of whether he had accomplished his mission, he was alive and calling for extraction. That meant Sarina had a new objective.

She made an abrupt course change, flipping the nose of her ship up and over and then veering away from her remaining three pursuers in a wild corkscrew evasive pattern. Reaching Bashir had become her only priority. She relayed the coordinates of his signal from her HUD to the fighter's navigational system.

Abandoning caution, she patched in every bit of thrust her ship could muster and set it all for an extended, nonstop burn. Multiple indicators redlined—hull stress, engine temperature, fuel consumption. The fighter shuddered with such violence that Sarina feared it might break apart all on its own. She pushed it past all its rated tolerances, setting it on a path of pure acceleration all the way to Julian.

Within a few seconds she was out of her pursuers' weapons range, and she noted that they didn't seem to be making an effort to match her speed. *They know this flying scrap pile can't keep this up for long,* she reasoned. *They're just waiting for me to fry its engines so they can swoop in and pick me off.*

She smiled as she triggered her own suit's recall beacon and hoped that Captain Dax and the *Starship Aventine* didn't keep her and Julian waiting.

Plates on her ship's forward fuselage spiderwebbed with cracks, and worry erased Sarina's smile. *Here's hoping I make the rendezvous in one piece . . .*

• • •

Bashir drifted alone in space, engulfed by silent darkness, a mote in the eye of the universe. The fire extinguisher had run empty, leaving him with no means of adjusting his course or speed, so he cast it away. The canister tumbled off into the endless night. *I know how it feels.*

The recall beacon's icon flashed in the lower left corner of his HUD. It had been several minutes since he triggered it. Dax had estimated the lag between signal and retrieval at five minutes, but that mark was past. Bashir tried to stay optimistic, but anxiety crowded his thoughts with worst-case scenarios.

Might the Breen be preventing the *Aventine* from coming after him? What if the ship had been destroyed? He shut his eyes and cursed himself for even contemplating the possibility. *Dax wouldn't let that happen,* he assured himself. *She'd find a way to survive.* He took a deep breath and cleared his thoughts, but other calamities rushed in to fill the vacuum. Even if the *Aventine* hadn't fallen victim to an enemy attack, what if it had been recalled by Starfleet Command or the Federation Council? It wouldn't be the first time that an operation was cut short in the service of a larger strategic goal or to advance a political agenda.

One paranoid musing led to another. *Is it possible,* he wondered, *that Starfleet abandoned this mission? What if they lied to me and Sarina? The Federation's never been fond of the genetically enhanced. What if this mission was just an excuse to get rid of us? Field agents are usually considered expendable. Why would we be any different? What if sacrificing us was the plan all along?*

His years of experience in Starfleet made him want to dismiss his suspicions as absurdities, but he was alone and drifting through Breen space with all his hopes linked to a recall beacon no one seemed to be answering.

With a quick twist of his torso he initiated a slow turn of his body so he could look behind him. As he finished the turn he jerked his arms in the opposite direction to arrest his momentum. The hollowed-out asteroid was far behind him and shrinking by slow degrees, but it was still the largest object in his field of vision. Its surface erupted with numerous small explosions, most likely precursors of the massive detonation soon to come.

Through the open doors of its hangar, he saw the sleek prototype vessel inching its way forward in a bid to escape. It was propelled by an assortment of small maneuvering jets. Though it seemed to be creeping forward, Bashir was certain it would clear the hangar's threshold in less than three minutes—well ahead of the explosion he'd arranged to destroy it.

He weighed his options and was dismayed to find he had none. There was no way for him to go back to the asteroid, and he had no weapons or munitions capable of affecting the ship's progress. All he could do was hang in space, watch, and wait. *I've failed*, he lamented. *I let Sarina sacrifice herself, I took lives in cold blood, all for nothing. Once that ship clears the hangar, it's over.*

Bashir prepared himself to surrender his last shreds of hope and accept the inevitable . . . and then a miracle happened. His visor's HUD lit up with an alert. A signal had been detected—Sarina's recall beacon had been activated, and it was on the move, heading directly toward him. Even if the mission failed, she was alive. He closed his eyes and hoped that his fears were baseless and that the *Aventine* was on its way. *Two miracles in ten minutes might be asking a lot,* he admitted to himself, *but it's pretty much all I have left.*

"The Breen ships are breaking formation," Lieutenant Kedair said. "They're leaving the blockade and setting course away from the border." She looked up at Dax with a conspiratorial gleam. "The road is open."

Dax watched the shifting icons on the tactical display beside her chair and tried to conceal the profound wave of relief she felt. Up until that moment she had been plagued by nagging doubts about the plan. As the *Aventine*'s commanding officer, she had to put on her bravest face for the sake of her crew. Moments of vindication such as this made all her hours of secret trepidation bearable.

Bowers stood at Dax's side and said, "Lieutenant Mirren, are the Romulan ships redeploying to cover the positions abandoned by the Breen?"

Mirren transferred her sensor data to the bridge's main viewscreen. "Affirmative, sir. Looks like they're scrambling, though."

Kedair tapped commands into the tactical console and highlighted several Romulan ship positions on the main screen. "Look at these maneuvers," she said. "The *Terrinex* made three rapid course corrections in under a minute— but for no apparent reason." Four ostensibly empty subsectors flashed red. "The only way her uncorrected position would've made sense is if those areas were covered. Her new position makes them look undefended, but I'll bet that's where the Romulans' cloaked reinforcements are waiting."

Keying in her own annotations on the starmap, Dax said, "This part of the grid has a lot of ships in motion, but it's completely chaotic. That's where we'll punch through— right now, before they get their bearings. Mister Tharp, set your course and confirm when ready."

Tharp entered the new flight path with a few deft taps of his blue fingers and turned his chair to face Dax. "Ready, sir. Just give the word."

"The word is given, Mister Tharp. Slipstream jump, maximum speed." She pointed forward as she added, "Engage."

The Bolian flight controller activated the slipstream drive, and the streaked starlight of warp travel became a bluish-white swirl twisting around the *Aventine*, whose hull rang with an eerie, almost musical resonance.

Dax imagined the stunned reactions of the hapless Romulans she and her crew had just left behind at the border and permitted herself a gloating smile. *Catch us if you can.*

42

The life-support module was the first system to fail inside Sarina's stolen Breen interceptor, followed half a minute later by the active sensors in the aft fuselage. Sarina didn't care as long as the engines kept going. Heat warnings lit up her console, and the fighter's flight controls were growing unresponsive. She could barely see through the cockpit's canopy, whose outer layer was splintering.

Her pursuers were still well behind her, but they hadn't given up the chase. They were waiting for her ship's inevitable engine failure. As the dartlike craft shuddered and sparks flew from beneath its forward console, Sarina suspected that fateful event was mere moments away. She checked her range to Bashir: ninety thousand kilometers and closing fast. Forty thousand kilometers was the maximum range of a Starfleet transporter. Because Sarina had no idea where the *Aventine* might be if—*when*, she corrected herself—it came to retrieve Bashir, to have a chance of being beamed up with him Sarina knew she needed to get to within ten thousand kilometers of his position, which was in the midst of an asteroid ring.

She was sixty thousand kilometers out when her starboard thruster started to sputter and lose power. To avoid being thrown into an unrecoverable spin, she cut power in the port thruster to match. Then the engine core of her interceptor seized, and energy levels inside her ship plummeted. She continued to hurtle forward, but the corrections she had made to keep her course steady as the engines quit had cost her a fair amount of her speed, and she was no longer capable of acceleration.

Her pursuers reappeared on her long-range sensors. They were flying at their top speed and gaining rapidly on Sarina's position. It took her a fraction of a second to calculate their velocity relative to hers and determine how many seconds it would be until they overtook her and entered optimal weapons range. In even less time she concluded that she would be just less than forty thousand kilometers from Bashir's position. Sarina frowned. *Not good enough.*

She armed her ship's forward guns and used her maneuvering jets to change her orientation, flipping her nose up and over to face her pursuers. When the maneuver was complete, she cut power to her ship's inertial dampers. Though the two incoming fighters were still out of range, she opened fire, holding down the trigger until the guns' heat warnings automatically shut them down. As she'd hoped, without the inertial dampers to counteract the weapons' effects on the ship, the steady discharge of energized plasma had imparted some small measure of thrust to her interceptor. Seconds passed while she waited for the guns to cool enough for her to resume firing. When the indicators turned blue again, she squeezed the trigger and hurled another stream of energy into space. Then the heat alarm went off and shut down the guns.

That'll have to do, she decided. Another tap on the sluggish maneuvering jets lifted the nose of her ship ninety degrees. Showing her ventral profile to her attackers was virtual suicide—it presented them with the largest possible target and exposed her ship's most vulnerable systems. Under the circumstances, however, Sarina saw no better alternative.

Her range to Bashir, displayed in her visor's HUD, ticked down past forty-two thousand kilometers. The sensor console inside the cockpit showed the pursuit fighters closing to weapons range in less than thirty seconds. At intercept-minus-twenty, her range to Bashir dropped below forty-one thousand kilometers. It broke forty thousand at i-minus-ten. Counting down the final seconds, Sarina closed her hand white-knuckle tight around her seat's ejection handle.

At i-minus-four her passive sensors detected multiple weapons locking onto her ship's ventral fuselage. At i-minus-two she pulled the ejection handle.

The acceleration was so fierce that Sarina thought she had struck something and was being crushed. The immense *g*-force of ejection abated as she rocketed away from her stolen vessel, the momentum of the escape system targeted to follow the same vector as that of her ship, increasing her velocity toward Bashir.

A searing flash of yellow-white light scattered her abandoned interceptor into scrap and free radicals. She caught a fleeting glimpse of engine glows from the pursuit craft as they raced by her.

Her visor's HUD confirmed she was less than thirty-nine thousand kilometers from Bashir and continuing to close the distance. Ahead of her she saw a dark lump of rock with a bright spot in its center, and she wondered whether that was the hidden shipyard she and Bashir had come to find.

Watching the kilometers tick away on her HUD, Sarina knew she would reach Bashir's position in less than seven minutes. Only then did she realize she had no means of slowing herself down. Which meant that in eight minutes she would be well past Bashir and hurtling away into empty space—and away from their planned rendezvous with the *Aventine*.

Bashir watched hope growing closer by the second. His visor's HUD registered the slow but steady approach of Sarina's recall beacon. He wondered what kind of ship she had commandeered. Whatever it was, he was certain she'd have a plan for retrieving him. Even if the *Aventine* never came back for them, even if Starfleet had cut them loose or some politician had written them off, he had faith that Sarina would find him and together they would escape and make their way home.

Home . . . He didn't know what that word meant anymore. Was it wherever he laid his head? Was it on Earth with his parents? Or on Deep Space 9 with the few familiar faces that still populated his increasingly lonely life? Or did he dare to imagine that "home" might mean wherever he could be with Sarina? The longer he entertained that notion, the more right it felt. She was his home. And if she wanted him to leave DS9 and go hopping through the galaxy on one covert mission after another, he knew he would follow her without hesitation.

A blinding flash of light made him wince. His visor compensated for the glare, enabling his eyes to adjust and see the final moments of a fiery explosion—which lay on a direct bearing to Sarina's last coordinates. Terror stabbed him in the heart, and for the span of one breath, he was paralyzed with dread and doubt. The burning cloud faded. Noting that Sarina's recall beacon was still transmitting, Bashir strained to pick out any sign of her, one tiny drifting figure against the endless expanse of deep space, but he knew it was a futile effort. He would have to trust his suit's sensors, which told him Sarina was still moving toward him.

New questions troubled him. *What if she's in the same predicament I am? If that was her ship I saw explode, how are she and I going to link up out here? And without a ship, what chance do we really have?*

His pessimistic musing was cut short as a pair of large, dark shapes zoomed past him, indistinct blurs in the darkness. Following their paths, he caught the bright glow of engine pods. *Looks like we're not alone out here. If those are patrol ships, they'll be able to pick us off with ease.*

He looked over his shoulder at the asteroid. The bow of the Breen's slipstream prototype vessel was passing through the hangar's main entrance. In less than two minutes it would be clear of the hangar and free to navigate. *That's it, then*, Bashir despaired. *Game, set, and match—we lose.*

High above him, a bluish-white storm of light erupted

as if from nowhere. It vanished in a momentous flash, and he felt a bizarre galvanic tingling on his skin. When he was at last able to relax and focus his eyes, he grinned at the most beautiful sight he could have imagined: the elegant, sharklike hull of the *Aventine* loomed a few kilometers above him, aglow from its own running lights.

Lieutenant Kedair's voice crackled over his helmet's transceiver. "*Aventine to Doctor Bashir. Do you copy?*"

"Affirmative, *Aventine*! I'm all right!"

"*Stand by for transport,*" Kedair said. "*We'll have you aboard in—*" Energy pulses slammed against the *Aventine*'s hull. Seconds later, two Breen interceptors streaked past the starship, passing over its primary hull and between its warp nacelles. As the fighters swung around for another pass, Kedair continued. "*Hang on, Doctor. As soon as we swat a few flies, we'll beam you up.*"

"Negative," Bashir said. "Ignore them and forget about me. You've got to stop that prototype from leaving the hangar inside the asteroid!"

"Incoming," Kedair said, sounding unfazed. Muffled thunder followed her warning, and she added, "More nuisance fire from the Breen fighters. No damage, shields holding. The Breen are breaking off and calling for reinforcements."

From the science console, Helkara said, "Jamming their comms now."

Bowers stood behind ops and asked Mirren, "What about the recall beacons? Do we still have a fix on Bashir and Douglas?"

"Aye, sir," Mirren replied. "Holding station three point two kilometers from Doctor Bashir, and Lieutenant Douglas's signal remains inbound at one hundred kilometers per second."

Dax stood up from the center seat and watched the real-time updates to the tactical displays beside the main viewscreen. "Mirren, give me an angle on the asteroid," she said. The image on the main viewer switched to show the Breen's prototype vessel emerging from its rocky cocoon. "We have to stop them, on the double. Sam, Lonnoc—suggestions?"

"If we open fire, it's an act of war," Bowers said. "The ship was supposed to be destroyed *before* we extracted Bashir and Douglas."

Kedair said, "If it never makes it out of the hangar, and the shipyard's reactor blows up, it'll be a moot point. The Breen can't make a fuss about a ship they deny exists, right? So we just have to get it back inside the hangar and keep it there."

Helkara turned from the science console and joined the discussion. "We can use the shields," he said. "Extend them in front of us, full power, and push the prototype back inside the asteroid. The only catch—"

"—is that we'll be right on top of the hangar when it blows," Bowers said.

"Make it happen," Dax said, returning to her chair. "Right now. Tharp, put us nose to nose with the prototype. Mirren, route auxiliary power to the shields. Kedair, reconfigure the shields for maximum forward effect. Sam, ready the ship."

Bowers nodded. "Attention all decks, this is the XO: Brace for impact."

The asteroid and the prototype filled the main viewer as the *Aventine* cruised toward its head-on confrontation. Dax felt the tension mounting on the bridge and noticed that she had reflexively clenched her fists on the armrests of her chair.

Mirren raised her voice: "The Breen fighters are moving into an attack profile against Lieutenant Douglas!"

"Warn them off," Dax said. "Phasers only. Shoot to damage, not destroy."

Kedair replied, "Aye, sir. Firing phasers." She tapped her console twice and was answered by soft feedback tones. "Two hits, one on each fighter. Minor damage to both. They're changing course and bugging out."

"Well done," Dax said. "Now for the *real* fun."

The deck lurched, and a calamitous boom of collision rocked the *Aventine*. "Contact," Tharp said over the din as he entered new commands into the helm. On the main viewer, the ship's normally invisible shields crackled with white lightning as they were forced into repeated collisions with the Breen vessel's bow.

"Now it's a battle of engines," Bowers said.

"Not exactly," Dax said. "Now it's a game of chicken. We're gambling that the Breen ship isn't armed because it's a prototype. Whoever's commanding that ship is probably betting we'll cut and run before the asteroid explodes."

Her comment provoked a worried look from Bowers. "Are you saying what I think you're saying? We're staying here through the detonation?"

"No," Dax said, "but we'll have to cut it very, very close. Mister Tharp, have you ever plotted and executed a half-second warp-one hop?"

"Yes, sir," Tharp said while keeping his hands and eyes on his work.

"Have you ever done one in *reverse*?"

The Bolian's eyebrows lifted in slow surprise. "No, sir. No one has."

"Well, then, get ready to make history. Lieutenant Mirren, how long do we have to reconfigure our warp-field geometry for reverse propulsion?"

Mirren replied, "Two minutes and forty-nine seconds until the shipyard's reactor core breaches and destroys everything within ten kilometers."

"Work quickly, Gruhn," Dax said.

"Aye, sir," said Helkara. The Zakdorn science officer turned back toward his console and muttered grimly, "Leishman's going to kill me when she hears *this*."

"Lonnoc," Dax said, "tell the transporter room we need to beam up two targets moving on separate vectors at different speeds just before we go to warp."

"I'm sure they'll be thrilled to hear that, Captain."

"I'm not here to make their job *easy*, Lieutenant. Just get it done."

"Aye, sir."

As the crew snapped into action, Bowers walked back to stand beside Dax's chair. Lowering his voice to a confidential level, he said, "Let me see if I've got this straight. You're risking the ship, the crew, and the mission on the assumptions that Helkara and Leishman are engineering geniuses, Tharp is a piloting savant, our transporter chief can work miracles, and the Breen are unwilling to sacrifice themselves in a kamikaze attack?"

Dax folded her arms, looked up at Bowers, and nodded. "Yup."

He grinned. "Damn, I *love* this job."

43

Thot Keer kept his curses to himself as he watched the Starfleet cruiser charging into a head-on collision with his one-of-a-kind prototype. He appreciated the irony and symmetry of the contest: the enemy vessel was one of Starfleet's new slipstream-enabled *Vesta*-class starships, whose designs the BID had stolen to facilitate Keer's work. *The parent comes to smother its bastard*, Keer fumed.

The two ships smashed together and filled the *Marjat* with a terrible sound of wrenching metal. The impact sent Keer and most of his crew sprawling across the *Marjat*'s mostly empty decks. He slammed against a bank of computer terminals, winced as he suppressed a groan, and scrambled to his feet.

"I need more power," he shouted to his skeleton crew. "Engage impulse drive on full—we need to push that ship out of our way!"

Jath, the foreman, replied, "Impulse coils are already at overdrive, sir!"

Keer seethed. This was no battle of equals. The *Marjat* was a shell housing an antimatter reactor and a propulsion system. Its greater power-to-mass ratio might have given it an advantage over the Starfleet ship had it been equipped with anything more than rudimentary life-support sys-tems. *No shields,* Keer raged, *no weapons, not even ablative hull plating. What am I supposed to do? Go outside and throw rocks?* Even the prototype's engines were not at full capacity. Someone—most likely the same saboteur who had killed the ops crew, Keer suspected—had crashed a work vehicle into the *Marjat*'s aft main thruster, forcing the ship to crawl out of its hangar on feeble maneuvering jets.

With the *Marjat*'s bow safely past the hangar's thresh-old, however, it was safe to engage the impulse drive. Push-ing the Starfleet ship aside would be a matter of raw force. "Patch the main reactor into the impulse coils," Keer said to Jath. "Disengage the safeties—if we achieve relativistic velocity after breaking through, all the better. But we *must* break through!"

After relaying Keer's order to the crew on the decks below, Jath approached the commander and said, "Even with all power to the coils, will it be enough?"

"I think it will," Keer said. "The Starfleet ship has com-parable engine power and greater mass, but it needs to ex-pend energy to keep its shields up. They know our base's reactor is critical, which means they cannot risk dropping shields to increase their engine output. That is our only ad-vantage, and I mean to press it."

Jath looked at the situation monitor mounted on the forward bulkhead. "What if the Starfleet ship opens fire? We have no defenses!"

"If they were going to fire, they would have done so by now," Keer said. "They need to destroy every trace of us in order to deny their crime. Even if we cannot save the ship, Jath, we must break free so that our deaths may be avenged."

The *Marjat* rang with the rising hum of engines being pushed past their safe operating limits, and its hull groaned. Together they made for a mournful sound, one that Keer regretted having to inflict on his greatest creation. It reminded him of his daughter's pained cries, the heartbreaking sounds that had issued from her dry, cracked lips as her illness wrought its final ravages on her tiny body.

I let this job consume my life, he reflected with bitterness. *I gave it all I had—my youth, my vigor, my imagination. When I lost my family I submerged myself into this. Now it is all I have left.* He would not let enemies of his people take the *Marjat* from him. "Jath," he shouted over the clamor of straining engines, "is the base's main computer still online?"

Jath spun and keyed commands into a terminal behind him. "Yes, sir."

"Get me a line to its command systems," Keer said. "We need to redirect the base's energy-dampening field toward the Starfleet vessel. If we match their shield frequency, we should be able to break through and ram them out of the way."

"Yes, sir," Jath said. "Accessing the command systems now."

It was a wild tactic, and Keer knew the odds were weighted against him. A glance at the chrono made it clear that escape was no longer an option; the best he could hope for now was to make certain the *Marjat* was not erased from history by an act of terrorism, and that the Starfleet crew that had come to seal his fate was forced to share it. *I will not go alone into the fire and the night*, he vowed.

• • •

"Sixty seconds," Mirren said over the shuddering and creaking of the *Aventine*'s hull, as if Dax and the rest of the bridge crew couldn't see the countdown ticking away on the main viewscreen.

Dax steepled her fingers in front of her. "Acknowledged." Looking over her shoulder at Helkara, she added, "Gruhn? Report."

"Calculations complete," the science officer said. "Leishman's making the hardware adjustments now. Awaiting final confirmation."

Bowers cast a tense stare at Helkara. "She knows we're in a hurry, right?"

"Yes, I made that quite clear, sir."

Kedair declared in a tone of alarm, "Shields are losing power!" Her hands flew across her console to summon new data. "It's the Breen base—their energy-dampening field is being recalibrated to cancel out our shields!"

Mirren swiveled her chair to face Dax and Bowers. "If we lose shields, the Breen ship'll ram us!"

"Thank you for stating the obvious," Dax said. "Lonnoc, switch to random shield-frequency nutation. Gruhn, pinpoint their energy dampener and knock it out with a feedback pulse. Tharp, if our shields buckle, dip our bow and try to come up under theirs—maybe we can pin them to the roof of their hangar."

Flashing a smile, Bowers said to Dax, "Never a dull moment, eh?"

"Not if you're doing it right."

The overhead lights, which were already dimmed, flickered and went out, leaving the bridge bathed in the crimson glow of its alert panels and the pale twilight cast off from its duty consoles and forward viewscreen. "Sorry," Kedair said. "That was me. I'm stealing every bit of power I can to keep the shields up."

"Core breach in thirty seconds," Mirren said.

"Warp coil polarity reversed," Helkara said. "Recharging now . . ."

A thin haze clouded the air between Dax and the main viewscreen, and she was fairly certain she smelled smoke. "Number One—damage report!"

"Overloads in the power-transfer system," he said, checking an aft engineering console. Keying open a priority channel, he continued, "Bridge to damage control! Plasma fire in deck one overhead. Respond RFN, that's an *order*."

Hunched forward over the conn, Tharp mumbled, "This is gonna be close."

"You have no idea," Dax said. To Kedair she added, "Lonnoc, as soon as we drop our shields, beam up Bashir and Douglas. I don't want them ending up as collateral damage when that hunk of rock goes boom."

"Aye, sir. Alerting Transporter Room One to stand by."

An alert buzzed on the ops console. Mirren silenced it. "The core breach is starting! Ten seconds to critical!"

Over the deafening rumbles rocking the hull, Dax said, "Mister Tharp?"

"The Breen ship is fully inside the hangar."

"Full reverse on my mark," Dax said. "Half-second warp jump!"

"Coordinates locked," Tharp said.

"Five . . . ," Mirren counted. "Four . . ."

"Standing by to beam up Bashir and Douglas," Kedair said.

"Three . . ."

"Drop shields," Dax said. "Energize!"

"Two . . . one."

Dax snapped, "Mark!"

Tharp tapped his console, and the asteroid vanished from the main screen in a blur of streaked light. Two seconds later, a flash of light filled the screen.

Turning slowly toward her tactical officer, Dax said in a quiet voice, "Lonnoc, I hope you have good news to share, or I'm going to be *very* upset."

Keer turned from one subordinate to another in search of good news but found only catastrophes. "Are their shields down yet?"

"No," said a newly hired engineer whose name Keer had not learned. "They changed the rotation cycle—we are unable to find the neutralizing harmonic."

Fists clenched in frustration, Keer bellowed, "Set the energy-dampening field to maximum power, full range—smother everything, us included!"

It was Jath who delivered the next bit of bad news. "The Starfleet ship generated a feedback pulse in the dampener," he said. "The system is offline."

Turning the dampener against itself . . . I have to respect their ingenuity. "Charge the warp coils," Keer said. "Prepare to ram them!"

"There is no time," Jath protested. "The core will breach any moment—"

Raising a hand to silence the foreman, Keer said, "I know. Belay my last."

On the master situation monitor, a countdown to the core breach dwindled to its final seconds. Keer had tried everything in his power, though he had hobbled himself by daring to hope he might escape with his ship and his life. *If I had chosen to sacrifice myself sooner, we could have charged the warp coils.* He bowed his head in shame and defeat. *It no longer matters. The fight is over.*

Behind him lay pandemonium. His crew was scrambling in all directions, their voices full of fear and desperation, each of them clinging to denial like drowning men to flotsam. Keer was determined to meet his end with more dignity.

On the main screen, the Starfleet ship vanished in a flash of light, and he knew he had been robbed of even his final act of spite. The enemy had escaped.

Keer dropped to his knees and, in defiance of all tradition and protocol, pulled off his helmet and cast it aside, revealing his true face.

"I have lived as a Breen," he whispered as the *Marjat* vanished in a flash of white heat, "but I die a Paclu."

44

No matter how many times engineers tried to convince Bashir that one was not able to perceive the passage of time while dematerialized inside a transporter buffer, he remained certain that he could feel the difference between a long transport cycle and a short one—and the one he had just endured seemed as if it had lasted an eternity.

He'd felt the immobilizing tug of the annular confinement beam, and then a haze of energized particles had surrounded him, scrubbing the starscape from view. In an eyeblink he had submerged into a sea of endless white light.

As the interior of the *Aventine*'s main transporter took shape before him, however, Bashir had the uncanny, mildly disoriented sensation of awakening from a long slumber. Feeling his feet on a solid surface, he wavered as he regained his balance and adjusted to being back in normal gravity. He spread his arms to steady himself, and his left hand touched something. He turned and saw another unsteady figure in Breen armor looking back at him.

Bashir unfastened the seals on his helmet and pulled it off in a fumbling rush as the person beside him did the same. He cast aside his Breen mask in time to see Sarina drop hers to the deck. They moved toward each other, half leaping and half falling, and collapsed into each other's arms.

Behind the transporter console on the far side of the compartment, a male Benzite chief petty officer nudged his enlisted female Orion assistant. "Not bad!" he exclaimed, oblivious of the heartfelt reunion transpiring mere meters away atop the transporter platform. "Wouldn't you say so, Taryl?"

The green-skinned brunette shrugged. "I guess."

"You guess? I, Neldok, with these two hands, successfully transported two subjects who were traveling with divergent velocities, acquired while the ship was moving at near warp speed, and rematerialized them together onto one pad!"

Taryl shot a bored look at her amphibian supervisor. "It's been done."

Neldok harrumphed. "I guess there's no pleasing some people." Belatedly taking note of Bashir and Sarina's continued silent embrace, Neldok pointed at the door and said to Taryl, "Perhaps we should step out and give them the room."

The crewman rolled her eyes. "You think?" She let Neldok usher her out the door. As the Benzite followed her out, he looked back and smiled with innocent admiration as he said under his breath, "What an adorable couple."

The door closed, affording Bashir and Sarina a moment of privacy.

He reached up with one hand and gingerly touched her bruised face. Her lips were brittle, cracked, and caked with dried blood. "You're hurt," he said, tracing the line of her jaw with his fingertips.

"It's nothing," she said, lifting her hand tenderly to his cheek.

"Who did this to you? The Breen military?"

She shook her head. "No, a civilian. A BID inquisitor."

He planted a soft kiss on her forehead. She winced. He pulled back and saw that she was trembling. "What did he do to you?"

"Went a bit overboard with his neural truncheon," Sarina said. "I'll be fine."

Taking her hand, he tried to lead her off the platform. "We need to get you to sickbay," he said. "There could be synaptic—"

"*Julian.*" She pulled him back to her. "In a *minute*. I promise I'm not dying." Offering up a bittersweet smile, she stroked his bearded chin and pushed her fingers through his hair. "I'm just glad you're not hurt," she said.

"Actually, I am." He averted his gaze, haunted by the memory of lives he'd taken in cold blood. *My wounds are just harder to see.*

She nuzzled his cheek. He saw no hint of judgment in her eyes—only compassion, affection, and under-standing.

He sank into her arms, thankful to be done with the mission but even more grateful to have her back at his side. "There's something I want . . ." He paused and reconsidered his choice of words. "Something I *need* to ask you."

Sarina nodded. "Okay."

"Now that this is over . . . what's next? For us, I mean?

Are you staying on with Starfleet Intelligence? Am I? Do you want me to put in—"

The door opened, and Dr. Simon Tarses entered, followed by a human nurse. Stopping in midstep, the young quarter-Romulan physician stammered, "Um, uh, sorry, Julian—I mean, Doctor. We, um, didn't—"

"It's okay, Simon," Bashir said to his former Deep Space 9 colleague. He masked his irritation at Tarses's unfortunate timing. "You're not interrupting."

"Ah, well, that's good to know," Tarses said with a nervous smile. "You two have had quite a rough week, I imagine."

Bashir nodded. "It had its moments."

"And then some," Sarina added.

"Well, tell you what," Tarses said. "Let's get you two down to sickbay, swap those pressure suits for new uniforms, run a few tests—"

Sarina lifted a hand to interrupt. "We know the drill."

"Throw in a hot shower, and you can run all the tests you want," Bashir said.

"Deal." Tarses stepped back and gestured toward the door. "After you."

Bashir and Sarina stepped off the transporter platform, and he led the way out. Once they were in the corridor, Sarina walked beside him and took his hand.

He threw her a sidelong glance, and she smiled and tightened her grip.

"In answer to your question," she whispered, "*I go where you go.*"

Bashir smiled. He didn't need to go anywhere ever again. He was home.

• • •

Lieutenant Mikaela Leishman stood in the middle of the *Aventine*'s main engineering deck. She was surrounded by loose parts, jumbles of cables, and several dozen frazzled engineers. The only thing she wanted more than a nap at that moment was someone else to take over her job as the ship's chief engineer.

Captain Dax's voice resounded from speakers in the overhead and echoed throughout the voluminous compartment. *"Bridge to main engineering."*

Leishman closed her eyes, swallowed a sigh, and in a bright voice intended to mask her fatigue, said, "Leishman here. Go ahead, sir."

"First, I want to commend you and your team for a fine job inverting the subspatial geometry of the main warp coils."

The compliment drew a weak smile from Leishman. "Thanks, Captain. It's always nice when someone understands the miracle."

"That said, I need to interrupt your victory celebration."

Turning her head to survey the engineering deck, Leishman saw only weary faces looking back at her as if to ask, *What ship is Dax serving on?* For the sake of diplomacy, she said simply, "We'll try, Captain. What's up?"

"Four Breen heavy cruisers are closing fast on our position. Whatever you did to make the warp coils go backward, you need to undo it."

"I presume this is a rush job."

"You've got three minutes."

"I stand corrected. No problem, sir. We're on it. Leishman out."

She waited until the channel clicked off. Then she squatted, picked up part of a plasma regulator from the deck, and held it over her head for her engineers to see. "Listen up," she said, addressing the entire team. "We set a record taking this apart. Now we have two minutes to put it back together—before the Breen kill us all." She added with a sweet but obviously insincere smile, "No pressure."

TWO WEEKS LATER

45

Dax sat at the desk in her ready room, sipped from a mug of *raktajino*, and faced the holographic comm display projected above her desktop. Looking back at her was the visage of Admiral Nechayev. The middle-aged, silver-blond human woman sounded apologetic. *"I know you thought this matter closed, Captain. I hope you'll forgive me if my next question comes off sounding . . . indelicate."*

"Go on," Dax said between sips of her drink.

"Have you ever known Doctor Bashir or Lieutenant Douglas to embellish *their accounts of events?"*

Dax set down her mug. "Why do you ask, Admiral?"

Nechayev sighed. *"Some members of the admiralty and the administration are finding it difficult to believe the details of Sarina's escape from enemy custody, or Bashir's debriefing with regard to how he reached, destroyed, and subsequently escaped from the target."* Holding up her hands, she added, *"I don't share their doubts, Captain, but without evidence to support—"*

"Admiral, we *do* have evidence: the solid-state drives built into Bashir's and Douglas's disguises recorded a complete log of their activities. But since Bashir's also contains secondhand recordings of the slipstream schematics, and both contain classified intel regarding Starfleet's preparations for the mission, I decided it was unsafe to risk transmitting them over subspace channels, regardless of encryption. I arranged with Starfleet Intelligence to hand over the drives to Commander Erdona once we reached Deep Space 9." She keyed in a command to relay a file over the channel to Nechayev. "I'm uploading the chain-of-custody log. It verifies that Erdona received the drives this morning at 0840 station time."

The admiral perused the data as it came up on her screen. *"So, Starfleet Intelligence has possession of the mission logs?"*

"Yes, sir."

Nechayev frowned. *"Nice of them to keep me in the loop."*

"Admiral," Dax said, "as long as I have your attention, I've been hearing chatter that the Typhon Pact is making waves because of what happened in the Alrakis system. And rumor has it the Romulans are especially irked about getting ambushed by the Klingons out by the Black Cluster. . . . I hope we didn't stir up more trouble than we were supposed to."

"No more than usual," Nechayev said. *"Stick to the version of events in your logs and there shouldn't be any problem. The Typhon Pact's ambassador will do her best to blow it out of proportion, but that's not your concern."*

Unsure whether Nechayev's nonchalance was genuine, Dax asked, "Are you sure, Admiral? I have enough commendations in my record that if adding a reprimand or two might help the diplomats back on Earth smooth things over—"

"Ezri, you and your crew performed commendably under near-impossible circumstances. Cut yourself some slack and don't worry about the political fallout. The wonks at the Palais put us in this mess—let them clean it up. That's an order."

"Aye, sir," Dax said with a smile.

"Nechayev out."

Dax's screen went dark as it shifted back into standby mode. She finished her *raktajino*, placed the mug in the matter reclamator, and walked out of her ready room.

The mood on the bridge was muted but busy. On the main viewer, Deep Space 9 loomed large, and the space around it was heavy with shipping traffic.

Bowers stood from the command chair. "Captain on the deck." The bridge crew snapped to attention.

"As you were," Dax said, continuing toward her chair.

Nodding at Dax as she approached, Bowers said, "Refueling operations complete, Captain. All requested provisions have been loaded and stowed, and Deep Space 9 has replaced our expired munitions with fresh ordnance. All personnel are aboard and accounted for. The ship is ready for service."

"That's nice," Dax said. "Give the crew three additional days of liberty and send them ashore."

The order caught Bowers off guard, just as Dax had intended.

"I'm sorry, Captain. I don't understand."

"Give the crew three more days of shore leave, Commander. Schedule it as you see fit—stagger it by shift, whatever works for you."

Bowers nodded once. "Aye, sir." Lowering his voice, he

added, "I still don't understand, sir. Did we receive new orders to stay at DS9?"

"No," Dax said. "I got something better—*slack*. And I intend to use it."

"For what?"

Dax shrugged. "Whatever."

"Can I get some?"

"What would you do with it?"

"I don't know. Catch up on personnel reports?"

"Then the answer is *no*, you can't have any."

"That doesn't seem fair."

"My ship, my rules."

President Bacco stood with a phony smile on her face as four of her protection agents escorted Tezrene, the Typhon Pact's ambassador to the United Federation of Planets, into her office on the fifteenth floor of the Palais de la Concorde. As usual, the Tholian diplomat wasted no time on courtesies; she launched into a tirade while crossing the room the moment she saw Bacco.

"Madam President, I hold you personally accountable for delaying this meeting," Tezrene said, her razor-screech of a native voice translated by her environment suit's vocoder into something that sounded equally sharp.

Bowing her head in a facsimile of contrition, Bacco said, "My apologies, Madam Ambassador. Pressing matters of state demanded my full attention."

The six-limbed crystalline arthropod parked herself in front of Bacco's desk. "To what matters of state do you refer, Madam President?"

Bacco widened her smile and narrowed her eyes. "I'm not at liberty to elaborate, Your Excellency. I'm certain you understand."

The squad of protection agents standing at the back of the room tensed as Tezrene gesticulated in a vaguely threatening manner with her two upper forelimbs. "What I understand, Madam President, is that your Starfleet committed acts of unprovoked aggression, and you, through your protracted silence over the past two weeks, have implicitly sanctioned it."

Stepping behind her desk, Bacco said, "That's simply not true, Ambassador. Captain Dax and the crew of the *Aventine* entered Breen space in response to what sounded like an urgent distress signal—one that was documented by the Breen Militia in that sector. Dax and her crew tried to confirm the signal, but the Breen Confederacy's local comnet had failed. In accordance with interstellar law, they crossed the border for strictly altruistic reasons."

"Doubtful," Tezrene said.

"Check the logs, Madam Ambassador. As soon as the *Aventine*'s crew determined there was no emergency, they withdrew from the Alrakis system."

Tezrene's vocoder voice crackled with anger. "Only after they sabotaged and destroyed the Salavat shipyard!"

"Once again, the evidence seems to disagree with your version of events," Bacco said. "The explosion that destroyed the shipyard appears to have been the result of an internal accident—a reactor core breach, if I'm not mistaken."

"Sensor logs show your vessel firing on Breen patrol vessels," Tezrene said.

"In *self-defense*," Bacco said. "Those craft fired first on the *Aventine*. Captain Dax's response was appropriate and proportional. Her vessel easily could have destroyed those interceptors, but it warned them off instead."

"You deny that the *Aventine* was sent to destroy the vessel being constructed at the Salavat yard?"

"I assure you, Ambassador, the *Aventine*'s crew had no such orders." Bacco leaned forward on her fists. "Why would I risk a war to destroy *one* vessel at *one* shipyard? What possible strategic or tactical value would such a mission have?"

It was a question that Bacco knew Tezrene could not answer in any way that would benefit the Typhon Pact. If Tezrene confirmed the Breen had been building a slip-stream-drive prototype starship, she would be divulging a major state-security secret. If she chose not to incorporate that information into her argument, however, it would be all but impossible for her to level a plausible accusation at Starfleet or the Federation. The fact that Bacco and Tezrene were both fully aware of what had happened at Salavat was beside the point; the game now was one of rhetorical one-upmanship—a battle to save face and amass political capital to spend on the next confrontation.

Tezrene inched away from Bacco's desk. "You and your Federation will pay for your arrogance, Madam President."

"So you keep telling us."

"No empire lasts forever." Tezrene turned and scuttled toward the door, flanked every step of the way by the team of protection agents, who followed her out. As that door slid closed, the one on the opposite side of the office opened, and Esperanza Piñiero walked in.

"How'd it go?"

Bacco shrugged at her chief of staff. "As expected."

"That badly?"

"Could've been worse. If I'd made her any angrier, she might have attacked me. Then my protection detail would've shot her, and Kant would be explaining to the press corps how a diplomatic courtesy call turned into an interstellar incident."

"Look on the bright side, Madam President: at least we're not at war."

Bacco heaved a sigh and sank into her chair. "Yes, we are. It's last century's goddamned Klingon Crisis all over again, except this time we have six enemies plotting against us instead of just one." Noting the smirk on Piñiero's face, she asked, "What's so funny?"

"A sixfold increase in enemies?" Piñiero said. "If that's not progress, Madam President, I don't know what is."

Bashir entered Deep Space 9's infirmary and found the place much as he had left it only a few weeks earlier: immaculate, quiet, and almost empty. He had reviewed his staff's recent case files and updates on routine vaccination procedures during his journey home aboard the *Aventine*, and for once there were no pressing emergencies or rude surprises waiting for him upon his return.

The lights in the main room were dim, and the air was laced with the sharp odor of disinfectant. Bashir unlocked the door of his office, stepped inside, and settled into his chair. His computer powered up automatically, and he glanced at the list of messages that had accumulated during his absence.

It'll take me days just to get caught up on all this. At this rate, I'm less a doctor than a glorified medical correspondent.

Looking out his office window at the rows of empty biobeds, he was struck anew by the feeling that he no longer had any reason to be there.

Bashir got up and moved with soft steps toward the intensive-care ward. He paused and peeked through its open entryway. Prynn Tenmei sat on a chair next to her father's bed. She held Vaughn's left hand with her own, and in her right hand she held a padd, from which she read to him. Even from across the ward, Bashir was able to hear her, thanks to his enhanced senses.

"'At the top of the altar, Wade saw the remains of the artifact,'" Tenmei read. "'It lay shattered and broken, its power and its promise sacrificed by men who had never understood it, never respected it, never used it wisely. In its runes they had read only the stories of their own ambitions, the tales of their own glory.

"'Wade pinched a few grains of gemstone dust between his thumb and forefinger. "It was our fault," he said. "Our magi and priests did this." He looked back at the men he had led around the world, over raging seas and blighted lands, only to bring them to this unholy place, and he felt sick with remorse. "It was Men who struck first," he said. "Men who rained fire on Scarden and laid it waste, and left the Wights no choice but to conquer new lands. Entire generations lost to war . . . and it all began with one decision, made here."'"

Tenmei stopped reading and looked up at Bashir as he approached. "You're back," she said.

"For the moment." Bashir accessed the biobed display to review Vaughn's chart and noted with surprise, "He's off the respirator."

"Nine days now," Tenmei said. "I thought about what you said—that maybe this wasn't such a bad time and place to let my father go. And I finally admitted to myself that keeping him alive just for me wasn't fair to him. So I signed the DNR and asked Nurse Richter to remove the respirator systems. But, as you can see . . ." She looked at Vaughn and smiled, though her eyes were wet with tears. "Still no higher brain activity, but something in him just refuses to give up."

Bashir nodded. "I have to admit, your father is one of the strongest men I've ever met. And one of the most stubborn."

Tenmei chuckled. "Oh, I know. Trust me, you don't have to tell me about *that*." She squeezed her father's hand. "I've been waiting for you to come back before I take the final step and have his feeding tube removed. I thought you'd want to be here at the end."

Standing at the bedside of his friend and former commanding officer, Bashir found himself thinking about the past few weeks of his life—in particular, the lives he had taken in the name of duty and country, and the stain that state-sanctioned murder had left on his soul. The notion of taking action to end Elias Vaughn's life, though it might be practical and even humane, no longer felt ethical.

"Let's not cross that bridge yet," Bashir said. "I don't think your father is likely to ever regain consciousness, but . . . something in him clearly isn't ready to die yet. And

I'm not going to take that away from him—or from you."

Tenmei brushed a tear from her cheek and shot a confused look at Bashir. "Are you sure about this, Julian?"

"No. But if I'm wrong, at least this is a mistake I can live with."

Sarina awoke from a dream whose details immediately faded from her memory. She drew a long, deep breath and listened to the sounds in Julian's quarters. The space station's ventilation system hummed overhead, and the angled windows above Julian's bed had been set to near total opacity to keep the room dark even as Deep Space 9's slow rotation brought the star B'hava'el into view for several minutes every hour. Beside her, Julian lay sleeping, his breathing slow and deep.

She lifted the sheet and blanket with care and slipped out of the warm bed. The air in Julian's quarters was chilly and filtered to the point of being all but devoid of fragrance—institutional qualities that did nothing to endear the place to Sarina, who had lived most of the first three decades of her life in just such an antiseptic environment. She gathered up her cashmere bathrobe from a chair in the corner and wrapped it around herself. Taking care not to wake Julian, she tiptoed toward the open doorway to his suite's main room.

As she reached the doorway, Julian mumbled from the bed, "Where are you going?" He was straining to see her through eyes heavy with sleep.

"To have some tea and check my messages," she said in a hushed voice. "I'll just be a few minutes. Go back to sleep."

Julian yawned, made a noise that sounded like "Umkay," and rolled over.

Sarina crossed the main room to its replicator, requested a Betazoid variety of hot herbal tea, and savored its floral aroma as she lifted the delicate cup from the replicator nook.

When she turned around, she was unsurprised to see her visitor sitting in a chair with her legs crossed, regarding her with a dispassionate stare. "Hello again, Sarina," said the black-clad Vulcan woman with a Cleopatra haircut.

"Hello, L'Haan," Sarina said. She set her tea on the low table between her and the Section 31 supervisor. "I've been expecting you."

L'Haan arched one eyebrow. "Naturally. I did tell you I would return." She leaned forward. "Section 31 is very impressed with your performance on Salavat."

"Happy to hear it." Sarina nodded toward Bashir's bedroom and whispered, "Aren't you afraid we'll wake him?"

"An acoustic-dampening field protects our conversation," L'Haan said, "and Doctor Bashir's dinner was laced with a mild sedative to deepen his slumber."

Sarina rolled her eyes. "Well, that certainly explains his diminished performance this evening. Glad to know it wasn't me." She focused her attention on L'Haan. "Why are you here?"

"To commend you. Your mission was a success—and, most important, the good doctor was forced to get his hands dirty. This was a major step for him, one whose importance is not to be underestimated."

Sarina nodded. "I understand. So, what's next?"

"Let your relationship with Bashir continue on its current arc," L'Haan said. "Whether he remains here or pursues a career at Starfleet Intelligence is ultimately irrelevant. What matters now is that you remain romantically enmeshed in his life—as intensely and as intimately as possible. When the time comes for his further development as an asset, your access to him and his talents will be invaluable. Do you understand?"

"Yes. That won't be a problem. He adores me."

"Excellent." L'Haan's mien took on a contemplative quality. "It is regrettable that my predecessors Sloan and Cole lacked this fundamental insight into Doctor Bashir's psychology. The doctor has no ambition to exploit his abilities for personal gain. The weak spot in his persona is not his pride or his ego—it is his unabashed *romanticism*." She stood, stepped around the table, took Sarina's chin between her thumb and forefinger, and lifted it so that their eyes met. "Make him *love* you," she said, "and then we will *have* him."

THE SAGA OF
DEEP SPACE NINE®
WILL CONTINUE

Acknowledgments

First, I thank my wife, Kara, for not strangling me or divorcing me or otherwise avenging herself upon me for being such a pain-in-the-ass recluse while I was writing this book during the first few months of 2010.

Also, my thanks go out to editor Margaret Clark, who commissioned this novel from me and guided its early development. Sadly, Margaret was laid off before the manuscript was written, so she did not get to complete the journey she helped me begin. Margaret, I hope you feel I've done this story justice.

My gratitude also goes out to Christopher L. Bennett, who took time out of his schedule to share scientific advice about real star systems that might serve to add verisimilitude to my tale's fictional setting, and to David R. George III, who valiantly agreed to serve as this book's beta reader, ferreting out its myriad flaws.

Last but never least, my thanks to you, the readers, who make these efforts of mine worthwhile. I hope we get to take many more literary journeys together.

About the Author

David Mack is the national bestselling author of sixteen novels, including *Wildfire*, *Harbinger*, *Reap the Whirlwind*, *Precipice*, *Road of Bones*, *Promises Broken*, and the *Star Trek Destiny* trilogy: *Gods of Night*, *Mere Mortals*, and *Lost Souls*. He developed the *Star Trek Vanguard* series concept with editor Marco Palmieri. His first work of original fiction is the critically acclaimed supernatural thriller *The Calling*.

In addition to novels, Mack's writing credits span several media, including television (for episodes of *Star Trek: Deep Space Nine*), film, short fiction, magazines, newspapers, comic books, computer games, radio, and the Internet.

His upcoming novels include the Mirror Universe epic *Rise Like Lions* and a new original supernatural thriller.

Mack lives in New York City with his wife, Kara. Visit his official web site, **www.davidmack.pro/**, follow him on Twitter.com **@DavidAlanMack**, and friend him on Facebook at **www.facebook.com/david.alan.mack**.